echoes OF BELONGING

VANDANA PRAJAPATI

INDIA • SINGAPORE • MALAYSIA

ISBN 979-8-89186-415-3

For Mom, who always reminded me
that words have the power to change the world.

You will always be with me.

Written with love, in the memories of Tara

Contents

Chapter 1

St. Mary College, day one—college number two for me. You'd think I might have gotten used to switching colleges by now, but being forced to transfer a few days into my senior year is next-level sucky. The Nandas—the family where I will be living in the coming years. I lost my parents three years ago in a car accident. My father and Amit Uncle were best friends from college days. Then, after completing graduation, my dad shifted to Delhi, and Amit uncle stayed in Dehradun only.

St. Mary's College is one of India's best colleges and is expensive and modern too. Most of the girls walking into this place are dressed like they are about to stomp down a catwalk. I do not fit the prototype in my old Vans, shredded hip-hugging jeans, and oversized black Nirvana T-shirt. After falling out of bed later than I expected to this morning, I made the decision to pull my wavy black hair into a low, messy bun. That was a mistake. Looking like a homeless street urchin is no way to make a good first impression.

I let out a breath that blew my scraggly bangs away from my eyes. Shift the strap of my ratty khaki messenger bag into a more comfortable position on my shoulder and zero in on the marquee sporting a gigantic black and orange paw print and the words HOME OF THE PANTHERS. That's when I hear someone behind me holler, "Hey, Vedika."

It's not like I have any friends in this town, so I have a pretty good idea who is calling my name: Tara, Amit's uncle's daughter. Like me, she is a senior, but I am certain that's where the similarities between us end. She seems to be made up of everything I am not. I am poor and mostly keep to myself. Her family is wealthy—Kavita Aunty is a lawyer, and Amit Uncle is the CEO of some gaming app company. She is a dancer, so she will have a ton of eager groupies in tow all the time, and she is beautiful in a high-maintenance movie star kind of way.

I turn around to find Tara coming towards me, her pink plaid sheet skirt and white crop sweater both riding up with every stride. There is a suggestion of frustration on her face. "Why didn't you wait for me? My mom said I was supposed to drive you."

"I felt like walking." I shrug. "Besides, you were taking forever to get ready. I didn't want to be late for my first day."

She runs a hand through her long, chestnut-colored hair and slings it over her right shoulder. "I am here, aren't I? You wouldn't have been late."

"Right. Thanks, anyway." I turn back to the school and start for the main entrance. She doesn't let me slip away unaccompanied—unfortunate considering I really don't feel like making small talk. Anyhow, I know she is only sticking close to me because her parents told her she had to escort me around.

"Do you have to get your schedule from the office?"

"Yeah."

"Okay. Let's go."

I picked up my class schedule, locker assignment, and map of the college from the admin office. "Block scheduling." I glow at the top of the paper. "I don't get it."

"Give me those." Tara snatches all three sheets of paper from my hands and scans them over. "What's not to get?" We have main days and elective days. They alternate. On most days, you have English honors, life skills, environmental studies, lunch, and then Indian literature. On elective days, you have partition, Greek mythology, and then study and tennis. Way to go on picking the lamest physical elective ever. Today is Main Day, so follow the schedule. Got it?" She hands the papers back to me.

"Thanks so much for being judgmental about tennis. And yes, I've got it."

"Whatever." She waves dismissively. "I am going to the arts wing. Come with me; we are in the same English class."

"You are in English Honors."

She leers at me. "What, you think because I am a dancer I must be stupid? Now who is being judgmental?"

I feel the heat of embarrassment bubbling in my chest and try to shake it off. "Touche."

She smirks.

We're about to head up the staircase to the second floor when she is ambushed by a group of girls whose barely there attire must push the boundaries of the college dress code. They ignore my presence and proceed to yammer at her, their voices meshing together in a wall of sound. She can't get a word in. "Guys", she says softly. When that doesn't work, she says it again, louder. "Guys!"

Everyone stops to focus on her.

She shoots me an apologetic look. "Everyone, this is Vedika. Vedika, this is Shreya, Avani, Meera, and Kritika." She motions to each girl as she introduces them.

They all looked at me, head to toe. I can tell they are appraising my coolness factors. I lose points for my clothing, but I suppose the fact that I am keeping company with Tara is enough for them to overlook the way I'm dressed because they opt to speak to me.

"Vedika, welcome to the college; where are you from?" Shreya asked.

"Delhi."

"She is staying with my family for a while, so you guys had better be nice to her," Tara replies.

Instantly, their demeanors soften. Interesting. She is the puppet master.

"So, Ved—I can call you that, right?" Kritika asks. I start to say, "I guess," but she doesn't let me finish. "Will you be trying out to join our dance group?"

Is she kidding me? Do I seem like I'm eager to join the Dazzel Brigade? "I was thinking about trying out for tennis, actually."

She sneers. At second glance, I see they all do—everyone except Tara.

"Just to let you know, all those girls are not straight," Avani said, making 'Not straight' sound like the most disgusting words in the English language—worse than'sewage,' or'maggot,' or 'pus.'

Should I blow their minds now or wait until later? Later would be better. I'd like to get through my first few days here unscathed. Maybe make some allies before I start making enemies. The problem is, on the rare occasion someone manages to piss me off, I'm really bad at keeping my mouth shut and really good at scathing comebacks. Oh man, do I have a comeback for this chick. Like, if you are going to be homophobic, I'd prefer it if you'd call me a 'dyke.' 'Rug muncher' is also a good one.

Tara comes to her friend's rescue without even realizing that she needs to.

"Avani, seriously, refrain from spewing your shit all over the place. You'll ruin my heels."

Savage

Avani's cheeks go bright pink.

The 9:10 bell rings; we've got five minutes to make it to class on time. Tara plasters on a pretentious smile and says, "We'd better get our asses to class. See you at lunch." She grabs me by the elbow and leads me up the steps. "Sorry. They can be bad sometimes," she says as we reach the second floor.

"I noticed."

"Did Avani offend you?"

Am I that transparent? Did she know that I'm bisexual? *Wonderful. That's exactly what I need—to live in a house with this girl until I graduate and get a job and have her feel uncomfortable around me the whole damn time—because,* of course, the system won't let me 'age out' until I finish my education or decide to drop out, despite the fact that my eighteenth birthday was last week.

"Did I seem offended?"

"Not really."

"Then why would you ask me if I was?"

"The rainbow patch on your bag, the one you were carrying when you moved in." She sucks in her bottom lip and bites down.

I forgot about that thing. "Oh."

"Listen, it's fine. I don't care." She sounds genuine, but I can't be certain.

"Are you sure?"

She laughs, which has to be the most inappropriate reaction ever. I'm aware that I'm glaring at her like she's high on something, but I can't help it. Before I can slip my features into a more innocuous expression, she reads me. It throws me off. You're losing it, kid.

She gathers herself and says, "There was a girl from my mother's side who was staying with us last summer who set fire to our garage. If the worst thing about you is being bisexual, I'm relieved, but you can't tell my parents about it. It's India." Her eyes go wide, as though she's afraid she may have said the wrong thing. "Not that being gay or bi is a bad thing. It's not. It's normal. I–"

"Tara, stop." I throw my hands up. I don't want her to have a political correctness-induced meltdown. "I can promise you that I'm not a pyromaniac, or a kleptomaniac, or any of those other words that have'maniac' as a suffix. I want us to be cool with each other. Can we try to do that?"

"Yes." She smiles. It's the first time I've seen her authentic smile. Pretty.

"Great. So, uh, will you show me where room no. 25 is, please?"

"This way."

"Caféteria is on this floor. Down the hall, make a right," Tara points out after English class is over. I follow her finger with my gaze, then settle on her face once she puts her arms down. Her eyes are blue, striking, clear, and crystalline, like photos I've seen in photography class. Another thing about her that's different from mine My eyes are a weird ochre color.

"Will you be okay with finding the room for the next class by yourself?"

"I think I can manage."

"We will have lunch together. Meet me outside the cafeteria at twelve."

Was that a command? I should probably make her clear that I have no intention of allowing her to become my puppet master. That stuff might fly with her mindless minions, but it won't with me. "Are you asking me or telling me?"

"I was asking, if you'd rather wander around the cafe looking for people to sit with like some pathetic freshman, be my guest."

No. That doesn't sound appealing at all. "I'll meet you outside the café."

"See you then." She starts to walk away. "By the way", she calls over her shoulder, "Tennis tryouts start today at three."

Apparently, she is unable to recognize sarcasm when she hears it. I wasn't serious about that. I only said it because I like the idea of becoming an actual athlete a lot better than the idea of becoming a dancer. I plan to avoid becoming either. "Thanks." I keep my eyes on her retreating figure until she disappears from sight.

BY THE END of the day, I've realized there isn't a single student at this school who wants to befriend me. NO one in any of my classes bothered to say a word to me unless prompted by the teacher. It was the same in the lunchroom, save for Tara, her surprisingly pleasant jock friend Jatin, and a few of his brothers from the football team. I know most of the guys only talked to me because they considered me fresh meat. They had the air of hungry predators who'd spotted prey. Tara shut that down real quick. "She isn't going to fuck any of you. She's not interested in trash." It was funny and preferable to her flat-out announcing my sexual orientation to the entire cafeteria. That would have been mortifying. I've been out to myself since I was fourteen, but it's something I like to divulge to people in my own time, on my own terms.

To add to what was probably the worst first day of school anyone has ever experienced, I didn't have enough time to make it to my locker at any point, so I'm dragging three thick-ass textbooks and a plethora of paperbacks courtesy of English Honors around with me. It's absurd that we're only allotted five minutes between classes to make our way through, like, two thousand students and four floors. What if your B Block classroom is on the first floor and your C Block classroom is on the fourth floor—the penthouse-like mine is on Pride days? There's no way in hell I'll have time to make a pit stop at my locker. Three days a week, I'll be stuck lugging every last thing I need for the day unless I cut into the forty-five minutes I get for lunch.

I find my locker, number 473, and give it an inspection. I'm not thrilled about the size of it—just high and wide enough to stuff a person into. My mind cooks up a vision of me crumpled inside, barely able to scratch at the metal, my face pressed against the grates as I gasp for every breath until I die. Get it together. I put my messenger bag down on the floor and proceeded to struggle with the combination lock that's built into the door. "Goddamn stupid thing."

"Only frosh have trouble with their locker. You look too old to be a freshman. That must make you a transfer," says a voice from off to my right. The locker next to mine bangs closed, and my observer comes into view. He's tall and muscular. His hair was a deep, lustrous black that seemed to absorb all the ambient light. Each strand was sleek and glossy, cascading in gentle waves that framed his chiseled face. The way it fell over his forehead and occasionally brushed against his piercing dark eyes gave him an air of mysterious allure. He turns toward me, and I notice his irises are the color of emeralds; they sparkled with amusement as they combed over me. I can feel my cheeks flushing. "No shame; we've all been through it. Let me help you."

I'm tempted to take him up on it, but I'm hesitant to give my combination to a complete stranger. There will never be anything worth stealing. "It's 27-9-35."

"Got it." He maneuvers into place between me and the door and hunches down to fiddle with the lock. I note the bold orange 22 and the name on the back of his black hoodie.

He opens the locker with such ease that it makes me feel twice as dumb. He moves away from it and gestures at the thing with a flat palm, like, 'Voila!

"Thanks, "I whisper.

"No problem." He offers his hand for a shake. "I'm Kanan. I'm a senior."

"Vedika, also a senior." I shake his offered hand, drop it a little too quickly, pick up my messenger bag, and start shifting books onto the top shelf.

"Vedika, sweet name. Where'd you transfer from?"

"Delhi."

"You're from the city? Why'd your parents move up here?"

I always dread this moment, having to explain to everyone I meet that I don't have parents. It hurts enough knowing that they are not there; telling other people about it is excruciating. Naturally, I have an alternative to the truth, a well-researched and complex lie: Both my parents are teachers who work for Delhi University. They went on a long tour, so I'm staying with family friends until graduation. with family and friends until graduation. For some reason, though, I can't bring myself to lie to him.

He contemplates me for a moment, bewildered by my silence. "Was that a hard question?"

"Mmm…"

"We don't have to talk about it," he says coolly. The softness in his eyes tells me he means it.

Pivot, moron. "The number is on the back of your sweatshirt. What sport do you play?"

He tugs his hoodie tight against his body. Below his left clavicle is a crest, the letters BHS, and a tennis ball emblazoned across it.

"Tennis. Nice."

"Speaking of, sorry to cut our conversation short; I have to go get ready for practice."

"Okay."

"See you, same place." He begins to saunter off, but stops a few paces in and turns shoes. "Do you have a study tomorrow?"

"Um." I scan my memory. "I do. Go Block 1."

"That's my study, too. Then G2 lunch."

"Same."

"Gotta love it; it gives us an hour and a half to do whatever. I'm psyched to use my off-campus privileges and the perks of surviving this shithole for three years."

This isn't a shithole. "Yeah."

"You want to come with me?"

I pause, weigh the invite, and then heI can already tell that I'll get along better with him than I ever will with Tara's friends.

"Sure."

"Meet me in the parking lot tomorrow at, like, 11:20? We can take my car."

I nod

"Dope," he says, then bounces down the hall toward the nearest stairwell.

"WHAT WERE YOU DOING WITH HIM?"

Tara appears at my side from nowhere.

Making out in full view of every passing student, duh. "What did it look like we were doing? We were talking."

She blinks at me. "He's trouble."

"Seems nice to me." I slam my locker door, turn to her, and sneer. "I'm going out to lunch with him tomorrow," I retort, then dash away from her.

She trails behind. Once she's close enough, she snatches my arm and stops me dead. "No, you're not."

Is it absolutely necessary for her to touch me? "Yes, I am." I yanked myself free from her grasp.

Her groan is almost inaudible, but it registers.

Deadpan. "What?"

Her face is a blank canvas. "I'm just trying to look out for you. You're new here, so trust me, you'd be better off staying away from Kanan."

Kanan, hun? "Why?"

She folds her arms across her chest and purses her lips together—secure as a dead-bolted door.

"I'd prefer to get to know him and decide for myself whether or not he's "trouble,' alright?"

"Fine." She rolls her eyes. "If you're not going to tennis tryouts, you'll have to walk home. I've got dancing," she says, then marches away from me.

"No skin off my ass," I mutter under my breath and embark on my long walk to the house.

Chapter 2

I'm sitting at the kitchen table reading George Orwell's *1984* for English class when Kavita Aunty arrives home from work. I look up from the book to find her overburdened by her briefcase and two brown paper grocery bags. I dog-ear my page and scurry over to help her. "Mrs. Nanda, let me get those for you."

"Oh, Vedika, thank you." She offloads the bags into my arms. "And stop calling me Mrs. Nanda. You can call me Aunty.

I sucked in a lungful of air. It's difficult for me to get comfortable with calling adults anything other than Mr. or Mrs. So-And-So.

Maybe it's a 'respecting my elders' thing. Hell, I think if I ever met my grandparents, I'd call them Mr. Sharma and Mrs. Sharma. God, that's pathetic on so many levels.

"Aunty." I let this word slide around my mouth, tasting tiny pieces of it as though it were a food I'd never tried before. I'm not sure whether or not I like it. I start to unload the bags and compel myself to concentrate on something other than any uneasiness.

"How was your first day of college?" She asks at my back as I'm putting a gallon of milk in the fridge.

"It was fine."

"Just 'fine'?"

Right? Should be an expert on the first days.

"Fine is better than shitty—uh, bad!" I spin around to gauge her reaction to my swearing.

She is as calm as can be. "You're enough to say 'shit.' You'll hear Amit say worse. He's a potty mouth, especially when he's testing a pre-release game." A little grin flickers into being.

To say I'm relieved would be an understatement. I used to get slapped in the mouth for cursing.

"Is there something specific you'd like for dinner? She asks, either not noticing or overlooking my reaction. " I was thinking of butter chicken and naan, Tara's favorites. Do you like chicken?"

"Yes, I do." A lot. "Butter chicken and naan sound great."

DINNER IS WEIRD. I haven't sat down at a table for a proper meal with my family in a long time. Amit's uncle is nice. I hadn't gotten the chance to talk with him much over my first couple of days here because he's been crazy busy with work. He seems pretty laid-back, precisely how I expected a guy who got rich designing video games to be.

Amit uncle and Kavita aunty are catty, talking about their day's grind: aunty had a debacle with a client who hadn't divulged his tendency to cheat on his wife, thereby obliterating the prospect of an amicable divorce. Amit uncle had to talk a graphics department intern through a mini meltdown after the lead designer told her to get the fuck out of the lead designer for being a prick to the poor girl.

Tara is silent throughout, sitting across the table from me. She's not spacing out, but she's not quite interested either. Now and again, I catch her watching me. Examining me? I wonder what's going on in her head. She's going to tell me, and I'm not going to ask.

She's different at home. Quieter. Is she more at ease here or less?

"Hey," Uncle says to his daughter, "does practice go well today?"

Tara rolls a few strands of her still-damp hair around her finger—she didn't bother to blow dry it after her post-practice shower.

"It was a dumpster fire. No one kept up with the routines over the summer. Everyone's out of shape. I'm quitting."

Kavita drops her fork. It tings against her plate. "You're what?"

Tara's shoulders are tense. She sits up straighter. Less at ease. Strange. "I'm quitting," she repeats deliberately. Defiant.

"That's not like you."

"Or maybe that's exactly like me."

Aunty frowns at her and puffs out an exasperated breath.

This got awks fast.

"If you're unhappy doing it, you should quit," Uncle interjects. "But if it's because you're frustrated—"

"I'm unhappy and frustrated. It's not fun anymore. It's a chore."

"It seems so sudden, is all," says Kavita Aunty.

"Sudden? I was miserable last season. I only ever thought it was fun because of—forget it. It's not my thing anymore, okay? I'm quitting."

Uncle reaches up, giving Tara's shoulder a gentle squeeze. "You do you, Kiddo."

Her posture relaxes. I see. She's a daddy's girl.

Aunty is placated. "You don't have to stay on the squad, but you have to do something. Join a club. How about the yearbook?"

Tara hitches her chin at me. “What are you going to do?”

“I, uh–”

“We need to have at least one extracurricular.” She looks daggers at her mom.

“House rules.”

That’s a new one for me. My uncle and aunty didn’t care what I did, as long as I stayed out of their way and refrained from any activities that might bring the cops to their doorsteps. I was staying with them after my parents’ car accident.

“Is there a photography club?”

The corners of her mouth prick up ever-so-slightly. “Mumhmm. I think it meets after school on Thursdays. I don’t know where.”

Tomorrow’s Thursday. Fantastic. “I guess I’ll check that out then.”

“Me too,”

I’m startled. She spots it. “You don’t have to.”

“It’ll be good for her to try something new!” Aunty exclaims. “And wouldn’t it be nice to already have a friend in the club with you?”

“Wouldn’t it?” Tara rests her cheek on her clenched fist. Neither of her parents catch her eyebrow wiggle.

I SCRAPE the dinner scraps into the garbage, and Tara begins the dishwashing. I offer to help. She shakes her head. I shrug and head for the hallway.

The house is large maharajah-style with two floors—common spaces downstairs, three bedrooms and a home office upstairs, and a bathroom on each level. The wooden ceiling beams are exposed in every room, and the walls are painted a calming pastel blue and eggshell white. My room—so to speak, I've never had a room to myself before—is next to Tara's, down the fall from Uncle and Aunty's. Overall, the place is nice—not just the size or the beachy décor, but the vibe too. More than a house, it feels like a home.

The wall along the wide staircase is lined with picture frames-art prints mostly, like Van Gogh's "Almond Blossoms" series, though family photos are sprinkled here and there. There's a recent one of Uncle, Aunty, and Tara in front of the India Gate in Delhi. I love Delhi. It's always beautiful. And consistent. With the best food and history. Sometimes I miss that city.

I stop to scan a photo of Tara when she was young, seven or eight. She's missing a front tooth, smiling—not at the camera, at something out of frame. She was adorable. Bright eyes and choppy bangs. Happy.

An unexpected heaviness blooms in my chest. I don't have any good photos with my parents outside of an old yearbook from middle school. I thought about tossing it a few moves ago, figuring it was just something that took up space in my duffle bag. In the end, I decided to use it as a reminder that it's okay for me to take up space.

"You good"? Tara's voice from behind me shakes me from my thoughts.

"Yeah, I'm good."

"Then, are you going to stand there all night or—should I, like, go around you?"

"Sorry." I continue the climb. She traces my footsteps. "You really don't have to come to the photography club with me," I call to her as she passes me to her bedroom. "I will be fine on my own."

"I want to. I wouldn't have offered otherwise. I will meet you there. I have to turn in my uniform at the Athletics Office first."

"Okay."

"Goodnight."

"Goodnight."

Chapter 3

The day drags on until the bell signaling my Free Study rings. Then it's as if I've entered warp speed. I haven't let myself get excited about anything in ages. If I don't get my hopes up, I can never be let down. Even though I've just met him, there's something about Kanan that makes

me want to take a chance on him. Whether or not that's a foolish notion remains to be seen.

The student parking lot is bigger than I realized. There are different sections for different grades, and they're haphazard at best. I decide to lean against a lamppost and keep my eyes on the entrance, so I'll see Kanan when he comes out.

A sea of kids floods the lot, seniors with G-Block lunch for free study exercising the hard-earned off-campus privilege on Thursdays and Fridays. They're all pumped to be outside. Most kids think of college as a prison. I've always felt my freest at college, where I know none of the

Adults can smack me around, and I'm guaranteed two hearty meals.

Kanan bounces out the door. He stops for a second and throws his head back toward the sky. His eyes are closed, and he is basking in the sunlight. charging his battery. He must think it's too warm out—he peels his letterman jacket off, folds it over his arm, and adjusts his T-shirt where it's riddled up his torso. Then he catches sight of me. His lips spread into a smile. "Yo!" He greets me, still smiling.

"Hey."

"Where do you want to go?"

No Idea. "Uh..."

"Ah, right." He gets it. "What do you feel like eating?"

"I'm down for whatever."

"Alright, alright, alright," He sings songs and signals me to follow him.

HERE SLIVER DODGE Charger suits him: a muscle car, though not overly flashy; four doors, long and lean. The windows are down, and the music's up—not so loud that we can't speak over it, but we're both content to listen to it for now.

He chooses a restaurant five minutes from college called Flip the Bird. Its logo is a pissed-off rooster, hunched over and scowling at the street from between its legs. I dig it. He knows you're here to devour him and is judging the shit out of you for it.

Kanan opens the door for me and ushers me through. He's got manners. A lot of people don't. "Thanks."

He nods.

It's not crowded, but there are two people in front of us waiting for their food. It gives me a chance to read over the menu.

"What are you getting?" He wonders.

"Mmm. The Ya' Basic! With a chicken burger," topped with an egg. "You?"

"Same."

I read its description aloud, "Chicken fried in a ghost pepper and habanero batter, lettuce, and red pepper jam. My mouth is on fire just from saying the words.

"I like things spicy."

I like things bland. The more boring, the better.

He tells the guy at the counter her order and mine. "And a Coke. Want a drink?" He asks me.

"Bottled water, please," I say to the guy. He rings us up. "Uh, sorry, separate checks."

"I've got it." Kanan glides his debit card through the card reader faster than I can protest.

There is plenty of time to blush, though. "Next time, it's on me."

"That's fair."

His first question for me after we've sat down and started eating is, "What's your favorite color?"

It's a sample getting-to-know-you question, yet I struggle with it. There are so many great ones to choose from. "I think grey, although technically that's a shade. I like it because it's neither black nor white. It's both simultaneously."

"A balance between light and dark. Like life," he says.

I'm amazed at his insight—wicked deep for someone our age. "What's yours?"

"Red. Not like the fire engine red. Blood red."

That, too, suits him: spicy things.

We talk and talk, mostly about inconsequential stuff. Until he asks about my parents again. He isn't trying to pry; he's curious because I was cryptic. I don't have to squelch my instinct to lie, but I do have to gather my guts to tell the truth. Sometimes people act weird around me after they find out. I don't think he will, but he could. " I don't think he will, but he could. "I don't have parents. They died three years ago in a car accident. That's why I moved here—to complete my graduation."

He digests the information with his last bite of sandwich, then slurps some soda. There was no visible reaction at all. "Do you like this place and college so far?"

He hasn't disappointed me yet. We could be friends. Not if you tell him that I'm staying with Tara. That might be true. She wasn't shy about her aversion to Kanan, so I'm sure Kanan must be aware of it. Maybe the animosity is mutual. Keep names out of it until you can't anymore. "Yeah. They're cool." From this point on, I speak about them with ambiguity, making sure not to give too much away.

*

THE PHOTOGRAPHY CLUB MEETS IN ROOM 321 every Thursday at three; I checked the BHS activities website during CompSci. Today is their first meeting of the school year. I'm relieved I haven't missed anything. I take a second to collect myself, never having been much of a joiner, then head in. I count seventeen kids. They're all already acquainted with each other. A few of them set their gaze on me, though their attention is fleeting. Their conversations and comparisons between cameras aren't interrupted by my arrival. The clock above the whiteboard reads 3:05 p.m. The faculty advisor hasn't arrived yet. Neither has Tara. She's not coming, stupid.

The door swings open behind me. Or is she? In walks a young-ish, black-haired teacher carrying a small blue bin and a clipboard in his arms. He's from the history department, I think. He makes his way to the front of the class, puts the bin and clipboard on the large rectangular desk, then leans against it. "Howdy, everyone. For those of you who don't know me, I'm Mr. Ravi. Welcome to the photography club." He removes the lid from the bin and plucks out a camera case. It's small—a point-and-shoot. "Anyone who doesn't have a camera is welcome to borrow a PowerShot. You can sign it out and take it home with you, as long as you promise to baby it." He cradles the camera case in his hand and makes cooing noises at it, eliciting a round of chortles from the students.

"Come on up if you need one."

Nobody moves. They all have hardcore Nikons, Canons, and Sonys on straps around their necks or in cases on their desks. Just me, then. Big surprise!

I kept my eyes trained on the floor as I got to retrieve my loaner. Mr. Ravi hands me the clipboard. I write my name and homeroom on the top line of the sign-out sheet. "Vedika Sharma," he reads my name back to me. "Good to meet you. Pick a camera, any camera." The one I chose is in a black-gray pouch.

I'm sliding into a combo chair-desk at the back of the room when the door swishes open again. Everyone turns to gawk at the straggler. Tara.

"I'm late, my bad." She isn't sorry; she's indifferent. "What's going on, Mr. Ravi?" She greets him as though they're

friends. She must've taken one of his classes before and liked it well enough.

He's as surprised to see her as everyone else is, like she's never shown as much interest in photography before. It could be that she hasn't, and she's only here because of me. "Tara, nice of you to join us. Do you have a camera, or do you need to borrow one?"

She rummages through her enormous white leather purse and pulls out her iPhone. "I'm covered."

Mr. Ravi sighs. "That's not a camera."

Her turn to sigh

She saunters up, fills out the form, takes a camera, and makes her way to the back of the class. She plants her ass in the seat next to mine and grins at me. "You thought I ditched you, didn't you?"

Yes and no.

Mr. Ravi clears his throat. "Alright, so let's talk about our first project: autumn landscapes."

THE CLUB WRAPS UP a little after four thirty. We hit the parking lot as the student's tennis practice was ending. Kanan is in his car, the driver's side door open. He tugs the strap of an orange Adidas gym bag from his shoulder and tosses the overstuffed thing into the front seat. He looks up, sees me, and sees Tara. I watch him grapple with whether or not he wants to wave. He decides to go for it.

I wave back. Tara can't subdue an involuntary flinch. There's definitely a history between them. Kanan hops into the car, turns over the engine, and reverses out of the spot. I follow the Charger with my eyes as it guns out of the lot and onto the street.

"I take it your lunch date with him went well," Tara comments. Her tone is neutral. I check her face—it divulges nothing. I'm starting to recognize that as a talent of hers, and it's unnerving. I'm good at catching glimpses of people's feelings, but it seems that when she wants to, she's better at hiding them than most. Perhaps she's even better at it than I am.

It wasn't a date. He paid, so it kind of was. "Yep," I respond as we slide into her azure BMW. I really don't feel like talking about it. I wish there were some music playing; she prefers to drive with the stereo off. "How did your friends react when you told them you were quitting the squad?"

She answers only after she's banged to the left onto Sohier Road. "Shreya was cool. Meera and Kritika were sad about it. Avani was pissed. She's the captain, and I've screwed up her roster. She and Coach have to find a spotter to replace me now."

"What does a spotter do?"

"Keeps everything from going to shit."

That makes me snigger. "How so?"

"A spotter always has to be paying attention, ready to react. They can't be afraid to catch a girl who's falling, and they can't be afraid of getting hurt."

Sharp and fearless. Hmm. That's fitting. "Sounds like an important job."

"I had to make sure no one broke their fucking neck, so yeah." Her words are flippant, though her expression is firm. She cared enough to want to do the job correctly and well. Why did she really quit?

I find myself yearning to get to know her. It's unexpected. I'm usually satisfied by passively coexisting with people. Rarely, if ever, have I sought any kind of relationship with any of them. Should I crush the bud or nurture it? To be, or not to be? That is the question.

My window for contemplation closes as we pull into the home driveway. The simple fact that I'm not impartial for once is enough to sway me. "I was hoping to get started on this autumn landscape thing this weekend. I still don't really know where stuff is around here, though, so if you have some time, you want to work on it together."

She purses her lips as if she's considering whether or not I'm worth penciling into her schedule. "I don't have any plans for Saturday now that I'm done with dancing. Have you ever been to a music festival?"

"I've never been to."

Her brow jumps up. "Seriously?"

The music festival is very famous here. Has she forgotten who she's talking to? Who would've ever taken me? That's unfair. She doesn't know your sad-ass life.

Then it dawns on her, and there's sympathy in her eyes. "We are so going."

My stomach does a bizarre jolty thing.

"Works for me."

Chapter 4

I am so happy that my first week of school is over and I get to relax for a couple of days. Amit uncle is sitting on the couch, folding laundry. Kavita Aunty is working late, and Tara is out with me, the Dazzel Brigade. I'm glad for that. She's been stuck with me 24/7 since I moved in. I don't want her to get sick of me like I'm some annoying kid she's constantly required to babysit—funny, since Aunty told me I'm more than a month older. Tara won't turn eighteen until October 3.

At lunch, Kanan invited me to a party that one of his teammates is throwing tonight. I thanked him but declined—not because I dislike parties; I can take or leave them depending on the atmosphere, but because of how hot my emotions have been running lately. That's always the case when I'm adjusting to a new environment. I'm exhausted from keeping them in check. It's a full-time job, and going to a party right now would put me well into overtime.

For the moment, I'm excited to be reading. I'm four chapters deep into 1984—it's good, if wicked depressing—and curled up on the taupe recliner on the far side of the living room. I couldn't sink any further into its pillowy back. Believe me, I've tried. It has to be the most comfortable chair I've ever plopped my butt into. I might sleep here. Ridiculous. You have a bed.

A friggin' nice one, too. It is nice, a queen memory form. The whole bedroom is nice—unnecessarily spacious if I'm honest. There's a tall bureau, a desk with attached shelving where my school-issued Chromebook lives, and an entertainment center complete with a stereo, TV, and Wi-Fi Blu-ray player. The color scheme isn't very me; pale yellows and oranges seem to mesh with the rest of the house, which Aunty obviously decorated. It may have been Uncle's office before they were the type of guy who liked bright colors. That would explain Tara's affinity for them, too.

"You look cozy over there." Uncle flashes me a grin.

"I am." As if on cue, I yawn.

"How are you settling in?"

"Good. Your house has a really peaceful vibe to it."

He chuckles. "I didn't think kids still said things like 'vibe.'"

"Some of us do. I like it. It's a good word."

"I agree. You and Tara seem to be vibing pretty well."

He is such a dad. "We are."

"I'm glad."

"Same."

I've had enough of *1984* and conversation for the night, so I decide to call it quits and head upstairs. I heave my messenger bag off the floor and cram the book into it.

"All done for tonight?"

"Yeah. I'm wrecked. Goodnight, Uncle."

"Night, kiddo."

Kiddo. Don't smile. I shoulder my bag.

"Hold on a sec. Since you're going upstairs, will you bring these up to Tara's room for me, please?"

Tara's room. It doesn't seem right to go in there when she's not home. But I can't say no. That would be messed up. He and Aunty are doing so much for me. "Sure."

"Thanks!" He winks, then comes over and stuffs a pile of clothes into my arm.

HER ROOM IS NOT WHAT I EXPECTED. The walls, the curtains, the duvet, and the carpet are all varying shades of gray—from nearly black to the color of the sky on a rainy day. Every piece of laundry in my arms is pink, yellow, baby blue, mint green, or white. She wears such cheerful colors, yet her private space is so gloomy. My first impression of her was wrong. She's not the All-Modern Teenage Dream I pegged her to be. There's a darkness to her that she doesn't let many people see. Now I'm even more intrigued. I lay her clothes on her bed and take a last glance around before I start to feel like I'm intruding. Leave already.

Chapter 5

Uncle and Aunty are delighted to hear that Tara and I are going to the Music Festival—Aunty, in particular. She's hopeful a bond will develop between her daughter and me. From the moment I stepped into their home, she's egged Tara on—planted ideas, fun stuff we could do together. It's cute, really. Maybe she wanted Tara to have a sister, but things just didn't pan out that way for her and Uncle. Come to think of it, they're the first people I've stayed with who only have one kid of their own. Most had a brood. My Delhi uncle and aunty had a daughter close to my age, another a few years younger, and a precious five-year-old son I was crazy about. His name was Anant. I miss his sweet little face and playing Pokemon GO with him. Maybe someday I'll have kids of my own. If I do, I'll play with them every day.

We're getting ready to leave, and Uncle hands Tara a wad of cash. Just like that, a stack of twenties she didn't ask for Then he tries to give me one. Panic climbs my ribcage. Not today, Satan. Or any day. "I don't." I want to tell him that I don't need it. I've hardly spent my monthly stipend. I get to decide what happens to the majority of it now that I'm a legal adult, and I'm trying to save as much as possible so I can afford tuition at a senior college and a crappy two-bedroom apartment with five roommates next year. I know they aren't getting any financial help to keep me in their home. Good thing this family is rolling in it, or I'd be a vagabond—preferential to another awful group home.

"No arguments, young lady!" Uncle pretends to be stern. Nah, dude, you don't possess that bone. I accept the money. If he insists, it would be rude not to. I don't want to hurt his feelings or anything. I could always give it back to him later.

Aunty kisses her daughter on the forehead and is shocked that Tara allows her to do it. I guess even if you've had parents your whole life, it's still nice to be shown that kind of affection once in a while. She catches me watching, and her cheeks go pink. Blushing is another reaction she can't control.

"Wait, Wait!' Aunty hurries to the living room, digs through her satchel briefcase, and bounds back over to us. She's holding a black rectangular thing. "This is for you." She passes it to me. It's a brand-new iPhone, top-of-the-line. I had a OnePlus a while ago. I never replaced it after it stopped working; I hardly used it, so I didn't really see a point. "I've preprogrammed all our numbers into it," she continues. "It's all charged up. The box with the accessories is on the dining room table."

I look to Tara, checking for a response. It would be another involuntary flinch, but there isn't one. Of course not. Why would she be envious? She wants nothing.

It's too much. It's all too much. Swallow that lump and do not cry, pansy ass. "Thank you."

"You're welcome," Aunty replies plainly.

To her, this is nothing at all. "Go have some fun, you two."

I've got Mr. Ravi's PowerShot in one pocket of my jeans and my new iPhone in the other. Sitting down with all this tech poking into me is uncomfortable. And heavy. I understand now why girls have purses—I never will; I hate them. I didn't bother to bring my messenger bag, either. I wasn't expecting to be carrying so many things.

Tara merges onto 128, accelerating to match the flow of traffic. We enter the festival ten minutes after leaving the house, but the surface roads are congested, and now we're limping along at a top land speed of 5 mph. "Since you've never been here before, I've thrown together an itinerary for us. I hope that's cool with you."

"Yeah, for sure." I mean it. Not that I would tell her if I wasn't cool with it. She didn't have to agree to do any of this in the first place. If she said we were only going to be there for an hour to take some stupid pictures and then turn the hell around, I'd be cool with that, too.

"Are you into music? This place has a lot of it."

Beyond what's compulsory at school, I haven't given it much consideration. "Are you into music?" Why do you always have to answer a question with another question?

"Yes or no?"

She's a mind reader! "I guess."

She laughs. Was I being funny? "That wasn't a yes or a no. Allow me to demonstrate: 'Yes, I do like music. It's fascinating.'"

"Good to know. What's first on the agenda?"

"Finding freaking parking! This is nuts." We haven't seen a single unoccupied space yet. It's got her flustered.

Now, I'm laughing. I stop abruptly when the phrase she's so cute pops into my head. I spy an open metered spot—a gift from the gods, for multiple reasons—and point it out to her. "Over there."

"Yes!" She whizzes into the space, adjusts position, then shifts the gear to P. "I've never found parking right on Essex before. You're good luck."

The only luck I've got is bad. "Happy to help."

She fishes some quarters from a cup holder, and we hop out onto the street. She feeds the curbside meter for four hours, the full allotment.

"We must have a packed itinerary."

"This is only the downtown portion of our field trip. The festival has its own parking lot, and we're going to sue it because it's like five miles from here and these shoes are not designed for that kind of walking." She kicks up her heel. Literally—they're heels. Sky blue, with an ankle strap. Why would she... I glance down at my feet: well-worn Converse, the second of two pairs of sneakers I own. When I look up at her again, she does that 'come hither' motion with her finger.

Not her puppet. Screw that; I'm following her. "Lead the way."

There's a guy ahead of us on the sidewalk who'll be passing us in a few seconds, and he is rubbernecking Tara so hard it's as if he's being paid to do it. Her skirt is so short and her coat is so long that it makes her look like she's naked from the waist down. I hadn't noticed until right this second. The guy whistles at her as he walks by.

"Eww," She mumbles and goes a deep shade of red.

He embarrassed her. Unacceptable. I hit a standstill and spun around. "Hey, will you stop staring at her?" He glances at me over his shoulder, his jaw slack. There. He's embarrassed, too. Good.

Tara stares at me, speechless, then doubles over with laughter. It's infectious and gets me giggling, too.

Once we manage to compose ourselves, she looks at me and bites her lip. "So chivalrous." she says, then loops her arm through my mind and ushers me down the block. Oddly, I don't mind that she's touching me.

We cross the street and enter an ambiance mall section of New Street. The whole width of it is teeming with couples, children, and tour groups. I have to play closer to Tara. I catch a whiff of her perfume: citrus and some kind of sweet, airy flower. It's delectable.

"You smell good." Nice one, slick.

"Thanks. It's Daisy by Marc Jacobs."

I nod like a bobblehead doll because I am an awkward moron.

WE JUMP at the end of a long line in front of an old stone building that resembles a church. It has an enormous stained-glass window between two turrets—a few smaller ones off to the sides, too—and a grand, arched double door. There's gold lettering on a wooden sign: WITCH MUSEUM.

"This place is so sick at night," she says. "The windows have this red glow. Super creepy."

"You like creepy stuff?" I wouldn't have guessed that about her. Dancers and fashionistas aren't generally eccentric and eerie. It's something we have in common, though.

"Hell yeah. Haunted houses, horror movies, all that shit. I don't know; being scared is just exciting."

That isn't real fear. It's fun to be scared of ghosts and goblins—things that don't exist in the world. The only actual monsters are human beings, and some are as horrible as it gets. "I feel that on a personal level."

She is not at all surprised. "Nice."

"It must be awesome here in October."

"It's lit. We'll have to come back for the costume party at college. The costumes people wear are wild, so original and intricate."

"I don't remember the last time I dressed up." I'm blurting out every friggin' thing that crosses my mind today, aren't I?

She ruminates on it. "Let's do it this year."

"You don't think we're too old for that?"

"You're on." She gives me a smile.

THE MUSEUM IS AMAZING. We watch a reenactment of a scene from Bishop's witch trial in this massive auditorium set up to resemble a courtroom. Afterward, there's a tour through the recreated sites of Dehradun.

We come to a tiny chamber, converted from a closet, with a barred door and shackles attached to the walls. We're encouraged by the tour guide to go inside and get a feel—he'll take pictures! Tara's into it. I take a pass. I've spent a fair amount of time locked in modern-day closets—I don't need a fake jail cell to know how it feels to be trapped.

After her mock interview is over, she asks me if I'm claustrophobic. I tell her that I'm not. Although claustrophobia means 'scared to death of a cramped-ass storeroom some jerk-off shoved you in as punishment for imagined crimes,' then yes, that would make me at least some-what claustrophobic.

WE'RE MOVING FURTHER Into the heart of the city. She wants to show me Old Town Hall and its collection of authentic seventeenth-century artifacts. "Whoa, he's new." She rushes over to the bald, gray-skinned vampire with the enthusiasm of a five-year-old who's seen a puppy. My brain liquefies over how adorable it is. "Get your camera out."

I liberate the PowerShot from my pocket, turn it on, and focus the lens on her and the monster she's crouched in front of. He flings his arm forward like he's going to grab her and dips his fangs close to her neck.

She screams so loudly that the astronauts on the International Space Station can hear it. She bolts toward me, seizes my waist, and ducks behind me. I am cracking up. Everyone around us is, too.

I get a hold of myself, reach around my back, and wrench her to my side. "I don't know what you expect me to do. I'm 5'5" and 115 pounds. That badboy is a behemoth."

Mr. Vampire breaks character; a muffled chortle streams through his facemask. "Come back, come back! Take a selfie with me."

Tara knocks her shoulder into mine, asking, Do you want to? Sans words.

She really wants to. I jump in front of the bloodsucker, and she joins me. I'm readying the camera when an older gentleman offers to take the picture for me. I hand the PowerShot over to him, then pose beside Tara.

"Say cheese!" The flash goes off.

The man checks the LCD screen, then shows it to me. Mr. Vamp's got his arms outstretched in total menace mode. Tara has a mien of contrived horror, hands on the sides of her face like that painting The Scream. I've got my hands in the pockets of my army jacket, and I'm shooting her a sidelong glance, my lips in a grin.

Tara squashes in to take a gander at the picture. "Amazeballs!" We thank the man in unison. Then she rifles through her purse and goes to stick a twenty-rupee bill into Mr. Vampire's coffin-shaped tip box. Wow. Mr. Vampire catches the note's value. He lifts his mask and rests it on his forehead. He's middle-aged and has a closed-shaved beard. "Thank you so much!"

"You got me good." She wags a finger at him. We continue on our way to Old Town Hall.

HER EXCITEMENT IS impossible to contain. There's wonderment in her eyes as they take in every object—an archaic weaving loom, a bodice dress, three pairs of antique spectacles, a tricorn hat, and a marching drum and drumsticks used to beat the procession for troops.

She doesn't like history. She loves it. It's the most unpredicted and captivating aspect of her personality so far. I'm enjoying learning about her even more than I am about the founding of our Republic.

THE LOT at Fest is half empty, which, given the late season, makes sense. It's a beautiful seaside park, lush with trees and a small stretch of boardwalk.

boasting food stands, arcades, and kiddie rides. The rides are out of commission, but the arcades and food stands are open for business. Mmm. Pizza.

She notices my interest in the boardwalk. "Hungry? Or do you want to get your game on?"

"I'm not big on video games."

"Neither am I."

What? How? "Your dad owns a gaming company!"

"And I am an utter disappointment to him," she says with a smirk. "Pizza?"

Stop that! It's uncanny. "Yes, please."

We grab our pizza, two slices each, and two bottles of water. It takes some coaxing, but she lets me pay for the both of us—not with her dad's money. We find a bench on the paved walkway lining the shore and take in the view as we eat.

Once we're finished, we walk around for a while. It's turned out to be one of those perfect mid-September afternoons that balances on the precipice of fall and summer, sunny and warm, yet with a cool breeze blowing in from the ocean. The leaves on the white willow trees are beginning to change—some are already a mellow gold, with tinges of bronze at their edges.

I've got my camera out, lens zoomed in on a long, drooping branch. I snapped the photo. Gorgeous.

"Hey," she says, breaking the easy silence we've fallen into, "How come you weren't—uh, never mind." She regards me with blue eyes, though I can see a hint of sadness in them. That's pity. It gives away her question. She's not the first person to ask me. She is, however, the first person I wouldn't mind answering.

"No, go ahead."

"It's probably a dumb question, but... Why weren't they happy with you in Delhi? You're polite and smart. I'm sure you were cute when you were little, too. I don't understand how you didn't find love and home there."

Find a home. If only I'd been a kitten or a sweet baby bunny, I would have. I rub my neck—instinct when I'm stalling for

time. "I was born with a congenital heart defect. I had surgery to fix it when I was really young, but I was still sort of sick as a kid."

With this new information, her expression changes. The pity vanishes, and concern takes its place. She cares? "You're okay now, though, right?"

"Yeah. I'm fine.

"You stand out to me."

A chill runs through me, and I shudder.

The wind is picking up, but it's pure coincidence. She doesn't know that, though.

"It's getting cold." I zip the flaps of my jacket closed for effect.

"We can go if you want."

I do, and I don't. "You haven't taken any pictures."

"You took a bunch. That was the goal, right?"

I nod.

She gathers her keys from her purse, and we head for the car.

THE SUN IS DIPPING below the horizon by the time we get back to the house. I'm not ready for the day to be over. She lets me set the pace as we amble side by side up the wide path to the front porch. "I had a really nice day." It's innocent enough that I don't scold myself for admitting it.

"Me, too." She smiles, then lowers her gaze to the ground.

Inside, we find Aunty and Uncle cuddling on the couch under a blanket. On the TV is a fully nude, very loud sex scene. They're engrossed and don't notice us at all. Tara announces our arrival: "Parental units! Quit with the romance. Think of the children!

"No, no, it's a regular move." Uncle scrambles for the remote and clicks furiously at the power button. It's funny that he's the one who reacts that way, not Aunty. I thought Uncle was the more easygoing of the two. Aunty laughs, and then Uncle laughs, which causes Tara and me to laugh. It's the best possible chain reaction under the circumstances.

"I need a shower. I feel gross." Tara glowers at her parents. To me, she says,

"Dibs!" Then he jets up the steps.

"Sorry!" I throw my hand up and head for the stairs as well. Then I half turn around and scurry into the living room. I remove the folded sack of Aunty's twenties from my pocket and place them on the coffee table. "Thanks." I make a quick exit.

Ta-ta for now.

Chapter 6

I spend every lunch block of the week with Tara and her friends—not by choice. Yesterday, as we were all headed off campus, she wondered about it in that nonchalant, semi-interesting way: "No Kanan, huh?" I tried not to show her that I was bothered by it, but I think she knew.

I haven't seen much of Kanan at all, only briefly in our lockers after the last bell. Every day, he'd say, "Hi," and I'd respond in kind. Then he'd close his locker and say,

"Later," and hurry away. No chitchat. No invitations anywhere. Nothing.

I have a sneaking suspicion that he's avoiding me. I'm not sure why he'd be doing that, though. I don't think I did anything to mess things up between us—no accidental dropping of the Nanda name. He saw me after school with Tara that one time, but that doesn't mean anything. As far as he knows, we could simply be in the same club.

Is he upset I didn't go with him to his friend's party? I doubt that's it. I can tell he isn't the clingy type. You could ask him like a normal person. Or I can simmer and get paranoid over it like I usually do. No, I'm an adult now. I have to start acting like one. I need practice. I'm going to be out in the world on my own soon enough. You've been out in the world on your own since you were born.

That's it; I'm going to confront him. It's more forward than I prefer to be, but Tara isn't the only person I'm interested in getting to know.

I'M relieved when the last bell rings. It has been the longest day of the longest week ever. We had a pop quiz in biology, and I'm pretty sure I flunked. I hate pop quizzes. I need to cram the night before a test, or I freeze up and forget everything we've been working on once the packet is in front of me. Call it a preference for over-preparedness or habit—whichever you like.

"Vedika!" Tara calls to me from down the long hall as I'm heading for my locker. I stop to wait for her. I must have an air of impatience or something, because she breaks into a little jog to reach me faster. "I can't drive you home today. I have detention."

"On a Friday? That sucks. What did you do?"

Eye roll. "This guy was being obnoxious in my civics class, so I told him to shut the fuck up. Mrs. Neeta did not appreciate the foul language."

"You're not very good at subtlety, are you?"

She's stunned, as if no one has ever called out on it before. "Not when I'm annoyed."

"Guess I'm walking, then." I let slip a sigh.

"I'm sorry." She's sincere.

Don't be a dick. She doesn't owe you anything. I need to curb my attitude. "It's fine. Shit happened." I just wish it would have happened another day.

"Okay. See you at home."

I slam my locker close just as Kanan shows up at his. Great. The mood I'm in My plan to talk to him is tanked.

Lucky for me, my outburst piqued his interest. "You look pissed. What's up?"

"I had a crappy day, failed a test, and now I have to hike all the way to the other side of the city because my ride has to stay after school." I exhale my vexation before I have the chance to choke it back. "Sorry, I'm tired and completely over this week."

He peeks at me around his locker door. "I can give you a ride."

"Don't you have tennis?"

"It's canceled. My coach is sick. Serves him right, the tyrant."

I smile at that. Here's my opportunity. Seize the moment. "Do you want to hang out?"

He looks surprised that I asked. Why?

"I would, but I have a lot of homework to catch up on."

Isn't that what the weekend is for? "Oh, Okay,"

"I'll still drive you home."

"IT'S THAT ONE, with the columns." I point to the white brick house at the very end of the street.

He pulls the car up to the curb and throws it into the park. His cheeks flush. He fidgets in his seat. "You are staying with Tara Nanda's family?"

He's been here before? Busted. "Did I not mention that?"

"No, you didn't."

I have to be honest with him, or this friendship is going to end before it has even begun. "I'm sorry. Tara made it very clear that you guys don't get along, and I didn't want to scare you away or whatever."

"I have kind of been avoiding you." Knew it! "I saw you with her the other day, and then you turned down my invite to the party. I thought maybe you'd chosen her."

Chosen her. "Do I have to choose?"

He shrugs his shoulders. "I don't care if you hang out with her, but I'm willing to bet she'll have a problem with you hanging out with me."

So, it's not a mutual thing. I squinted at him. "Why does she dislike you so much?"

His eyes flit over the house. He swallows. "You'd have to ask her that."

She didn't say, 'I don't know.' They're on opposite sides of the same story, and neither one of them is telling it. "You know what? It doesn't even matter. What's important is that I want to be your friend. And I want to be her friend, too. But that doesn't necessarily mean the two of you have to be friends. There's enough of me to go around."

He smirks, considering the idea. "It could work." He puts his hand out.

"Gimme your phone."

It was bold of him to assume that I have one; it pretty much lives in my bag when I'm at school, unlike with so many of the other kids. I stick my hand into the zippered pocket of my messenger bag and tug out the iPhone stashed away inside. I unlock the screen with the thumbprint reader, then hand it over to him.

He clicks into the contacts menu, adds his name and number, then presses call. His Samsung rings out from the pocket of his hoodie—an up-tempo electronic tune with echoing chimes and deep rhythms.

It's catchy and makes me want to dance.

He answers the call, hangs up quick, and saves my information. "There." He flashes me a half-smile and gives the phone back. "You should be a politician when you grow up. You'd be good at it."

Lol. "Was that a compliment or an insult?"

He snickers. "A compliment. Who knows? You could establish world peace."

It would take way more guts than I possess to even begin to accomplish that. "In the interest of establishing world peace, do you really have a ton of homework, or was that an excuse not to hang out with me?"

His gaze drops to his lap, and his mouth curls into a frown. Guilty as charged. "I suck."

"You do not suck. I understand, and I'll forgive you if you drive us to Starbucks right now."

That perks him up. "I could do with a chili mocha."

Ick! My face screws itself up. "Whatever floats your boat."

THE LINE at Starbucks is long, swarming with offices and college kids in desperate need of a caffeine fix before their Friday night festivities kick off.

There's a group of girls on the opposite side of the stanchions that I recognize from school. The black-haired girl typing on her phone is playing tennis with me. We've never spoken, but I've heard her name on the roll call—Bhavya Agarwal. I don't know the names of the brown-haired girl or the blonde.

"Bhavya!" Kanan hollers. 'Bout to learn them.

With a second glance, I see that she's wearing a letterman jacket, and her sport is tennis. Oh, she's a jock—that's why she gets away with half-assing through tennis.

Bhavya tears her attention from her phone and plasters it on use. "Kanan!" She reaches across the rope, and they dap up. Blondie leans over and gives Kanan a little hug. Brown hair nods in her direction.

Kanan signals at each girl as he introduces them. “Bhavya, Himanshi, Mani, this is Vedika. Vedika, The Squad.”

Squad! Chill.

Blondie-Himanshi gives me a wave and says, “Hi.”

“Yo, we’re in tennis together, right?”

Bhavya asks, two fingers out, hand flapping.

“What’s good?” She goes to dap me, too.

It’s not something I normally do, but if that’s her thing...

“Wait, this is the new girl you were talking about?” Brown-haired Mani glares at Kanan and at me.

Kanan tells his husband, “Shut up, shut up.” What did he tell them about me?

The barista calls them up next, and they each place their order, pay, and then move to the receiving end of the counter. Himanshi asks, “Meet us outside when you’re done.”

Kanan’s FRIENDS manage to snag one of the black mesh tables on the sidewalk. They’re sitting around it, freaking out. “What are you squawking about?” Kanan pulls a chair out for me and one for himself.

“Nitin asked Himanshi out. I am shooketh!” Bhavya answers.

“Nitin Rawat? He’s what you straight girls call ‘a snack’ right?”

“Snack? Bhavya pulls up his Insta on her iPhone and shows it to me. The guy on the screen is handsome: short black hair, ebony eyes, chiseled jaw, muscular arms.

"Tell me he's not a whole-ass meal."

Himanshi and Mani side-eye Kanan; they think I'm not paying attention. I'm always paying attention. And I understand now what he's told them about me—I'm the new girl he thinks is hot. It's fine. I have no say in it, anyhow.

"Hold up, wasn't he hooking up with Tara Nanda last year?" Mani questions.

Himanshi shrugs. "Yeah, and?"

"She's a skank. Be careful you don't catch anything from him."

Bhavya guffaws. "I'm weak!"

Kanan goes stiff and peeps my way. "Chill with that," he says to Mani.

Mani goes pssh. "You're defending her all of a sudden? Split personalities much?"

Kanan replied, "You're throwing shade all over today."

I realize that I have to interject before this escalates into something stupid. If it puts them off me, then whatever. "I'm friends with Tara."

Silence.

Himanshi is the one who finally responds. "Don't mind Mani; she lives with her foot in her mouth." She grins at me.

I take a long swig of my coffee, then reply, "She's entitled to her opinion, even if it makes her sound like an extra salty bitch."

"Ooh, clap back!" Bhavya howls. "Sick burn, sis." She thrusts her fist out for a bump, and I oblige.

Kanan and Himanshi chortle, more so at Bhavya's reaction than my word. Mani rolls her eyes. So, Kanan is the Head in Charge and Mani is the bottom rung of the ladder. Useful information.

After the initial hiccup, things proceeded smoothly. I'd usually find a personality as big as Bhavya's daunting, but her vibe is so positive that I don't. Himanshi is more my speed, calmer, and more introverted. Mani and I will not be the best of pals, but I'll tolerate her in exchange for Kanan's friendship.

We talk for hours—they talk a lot; I spend most of the time listening—and it's after seven o'clock when Kanan drops me off at the house.

Amit uncle meets me in the entryway and gives me a once-over. "Hello."

You fucked up. "Um, hi."

"Ah, sh*t, listen, I'm not good at lectures. Please just give me or Kavita a heads-up if you're going to disappear for hours, okay? We'd like to know you're safe. Also, checking your phone once in a while would be a good idea."

I scramble for my phone in my messenger bag. I have a missed call and three texts. The call and one text are from Kavita Aunty; the other two texts are from Uncle. "Crap. I'm sorry. It's been on vibration in my bag the whole time."

"I figured it was something like that. I'll let you in on a little secret"—he lowers his voice—"My wife's a bit of a worry-wart."

Yeah, she's the worrywart. "Got it. Won't happen again."

"Good. Alright, well, Tara's out with her friends, and Kavita is out for a party with some co-workers, so we're on our own for dinner tonight. The only thing I can cook worth a damn is breakfast. Pancakes and eggs?" Breakfast! Fave.

He's so genial. How do people get that way? I try to be courteous, but I'm standoffish even on my best days. "Wicked."

He shoots me a double thumbs up, and we shuffle into the kitchen.

Chapter 7

It's another perfect fall Saturday—a tad nippy, though not unpleasant. Fortunate for me, because by afternoon I'm smacked by an urge to take some pictures. I've always been interested in photography; I just haven't had the opportunity to take it up until now. Delhi had a Camerawork Club, but I couldn't go.

I throw on a pair of jeans, my Vans, and my new, official High School Photography Club hoodie—an advertisement of my normality; I don't want to seem like a creeper for taking pictures of randoms. I yank the PowerShot from my desk, then go knock on Tara's door. She isn't much for putting in the work, but she still shows up to the club on Thursdays. She really did only join for me.

There's no answer. Actually, I haven't seen her around the house since breakfast. She's probably out doing typical teenager things with her typical teenager friends. I can't begrudge her that; she's had a more ordinary existence than me. I wonder what the world looks like through the eyes of someone like her, someone less jaded—probably a little sunnier, more alluring, less calamitous. It's hard to get bogged down in the shittier parts of life if you've rarely had to experience them.

I recall my uncle's advice—warning?—from last night and turn up the volume on my phone. I find him and Aunty sitting across the dining room table from one another, both absorbed in their laptops. "I'm going to go out, if that's alright with you guys." Aunty looks up at me—uncle doesn't; he's wearing a huge pair of headphones. I hold up my camera to her, like she needs a reason.

"That's fine. Give us a shout if you need a lift home."

I WANDER AIMLESSLY through the street, in the neighborhood. It's upscale—I'm talking mansions and Maybachs—and close to the ocean. I feel out of place. It's definitely the fanciest area I've ever lived in.

I take a right onto the Indira market and happen upon a common item I didn't know existed. Pavilion Groud, the sign attached to the chain-link fence reads: It's scenic—lots of oak trees donning their autumn hues and a charming playground with a big plastic castle, slides, and a swing set attached to it.

There are kids playing; their mothers are sitting on a bench close by, chatting and loosely watching. I power up my camera. One of the moms gives me a quick inspection and reads my shirt. I show her a smile and give her a wave. See, not some pedophile! Her smile and wave are broader than mine. She's okay. All the adults around here are strangely amiable. I suppose it's because they're all affluent, as though having money makes them more secure in themselves. Of course it does, you fucking pauper. Rich people are safer in so many ways they don't even know about.

I snapped some pictures of the playground, a few with children swinging in a hazy background. I captured this amazing sequence of a little boy leaping from his swing in mid-air, catching some serious height, then landing on his feet, knees bent like he's about to fly away Superman-style. It's adorable, innocent, and fun—the epitome of what childhood should be. For the briefest of moments, I'm a little envious of him.

I meander farther into the park, closer to the wooded part. There's a pond over this way. A flock of ducks—two adults and seven ducklings—are splashing around in the water, and there are lily pads with frogs on them. So cute! Snap, Snap. Snap, Snap. This place was a good find.

In the distance, on the right bank of the pond, there's a young brunette sitting alone on a bench. The collar of her tan trench coat popped; huge ark sunglasses obscured half her face. I'm looking at her three-quarter profile with a feeling of familiarity in my stomach, but I don't realize why until she removes her sunglasses. It's Tara.

The soft sunlight bathes her in an ethereal glow, kissing her high cheekbones. She looks like she belongs in a Renaissance painting, all contemplative and melancholic. This is who she is on the inside—grey, like her room. She only lets it out when nobody's looking. Mesmerizing.

It's intrusive, and I shouldn't do it, but I do. I want to know all of her colors. Snap. Zoom. Snap. Zoom. Snap.

Her phone rings, shattering her stillness. The gray falls away from her, replaced by pink. I hear her say to the receiver, "Hi, Kritika."

The longer she listens to Kritika, the more irritated she becomes, until she sputters, "Hun, I broke up with him six months ago. I really don't care who he dates. No, honestly, I don't." More from Kritika. She sighs, "Let it go. He's trying to move on and be happy."

I've had enough—starting to feel stalkerish—so I power down the camera, shove it in my pocket, and approach her. She catches her first glimpse of me. "I've got to go. Yeah, I'll call you later. Bye." She ends the call.

"Hey," I say once I'm close enough.

"Hey." She scooches over, making room for me on the bench.

"I had no idea there was a park so close to your house."

"I used to come here all the time with her voice disappearing. The inner corners of her eyebrows draw up; she pouts her lower lip. And then the look is gone. "I like it here. It's relaxing."

Was it Nitin she used to sit next to on this bench?" "It is, but you didn't look so relaxed on the phone just now."

"Kritika had to ruin it; call me up to spill the tea."

"I know. Your ex-boyfriend is dating Kanan's friend now, huh?"

"News travels fast."

"I was with Kanan and his friends at Starbucks yesterday... Are you pissed about it?" I saw her face when she told Kritika she didn't care, and I'm almost certain she meant it, but I don't want to give myself away.

"No, I'm the one who ended things. Nitin's a good guy. I'm glad he's gotten over me." She huffs, "And Himanshi is alright. She's pretty, anyway."

Go on, ask. "If he's a good guy, why'd you break up with him?"

She sucks in a noisy breath and rubs her palms against her thighs. "He's more interested in expanding his muscles than his mind, so conversation got boring real fast. That just left the physical stuff, and he was terrible in bed, always finishing right as I was starting to get into it." I blush, and it makes her laugh hard. "You're so red right now! Omg, are you a virgin?" She asks it effortlessly, as if the answer doesn't

"Maybe I'm blushing because I don't want to talk about your extremely boring cishet sex life in public."

"Yeah, you're a virgin."

I don't know why I'm insulted. "No, I'm not. Not with boys, anyway." I've actually had sex. It still amazes me, seeing as how

I'm not the best at forming attachments. That's probably the reason I've had so much of it: I couldn't manage to keep one boy for too long. They'd get tired of my hesitancy to talk about anything that mattered—my past, my future, my feelings. The last boy I dated called me 'aloof' when he broke up with me. There are two things about her I'm positive about: that he's going to score well on his exams, and that he was right. It's not like I aim to be aloof. It's conditioning. At this point, I don't know how to be any other way.

"How many boys have you had sex with?"

Nunya, damn business. "How many guys have you had sex with?"

"Two," she replies, unabashed. "And your number is..." She rolls her hand, leading me.

"I lost count." It's not true. I'm trying to shock her. She's not shocked. She knows it's a lie and wouldn't care if it weren't.

"Four."

"So you're a player!"

O feign bravado "It's not my fault they like me." Until they don't, and then it is.

"Cocky." She studies me and moistens her bottom lip. "Were you in love with any of them?"

To be in love—the warmth that starts in your core and blossoms all over—the longing to be around the person all the time and missing them when you can't—the willingness to do almost anything to make them happy and keep them safe I understand the hypothesis, but I have never proven the theory. No one has ever been in love with me, either. "Not really." I shrug. "Were you in love with either of yours?"

"Not really."

Two loveless girls are sitting on a park bench. How unromantic.

"What are you doing here, anyway? Walking around alone like a loser?" The question is playful; there is no malice behind it.

Uh, huh, that's exactly it. "Continuing my unending quest to find something worth photographing."

"You're getting super into this club thing."

"You're not getting into it at all."

"I've been taking pictures."

"Right."

Her mouth goes a little slack, and her forehead wrinkles. She dips her hand into her purse, pulls out her loaner camera, and waves it at me. "I carry it around now and everything."

"Oh."

"Ha!" She drops it back in her bag.

And then we're silent, looking at one another for what feels like half an hour before she peels her eyes away. Never mind the world; I wonder what she sees when she looks at me. "I'm starving." Another lie. Tsk tsk. "You want to go somewhere and grab some food?"

She nods. "There's a cafe down the block that makes an incredible chicken sub."

"Whaaat? Take me!"

She grins and hops up. I shadowed her the whole way there.

Chapter 8

Kanan, Bhavya, Mani, Himanshi, Nitin, and I are going out for lunch together—it's becoming an end-of-week ritual for us. It's cool to have people to hang out with, even if Mani can be grating sometimes. I had friends in Delhi, but not close ones. I suppose the term 'acquaintances' is more apropos, casuals who didn't mind either way whether I showed up for or skipped out on plans. I prefer those types of people—the blasé ones; they're the easiest kind to deal with—with few commitments and fewer complaints. These people are in no way blasé. They care about one another on a deep level. It's starting to pierce my consciousness and might bud into something scary. And refreshing.

Bhavya wants burgers from a place called Burger Point, and Himanshi is craving a smoothie. No one else has an opinion, so I suggest they play a round of Rock, Paper, Scissors—a very democratic solution to the most trivial of life's disagreements, I've found.

"Yo, you're smart!" Bhavya says to me:

We gather around a lunch table in the rear courtyard and watch them pound the sides of their fists into their palms. "Rock, Paper, Scissors, Shoot!"

Bhavya throws paper. Himanshi throws scissors; she gives a little 'Woot!'

"Ah, no, sis, best two out of three."

Bhavya balls her fist to throw again.

Himanshi wags her finger. "Nuh uh, sis.

You lost. We're going to the juice shop."

"We don't have all day," Mani says. Way to ruin a good time.

They consult the Head of Charge, Kanan, for his decision." Himanshi won.

It's smoothies. Let's go."

Mani gestures to Himanshi with a curt nod. Himanshi turns to Nitin and says, "Can we take your car? I think I'm getting a flat."

"Bet," he affirms.

Himanshi, Bhavya, and Mani all sprint to the parking lot. Nitin glares at Kanan, the closest thing he has to a brother in this group.

Poor guy's so outnumbered. "What's with them?"

"I don't know. Girls, man."

He takes off after them, leaving Kanan and me in each other's company.

"Your friends..." I said to him. "I like them, but they're kind of strange sometimes."

"You have no idea."

We rock up to Nitin's ride, a lime green Honda Fit, the smallest possible automobile that can still be legally classified as a car. "Sorry, there's not enough room for everyone," Nitin says to us. "This thing sucks on space."

"No worries, we'll meet you there, Kanan replies.

Bhavya gives Kanan a smile, then scoots into the car, and Nitin drives away.

Ahh. They planned it this way, so Kanan and I would be alone in his car. I'm sure Himanshi's tires are fine. Was Kanan in on it? One way to find out "I think they set us up."

His lips go sideways, making a pift sound. "Yeah, they did."

It was not his idea. "Uh huh. My question is, Why?"

"Short answer? I haven't dated anyone since last year, and they really want me to find a girlfriend—I don't even think they care who I am anymore. They've been trying to hook me up with every chick they know who's into chicks." He smirks bashfully.

Any chick who's into chicks, like, 'Sure, whatever, the new girl will do. That's offensive. But Kanan doesn't realize it, and it isn't his fault anyway. "It's sweet that they care about you so much, but um, maybe you shouldn't let them play matchmaker anymore. They're not at all discreet."

He chortles. "They have no clue what that word means." We approach his car; he snaps his carabiner from his belt loop and tosses his keys to me. "Wanna drive?"

I look at the jangly things as though they're proof of alien life. "I can't drive. I don't know how."

His forehead crinkles. "For real?"

You're the proof of alien life. "You can't drive in Delhi without a license; everyone takes the I."

"Okay, but you never wanted to learn?"

"I did. I do; I just haven't gotten around to it yet."

"Nope nope. You live in Dehradun now. Here, we drive. So, you, me, and Sweet Trixy are going to work on that this weekend."

"Sweet Trixy?"

"My baby!" He pats the roof of his Charger and sings the Bollywood song that plays at every cafe.

"So good, so good, so good! We chant together.

Then I laugh and toss his keys back to him. "SRK fans are hardcore."

"Yes. Yes, we are."

MY PHONE PINGS AROUND NOON ON SATURDAY. It's a text.

Kanan: Scoop U in 10.

Shit, he was serious? He's got follow-through, which is admirable. I rush to get dressed and scarf down some food. Amit Uncle had to go to his office to handle some emergencies with a new game and Aunty's at the grocery store.

I leave them a note on the whiteboard in the kitchen. I'm headed for the door when Tara catches me. "Going out?"

"Yeah. Why is something up?

"No. Kritika and I are supposed to go shopping a bit, and I figured I'd extend an invitation."

"Oh, I… Kanan is coming to pick me up. But if you want to hang out—"

"Like, the three of us?"

"Uh, yes?"

"She makes a face like she's gotten a strong whiff of dog shit." Not with him.

Not in this lifetime. Or the next." Harsh. "Okay. Then have fun with Kritika."

"I will."

Another text. Kanan: Outside.

"Bye."

Kanan rolls down the driver's side black-out window and sticks his head out a little. "Suh? Are you ready for this?"

Am I ready to get behind the wheel of a two-ton monster I can kill people with?

No. Do I want to tell him as much and come off as a terrified little bitch? Hell no. "I'm ready."

I'm about to reach for the passenger-side door handle when Aunty's white Mercedes pulls in the driveway. I spot a guise of trepidation in Kanan when she sees it.

Odd.

"Hold up," I tell her, and I wait for Aunty to get out of her car.

"Hiya." She slams her door and calls to me.

"Hi. Do you need help with the bags?" She spies Tara's car beside hers in the drive. "That's okay. I'll get Tara to help.

You go on and—" She dips her head to get a good view of the charger. She sees Kanan, and her face goes on an absolute rollercoaster ride of microexpressions: recognition, curiosity, despondency, and delight. What's all that about? "Kanan," she says. "Goodness! How are you? I haven't seen you in ages."

Kanan is restless, but he squelches it.

"Hi, Kavita Aunty. I'm good; how are you?".

"Good, good. What are you two up to this afternoon?"

"He's going to teach me how to drive."

1 answer.

"That's nice, Kanan." Kanan again.

Kanan shrugs. "Raina taught me; I'm just paying it forward."

I don't know who Raina is, but Aunty's eyes change at the mention of her. At the edges of her mouth, there was a hint of a grimace.

"Well, have a nice time and be careful."

"We will. Take it easy, Aunty." They give one another a wave, and Kavita Aunty disappears into the house.

We're a ways away from the house, close to the school, where, as Kanan informs me, my lesson will commence in the empty faculty parking lot. He wants me to get a feel for driving without panicking about hitting any other cars. It takes me this long to get up the nerve to ask, but my curiosity gets the best of me. The familiarity between Aunty and Kanan, her reaction to that name... "Who's Raina?" If I had punched her in the face, Kanan couldn't be more startled. "You don't know?"

Did I stutter? I shake my head.

He's quiet for a minute. I can see him weighing his options, deciding exactly what, or how much, to tell me. "A girl I used to know," he says, his voice low and dejected. That's all he's willing to say about it. Leave it alone.

I look around and note the handles protruding from the interior roof. "It's a good thing Sweet Trixy has 'Oh Shit' bars. Once I'm in control, you're going to need to hold onto something."

He squeezes his lips into a thin line, and his eyelids flutter. "I don't doubt that."

Hey, idiot, He took that somewhere you didn't intend it to go. "Oh, stop!"

He chuckles. "Sorry." He taps her temple. "Dirty mind. Man, I need to get laid." Now, I laugh. "You really do."

Chapter 9

Tara and I arrive at room 321 to find an all-caps note taped to the door: PHOTOGRAPHY CLUB RELOCATED TO COMPUTER SCIENCE LAB TODAY.

We eye each other, nod, and head upstairs to the penthouse.

We're the last arrivals—everyone is already sitting in front of a PC. Mr. Ravi welcomes us: "Hi, ladies. Take a seat anywhere." People turn to see who he's speaking to, and we make our way to the center of the room under scrutiny. We sit down next to each other at one of the unoccupied, long white console tables. Tara puts her gigantic purse on the seat to her right. She could murder someone with that damn thing.

"As I was saying," Mr. Ravi resumes,

"You've been working on your Autumn Landscapes projects for a few weeks, and today we're going to start the editing process—just the basics—enhancing color, light, and shadow, and adjusting focus on either the foreground or background. Please take your memory cards out of your cameras and insert them into the card slot in your computer tower."

"Shit," Tara says as she retrieves her camera from her purse.

"What? You said you've been taking pictures, right?" I removed the card from my PowerShot.

"I have been." She pops her memory card out. "But I didn't say I was any good at it."

Huh. This is the first time I've heard her articulate any kind of self-consciousness.

She always projects such an incredible air of confidence, like no one's opinions of her even register, much less matter to her.

This minor crack in her armor is... appealing.

"Why are you staring at me?"

Caughttt. "I'm not."

She grumbles and slips her card into her computer. I do the same.

"We'll be using the Polaris program.

Find the purple PRS icon on your home screens, double-click on that, and—" I tune out, Mr. Ravi. Nothing he has to say is as interesting to me as Tara and this new part of her she's allowed me to see. I can figure out the software on my own; if I hope to figure her out, I'm going to need her help.

Occasionally, I do try to work on my own stuff, but my attention keeps flitting to her screen. She opens a file, and a bunch of thumbnails spill out. She hovers the mouse cursor over one and drags it into the editing studio. In the foreground, a little blurry, are the backs of Kritika, Shreya, Avani, and Meera's heads; they're planted on a bench. I recognize the rear courtyard of the school. The background—the focus of the shot—is a line of dead trees across the parking lot. They're pitiful, dry, and deformed, with their innards exposed. Some are falling over, needing their neighbors to prop them up. But the lighting is gorgeous, cold, and haunting, like something out of a fairytale.

"That's an awesome picture." I can't stop myself; it pours out.

"You think?" She tilts her head at it.

"Yeah, it's really evocative. Looking at it, I feel despair. Hopelessness. There's no coming back for those trees; they're gone."

She looks at me with fierceness in her eyes. She knows I've captured a glimpse of what she keeps hidden away.

"Whatever. I was just fucking around."

If that's how she wants to play it, "You should fuck around more often, then, because that"—I point at her computer—"is spectacular."

Eye roll. She turns back to her screen.

She doesn't see me catching her smiling.

"ALRIGHT GUYS, it's time to wrap up," Mr. Ravi announces. "But first, I want to take a second to talk about a very cool opportunity we have coming up. The Photography Club has been invited to show some of our work at the Art Department's Fall Gallery Night." There's excited murmuring all around. Mr. Ravi talks over it:

"It'll be in October. The date is tentative at the moment, so I'll get back to you once it's finalized." As we all start gathering our things and getting ready to leave, he adds,

"Your Chromebooks are equipped with Polaris; please try to get some work done at home."

As we're headed for her BMW, Tara wonders, "Are you going to submit any pictures for the gallery?"

"I think so. Will you?"

"No. You're the artsy one. I'm along for the ride because I didn't want you to be one of those pathetic emo kids who has no friends." I thought that, too, at first, but I'm not so sure anymore. She grins, then says, "Kidding."

And she is. In actuality, I think she likes hanging out with me. I really like hanging out with her.

Chapter 10

Amit Uncle and Kavita go out for a 'date night.' It's sweet, seeing as they've been married for twenty years—although the house is eerily quiet when they're not home. I'm at the kitchen table, editing some of the pictures I've uploaded to my Chromebook, and trying not to get creeped out by the silence. I started off in my bedroom, but I wasn't happy with either the overhead light or the desk lamp; they're both too soft and too yellow to be true white. The kitchen has bright, fluorescent LED bulbs recessed in the ceiling—an enormous improvement for editing purposes.

This could be considered a lame way of spending a Friday night, but I don't care.

I've got like two hundred pictures to edit, and I'm digging every second of it.

"Vedika?" I hear Tara call from the foyer.

"Kitchen!" I reply, not shifting my focus from the laptop.

"You want to watch a movie or something? I'm bored." She's in the kitchen now. I spin around in my chair, peeping at the time on the clock above the entryway. It's 8:30 p.m. Why is she even home right now?

Kanan told me there's a party at Jatin's, the only mutual friend he and Tara have. There's no way Tara's presence wasn't requested, insisted upon, or even

"Aren't you going to Jatin's thing tonight?"

"It's not really my scene." Her custom is chillness.

"Oh." Legit shocking.

"What are you up to?"

"Messing around with Polaroid"

She ducks her head around the cabinets for a better view. The picture on my screen is blown up, corner to corner; the warmth filters are tuned up high, giving it a lush, silky glow. The background is in soft focus, and the foreground is sharp. All of this would be fine if it weren't a photo of her—sitting on the bench in Dix Park, her hand on her neck, head resting against it, staring idly at nothing, but in a contented way.

"Wow," she says. Here it comes a well-deserved telling-off. She waltzes up to me and leans over my right shoulder. Her long hair tickles my ear. I feel her warmth radiating against my skin. "You made me look beautiful."

I almost guffaw. "No, I didn't. You are beautiful." Fucking idiot, that's an inside thought! I watch for her reaction. She opens her mouth to say something, then snaps it shut. We lock eyes. Those eyes. She bites her bottom lip. That lip thing, God.

"Uh, what movie did you want to watch?"

She stands up straight. Too straight.

"Something with zombies."

That's all she needs to say. "I'm in."

WE'VE TURNED OFF EVERY LIGHT. Tara made a giant bowl of popcorn that neither of us is interested in. We're sitting next to each other on the cushy blue sofa.

—closer than is necessary, considering the size of it. It's too late to move now. We've been scrolling through Shudder for a good ten minutes, and she still hasn't settled on anything. "How 'bout this one?" She hovers on the preview screen of a film called Extraction.

"It looks good to me."

She presses play.

******

WE'RE two-thirds of the way through the movie, and she's fallen asleep. How?

There's been screaming, explosions, and gunfire gushing from the TV speakers this entire time. My mind flashes back to the conversation we had about her being a spotter. Brave. Then I think about her reaction to Mr. Vampire and her smile. Maybe not so much.

Her head is resting on my shoulder. She nuzzles into me and makes this low 'mmm' sound. She has a little subconscious jerk, and her hair falls into her face. I inch across to brush it behind her ear—try to do it as gently as possible, but end up waking her anyway. She sits up, yawns, and stretches. Then she's wracked with an expression of pure alarm. "Was I sleeping on you?"

"Yeah."

Her cheeks go rosy. "My bad."

"I don't mind." Shut up, stupid.

'Kay, I'll get right back to it, then."

"You can if you want." I pluck the remote from the table, lower the volume, set the thing down next to me on the arm of the couch, and recline, all easy-like.

"There."

She sniggers, and her head falls back against the cushion. "I missed too much; what happened?"

"You didn't miss anything. Most of the group is dead; that big dude with the machete was bitten but is sticking around to kill as many people as possible before he turns, and in about twenty minutes, the final girl will be the only one to make it out of the building alive."

"Argh! Predictable."

Snort. "Were you expecting a twist?" She shakes her head. "Wrong genre for a twist; that's suspense thrillers, sometimes romance."

"A romance with a twist? Right! I could be into that if they existed."

"Ooh, Imma, hook you up!" She leans across me and snatches the remote. So warm.

"*Big Time Love* is the best rom-com ever." She scooches herself up and folds one leg under the other. Then she yawns again.

"We should finish this movie and call it a night. I think we're both too tired to start another one."

"You're right. Raincheck on the rom-com."

Definitely. "Sure."

THE CREDITS OF *The Horde* scrolls up the screen. She pushes off the couch and goes for the bowl of popcorn. "I'm going to toss this."

"I'll take care of it. You're beat; go to bed already."

"Thanks." She grins. "Night."

"Night."

When she's gone, I google the trailer for *Big Time Love*. It's a US movie. The movie's a few years old, starring Kendall Bettencourt—wicked hot—and some other actress I don't recognize. and the twist is totally homo. The best rom-com ever, huh? Straight girls are allowed to like LGBT movies; it's not illegal!

I pick up the popcorn, bring it into the kitchen, and dump it in the garbage.

Chapter 11

"Ved!" Kritika calls to me from the far end of the hallway as I'm twisting my combination lock. She's got Shreya and Meera in tow.

They've been warming up to me, despite my not giving them much reason to. Still, they don't usually bother with me when Tara's not around—only ever on the days I eat lunch with their group, so I'm caught off-guard. They are too damn cheery for this ungodly hour. I'm barely functioning with one open, bloodshot eye. Adding to the oddity of the scenario, they're acting sketchy, huddling in close to each other and scheming in whispers as they sidle toward me.

"Uh, hey, good morning."

"Morning," they all say. Meera gives me a smile. Kritika and Shreya look at me with uncertainty in their eyes, evaluating whether or not to say whatever it is they want to say to me.

If we ain't going to talk, skurt. "What's up?" I open the locker, sift through my stuff, and start pulling out textbooks and binders.

"You know how Tara's birthday is next Saturday?" Shreya asks. She brings her high ponytail over her shoulder and plays with the ends of her bleached platinum hair.

"Yeah." I shove a book into my messenger bag.

"We were thinking about throwing her a party—not like, a surprise party or anything—that shit's dumb. Jatin's got a madly nice house, and his mom is never home, so..."

"Okay." That's actually really thoughtful, but what the hell does it have to do with me? Godspeed, ladies. "I'm sorry, is there a question here somewhere? Because I'm not sure how much help I can be; you guys have known her way longer." Probably not any better, though.

"It's just," Meera starts, "She doesn't really do parties. But we've been thinking she might be okay with it, since it's a special occasion."

"And if you talked to her about it, she'd be more receptive to it," adds Kritika.

What, me? "Where'd you get that idea?"

"If you told her you wanted to go to a rager, she'd take you to one."

Is she for real? "How do you know that?"

"She told us when Jatin invited us to his last week. We expected her usual 'hard pass,' but she said if you wanted to go, she'd be into it. And then Jatin never got around to asking you, so she obvs let it drop."

Wow, okay. So, she does like chilling. "I mean, I'm not sure she'll be down, but I'll ask her. I'll let you know her answer either way."

All three of them squeal, their faces alight with excitement. Kritika throws her arms around my neck. It's a quick hug, but I still go stiff.

The first bell rings, and I catch Tara in the corner of my vision. She's approaching fast. Mmm, English class. "Guys, she's coming," I whisper.

"Hi, Tara!" Meera waves to her as she reaches us. "Come on, Shreya, Mrs. Anita will kill us if we're late again." The three of them blow past Tara without so much as a goodbye. Why don't any of these kids comprehend the concept of finesse?

Because they've never needed it, dumbass.

Right. Their parents probably encourage honesty and openness—the kind of guardians who'd never hurt a child for saying something they didn't like or speaking out of turn.

Tara gawks at her friends' backsides, then glowers at me. "What the hell was that?"

"Your friends asked me to convince you to let them throw you a birthday party. I don't know why."

"No," she says without hesitation.

"Alright. I've been instructed not to ask, 'why not,' after you inevitably say no, but it's going to eat at me, so why not?" Fully fabricating stuff now...

"I told you I'm not into parties."

"But you're turning eighteen. It's a milestone."

She gives a fervent headshake. "I said no; I meant it."

New tactic. "I really would have liked it if I had friends who cared enough about me to throw me a party for my eighteenth, but I didn't." I soften my eyes, pout my lips, and let them quiver just a touch—the most adorable sad, homeless puppy face I can muster. It's a valuable skill: manipulation through guilt. It's not a muscle I'm particularly proud to flex, though.

"Oof." She grimaces as though my words were a wasp sting. "That's not fair, and you know it."

Right in the feels! I go from puppy face to serpentine grin in two seconds flat. "It might not be fair, but it's true."

She groans. "If I say yes, will you come?"

Abso-friggin-loutely. "If you want me to."

She's bewildered or insulted—she's faltered just enough to let something show. "Don't be stupid. I wouldn't have asked if I didn't want you to."

"Then say yes, and I'll be there."

She nibbles on her lip. They do look scrumptious. "Whatever. It had better be the most fire event of the year." Snicker. "I'll stress that to them."

"Good," she sneers. "Class?"

"Yeah."

I hang around near the cafeteria doors, waiting for the Dazzel Brigade. Don't be a douche; they're okay. The lobby is filling up with kids. Even so, I'm confident I can catch them. They're unmissable; the energy they exude is palpable as soon as they enter a room.

I spy Shreya and Kritika in the crowd. I kick off the wall and head them off halfway to the café. We gather in the alcove of an empty classroom. Kritika's hazel eyes are full of anticipation. Shreya is a bit calmer.

"It's a go."

"Yas!" Kritika replies.

Shreya says, "I knew you'd come through."

As promised, I add, "I cannot stress enough how imperative it is that you throw her the most incredible party ever thrown."

"Thread that," Kritika says.

Shreya nods. "Bet."

"Cool."

They bounced to the cafeteria. I stay put, standing against the wall, wondering whether it was a smart move to get involved. It's my ass on the line, even though it's their brilliant idea.

Tara, Avani, and Meera are approaching, beaming at whatever funny thing Tara said. They're about to walk right past me without even noticing that I'm there.

At the last second, Tara's gaze flitters over me. She shoos the others on, then squeezes into the nook across from me.

She slips her purse off her shoulder and dangles it in her hand. She rests the back of her head against the wall, closes her eyes, and exhales slowly. I have no idea what's happening. "Are you okay?"

"Do you ever wish—" She opens her eyes, and I'm sure they're bluer than I have ever seen them. "You want to get out of here?"

"Er, it's Wednesday." No off-campus privileges until tomorrow.

"I didn't mean for lunch."

"I'm supposed to meet Kanan inside."

"Right." She starts to move away. I grab her wrist and pull her back, willing her to stay here with me at this moment for a little while longer. She stares at my hand, at my hand holding onto her. And then her eyes are glued to mine. They're pleading with me: 'Come with me or let me go.'

"Let's get out of here."

She's so eager to escape that she bolts.

I tail her up the steps, out one of the side doors, straight to the parking lot for her car.

No one tries to stop us.

"WHERE ARE WE GOING?" I wonder out loud once she's jammed the keys into the ignition. I suspect she hasn't thought that far ahead.

"I don't care, as long as it's someplace you've never been before."

"There are far too many of those for me to choose from."

"Name one. We can go anywhere."

Make her smile and pick someplace ridiculous. Straight-faced, I say, "The Grand Cafe."

She cackles. And suddenly, she's okay again. I see the tension leave her body as though it has tangibility, a molecular structure of its own. "You're really funny. I feel like I've laughed more in the time I've known you than I have in years." Ah, yes, humor—one of my special skills and one of a handful of coping mechanisms I've developed. At this moment, it's by far my favorite. "That's a good thing, isn't it?"

"So good." Her expression… Again, I can't name it. I like it all the same. "We can go back inside if you want."

"Back inside, hell! You promised me the Grand Cafe."

That gets her laughing again. "How about we go to Japan instead? The café is serving sushi today."

"Yes, sushi! Ugh, I should weigh as much as a whale with how much I love to eat."

She gives me a thorough examination.

"You're good." A redness creeps up her neck, and she adds in a hurry, "Sorta scrawny."

Jerk. "In that case, I suppose I'd better get some sushi into me."

She flashes a smile. "You simply must."

AS WE'RE PAYING for our food, she says,

"Sorry, I cut into your time with your friends." I try to say, "You're my friend, too," but before I can get the words out, she's already saying, "I'll catch you later." Then she takes her tray and goes to find the Cool Kids table.

I yank my phone from my pocket and type a text to Kanam: Change of plans. I'm going to eat with Tara. Sry. The 'read' notification pops up next to my text bubble. I wait a few seconds but don't get a reply.

I shuffle over to Tara's group. When she sees me, the corners of her mouth slip into an understated grin. She elbows Avani and says, "Slide over." Avani looks up at me.

There's disbelief on her face as she vacates the stool beside Tara—I've stolen her position in the starting lineup, and she's been relegated to the sidelines. Tara either doesn't notice or doesn't care. I decide not to care either and take a seat.

Chapter 12

There's a knock on my bedroom door. I open it to find Tara standing way back in the hallway. She's so far away from the threshold that she's almost in the bathroom. What is this, a fresh version of ding-dong-ditch? "Hi."

"Hi." Her eyes darted around my room.

She's standing stock-still and perfectly straight—a sunflower stretching toward the sun. Or a deer about to be run over by a tractor-trailer. She's looking through me, not at me, and it's making me squirm inside.

"Do you want to come in?"

Her shoulders go taut, and her lips downturn.

"Really, you can come in. I won't bite you or anything." Thinking about it, she has never knocked on my door. Seriously, not once. It's been Aunty or Uncle every time.

Did something crazy happen to her in this room before? Could it be that her pyromaniac girl from her mother's side attacked her over something as innocuous as a knock on a door? I would never do that to her or to anyone.

Without parents, kids can be extremely messed up.

Most of us have been through some sh*t.

I know how fortunate I am never to have been raped or beaten half to death by a relative.

She takes a step forward. That's right, I won't hurt you. "Dad sent me up here to get you. Family meeting in the living room."

Family meeting. What the hell did I do now? "Okay."

Aunty and Uncle are on the love seat. The TV is on, but muted. The TV being on is a good sign. Whatever's happening isn't so grave as to require my undivided attention. I'm not going to be screamed at or slapped. Although I'm almost positive that neither Aunty nor Uncle are the type to set me straight with violence, it's always a situation I'm prepared for. They could stuff you in the kitchen cupboard. Fucking hell.

Tara takes a seat on the couch, and I join her. The closer I stick to her, the safer I'll be. It's hardly ever the biokids who get the brunt of things, and once in a while I've known them to step in if the situation gets too out of control.

My focus is fluttering back and forth between Kavita Aunty and Amit Uncle. Neither of them seems annoyed or angry. They look unperturbed, like this is a totally normal thing.

Tara leans forward, resting her elbows on her thighs. She lets her hands loll over her knees. "What's good, parental units?"

I feel my muscles relax.

"So. Uncle drags out the 'o.' "I have to go to Japan for a week; see what it'll take to get the Asian market interested in our first shooter game."

Tara is surprised. "You haven't gone on a business trip in a long time."

"I know. I don't like to leave you guys alone. I've been able to send Uncle Jagdish to most places, but our new PR partners will only deal directly with me. I'm leaving Monday."

Tara doesn't know how to feel about it; Uncle is upset. "I've tried to put it off until after your birthday, but I can't swing it. I'm really sorry, kiddo."

She sits up, scrunches her lips to the side, and steals a minute to collect her thoughts on the issue. "It's cool, Dad.

You've never missed any of our birthdays before, even when you were traveling all over the place. I can let this one slide as long as you promise to get me turned up for my twenty-first." Her smirk is straight-devilish. This girl is unreal!

Uncle and Aunty both chuckle, and so do I.

"Do you think I'd have it any other way?" Uncle replies. "But since I can't be here for this birthday, I'd like to have a daddy-daughter day this weekend, like we used to when you were younger. I thought maybe the three of us could go to Jim Corbett on Sunday."

Tara splutters, "Jim Corbett?"

"Wait, you want me to come?" Everyone's gawking at me. Was that a stupid question? "Of course!" He says it like it's the most obvious answer in the world, as if the alternative never crossed his mind. "That is, if you want to. You don't have to."

"She absolutely does have to!" Tara exclaims. We look at each other. "If my ass is getting dragged to Jim Corbett, so is yours." She gestures between us.

I have no objections. I went to Jim Corbett once on a class trip in fifth grade and really liked it. Maybe Tara is too cool for that now, but I'm not. "I'd like to go."

"Great!" Uncle's eyes sparkle.

Tara peeps at me and shows me the suggestion of a smile. I've let something novel slip, and she finds it amusing. There's nothing I can do about it now.

Chapter 13

Kanan is uncharacteristically quiet at lunch. That isn't to say he's ever rambunctious or even loud; he's sociable, doesn't have to search for words, but is also very good at listening, which is why I'm worried. I don't want him to shut down on me. We've had a few driving lessons now, and I've enjoyed them a lot. He's patient and kind; he never gets flustered, even when I stomp too hard on the brake or catch some air over a speed bump. If I'm honest, I don't care if we're sitting around doing nothing; I like his company. I don't need anything more from him than that.

So observant, yet so staggeringly obtuse.

Oooh, that's it! He feels the same way, and he's being weird because I blew him off for Tara the other day. Our friendship must bother him more than he's willing to admit. Sometimes I hate that I can be so crappy at grasping normal social mores.

It's hard not to cave to my impulses when one grabs me by the crotch—it's such a rare occurrence that I have no defense against it.

How do I fix this? "Kanan, do you want to go to a movie or something on Saturday?" The conversation going on around us screeches to a halt. Bhavya, Himanshi, and Mani all glare at me and Kanan. It did sound like I was asking him out. Whatever. I can't afford to obsess about verbiage right now. There'll be time for that later once I've salvaged this, wrapped some insulation around it, and given it the warmth it deserves.

He deadpans, "I don't really like movies."

Denied. Everyone else goes back to chatting, embarrassed for me. Be suave.

"That's why I said, 'or something? We can do whatever." I don't add; I just want to hang out with you, despite wanting to.

He smiles. Got him. "Ever been rock climbing?"

Say what now? "Um, like, up a mountain?"

He titters. "No, indoor. At a gym."

"I have not. It sounds fun, though." No, it doesn't. But if that's what he wants to do, I'll get up and do it.

"Want to try?"

"For sure."

"Dope. I'll pick you up Saturday at like, one?"

"Perfect." I catch Bhavya leering at me as I say it. Oh God, okay. She for sure thinks I've asked Kanan out. Bookmark it. Address it in the future.

I DON'T KNOW what the appropriate attire is for scaling rock walls. I could ask Tara.

She's an athlete; she'd probably have a better idea. But if I do that, she'll ask me why I'm asking her, and I don't feel like playing twenty questions. The hassle. She isn't home, anyway. She went to the cricket game. She asked me to come with her, but obviously, I couldn't. I didn't tell her I had other plans; I just said, "Maybe next time." Yo, dummy, Aunty goes to the gym. Problem solved. I find her and Uncle in the living room watching TV. No sexy stuff this time around, thank God. "Aunty, can I ask you something?"

"Shoot."

I do this awkward shuffle thing for a second. I'm not one to seek advice, especially not about stupid stuff like clothes; it feels weird. "Do you know what a person should wear to go indoor rock climbing?"

"Hmm." She sits up. "That depends. Is the person going for a workout, or is it a date sort of thing?"

This is too complicated. "It is a non-romantic one-on-one hangout thing." Could you be a bigger loser?

She chortles. "Let's take a look at your wardrobe."

"Uh, cool."

Aunty and I pick out a heather gray, loose-fitting racerback tank with an outline of Massachusetts on it, one of my nicer zip-up hoodies, and the only pair of leggings I own—black. We hit a snag on the shoes.

"Vans aren't made for climbing. You don't have sneakers with better grip?"

"No."

"That's a problem." She taps three fingers against her lips and makes a humming noise. "What size shoe do you wear?"

"Seven."

She snaps her fingers and says, "Wait here." And then she's gone for maybe two minutes.

When she returns, she has a pair of black and pink Nikes in her hand. "You can borrow these."

She actually wants me to put my funky-ass feet into her nice-ass sneakers.

Is this something that moms and daughters do—swap shoes whenever? I take them from her.

"I think you're good to go." She winks at me.

"Thanks for your help and for the sneakers."

"Anytime."

Kanan RINGS THE DOORBELL. Why not send a text? I fly down the stairs and reach the door half a second before Aunty can get to it.

—not that it helps at all; the windowpane is only slightly frosted. "I won't be out late."

"Have a blast," Aunty sings.

Kanan is in a very tight maroon Metallica T-shirt and grey cargo pants. His hair is neatly combed. And… Shit. He thinks it's a date, too.

"You look nice," I say without thinking.

Hey, asshole, Is this or isn't this a date?

He gives me a half-smile and makes a quick assessment of my attire. "So do you."

Gulp. "Listen, I have to tell you that if I die today, I'll be very upset about it." That earns me a full smile. "Not going to happen." He gestures toward Sweet Trixy, and we're off.

WE ARRIVE at an enormous warehouse that's been painted an obnoxious purple.

There's a yellow sign above a set of glass doors: Rök. I tug one of the doors open before Kanan can reach for the handle, and he's taken aback. He likes being the one to do the chivalrous stuff, like holding open doors and pulling out chairs. To reiterate, is this or is this not a date?

Inside, there's a large reception desk manned by two women. I'm ready to pay them the price of our admission when Kanan takes a membership pass from his pocket and presents it to them. They wave us through to the gym.

The climbing area is sprawling. It has twenty rock walls of various heights and difficulties, along with five small ones for the kids.

Kanan leads me to this colossus of a wall, with hundreds of colorful feet and handholds protruding from it. There's a warning on the red plasterboard at its base:

RECOMMENDED FOR EXPERT-LEVEL CLIMBERS

No. Nope. Fuck that noise. "You told me I wasn't going to die today!"

"And you won't. I guarantee it."

A muscular guy in a purple Rök-branded polo comes to greet us. "Kanan!

Back again, huh?"

"You know it. Rohan, this is Vedika."

"Hi, Vedika." We shake hands. "I'm going to be your instructor for today." He regards Kanan. "What are we doing this time, bouldering? Lead?"

"Top rope, my dude. Vedika's a noob."

"Let me get the equipment." He heads over to a storage bin, removes two harnesses and two helmets, then comes back to us and hands us one of each. "Here you go."

The helmet is straightforward; I pop it on and fasten the clip. The harness has too many straps for me to know where to begin. Kanan hops into it and secures it with no problem. I'm still standing in the same position, my harness hanging from my hand. "I don't usually have such a hard time strapping things on."

He snickers at me and goes, "Need some help?"

"You have to ask?"

"Come here." He takes my harness from me and gets down on his haunches.

"Step in." I steady myself, my hand on his shoulder. I put my right leg in—shake it all about—then my left. He slides the contraption up my thighs, adjusts the straps, and then clicks the snap-clips in place around my waist. He tugs on the belt, and I jolt toward her. "How's that?" He's so close to my face that I can feel his breath, balmy on me—minty, hints of vanilla. How smooth.

"Good," I responded evenly.

I've got to give it to him; the boy's got a game. All I have to do is refuse to play. Or not.

I'M STUTTERING through my climb, slow as a snail. Up a goddamn baby wall. Almost there. Keep going. True to his personality, Kanan has infinite patience with me.

He's belaying me, shouting words of encouragement with every new handhold I grab.

I really want to like him. I like him.

I don't know if I can. He's attractive; there's no question about that—an Amazonian stunner. But something's missing... the spark, or whatever other dumb cliché they use in love stories.

And... I'm falling. Oh fuck! I bang against the wall and scrape my shoulder.

"Whoa! I gotcha." Kanan takes all of my weight and stabilizes me.

"Damn it! Sorry."

"It's okay. Want me to bring you down?"

"Please!"

When I'm close enough to the bottom, he catches me and helps me plant my feet on the ground again. He holds me a second longer than I need him to, and I let him.

Come on, spark! I gaze up at him, seeing the concern in his viridian eyes.

"Are you hurt?"

Nothing. Damn. "I'm fine. Thanks." I step out of his arms.

No, this is not a date. Aloof. No shit.

Uncle AND Aunty are out when I get back to the house. Tara's lounging on the couch, reading 1984, wearing glasses. They're square, pink and black, and semi-rimless. How is she even better-looking in specs? It's not fair. "You wear glasses?"

Her head snaps up from the book. "My contacts were bothering me. How was your date with Kanan?" She's irritated.

"It wasn't a_"

"Please. My mom was gushing about how adorable you were, making a big deal over what to wear."

"That's not… I'm not used to athletic activities, that's all."

"If you say so."

Pivot. "How was the game?"

"We lost—a big surprise. Our cricket team belongs in a dumpster, not on a field."

Ha! "Then why'd you go?"

"For the squad, not the team." She's a good friend. I wouldn't go to a cricket game to watch the dancers.

The hell you wouldn't. Okay, fine, but I'd go for the skirts, not the sport. "You still owe me a raincheck on that movie. Can I cash it in?"

She closes the book, tosses it onto the coffee table, then sits up straight and pats the couch beside her. I plop down and watch her set up the TV. She's not even doing anything out of the ordinary, and I feel like I've got a bunch of Cirque du Soleil acrobats in my stomach. What was that about sparks?

No! She's straight, and it wouldn't matter if she weren't because she's so off limits that she's the human equivalent of Chernobyl.

THIRTY-FOUR MINUTES AND FORTY-THREE SECONDS—THAT'S the build-up to the first kiss between the two leading ladies, though I knew it was coming right at the start of the scene. It's tame, yet I'm fidgeting like a total prude. I take a look at Tara. Okay, so she 'sparks' me. Thank God it's one-sided; I don't want it to be mutual. That would complicate the shit out of everything, and I really don't need that kind of aggro. I just want to ride out this year, nice and easy, so I can get on with adulting.

Sixty-five minutes and seventeen seconds: next-level lesbian love scene, crazy for a rom-com. Everything about it is sensual: the soft lighting and lingering close-ups, the hair-tugging, and the tongue action.

I know I'm redder than a baboon's ass. I don't dare glance at Tara, not this time. If she were to catch me, she'd be able to read me, for sure.

I don't breathe until it's over.

Yeah, this year isn't going to go smoothly at all. Somebody killed me.

"WHAT'D YOU THINK?" she wonders as the credits roll.

"I didn't expect the ending. I thought Allie was going to go through with marrying Heather's brother."

"No. They were meant to be friends.

She was always going to end up with Heather."

Hmm. "It was good. I like happy endings." There aren't enough of them in real life.

"So do I. But things don't work out that way." Alright, seriously, she is psychic.

"They did it for Kendall Bettencourt. She and her wife have been together for years, since they were, like, our age. I read online that they're having a baby soon, too." She grins. "Fine. I guess sometimes they do."

Chapter 14

Amit uncle is more excited about heading to Jim Corbett than either of us actual kids. It's about a half-hour drive home given the traffic, and he is giddy the entire way.

Tara is in the front seat, being so cute about it—indulging him as he relays every part of the afternoon's schedule, guiding him on Google Maps.

It's sweet; these two are wicked close and have such a strong bond. I haven't witnessed a connection like this between a dad and daughter since my friend's home in Delhi.

Uncle PARKS THE CAR. The lot is packed, with tons of people trying to cram in a visit before the weather turns bitter. There are families with little kids all around us as we head to the ticket booth. Not too many teenagers, I notice.

The line is longish, though it moves fast.

When it's our turn, Uncle purchases three tickets. I am prepared—Kanan stopped at an ATM for me on the drive back yesterday.

I take my wallet out of my pocket, flip it open, snatch a twenty, and go to hand it to him.

Tara shakes her head as Uncle turns toward me. His eyebrows squeeze together as he catches sight of the money.

"What the hell is that?"

What kind of response? Just like his daughter, it was funny and unbefitting.

I'm frozen. Speak, stupid. "It's for my ticket."

"That's not how it works, kiddo. I give you money, not the other way around." His smile is so kind. So are his eyes. Tara's got his eyes, brilliant and lovely.

Say thank you. "Thank you!"

He hands a ticket to Tara and one to me. I slide it and the twenty into my wallet, then the wallet into my back pocket.

He claps his hands and rubs them together.

"Let's do this!" He scurries through the gate with extra springy steps. Tara and I ogle each other. She huffs. Then, we scramble to catch up.

WE see so many exotic animals from all over India.

Tara is blah about everything, save the big cats. I saw her face when the tigers were playing with these huge cardboard boxes all around their enclosure. It was pure delight. She must be a cat person, which would make sense—she's sort of cat-like herself, sweet when she wants to be, surly when she's aggravated, and preternaturally untouchable in comparison to most other creatures.

As for me? I am in awe of every single beast we come across. Lions, zebras, tigers, birds, and a lot more. They're all exquisite in their own ways. But when we enter the Aviators exhibit, I know that it's going to be my favorite part of the day. There's an entire section dedicated to birds of prey: hawks, harriers, falcons, and owls. Indian bald eagle! I scamper over to the bird and snatch my camera from my jeans. Pictures! There are lots of them. Snap.

Snap. Snap. "You're such a handsome boy," I murmur to him between shots. "Can you spread your wings for me, bud?" He does it!

Tara pops into place beside me. "I see you like birds."

"Mmhmm." I love birds. Peacocks and white parrots, specifically They're so majestic and so untamed. Imagine having that kind of freedom—the ability to soar high above the earth on the winds and go anywhere I please." If I could've chosen to be born as anything, it would have been a peregrine falcon." Why'd I tell her that? Embarrass yourself as usual.

I can sense her grinning. "They have one here."

My head snaps to the side, and I see that she is grinning. "No..."

"Oh yeah." She reaches out, wraps her fingers around my wrist, and drags me clear across the exhibit. It happens with such swiftness that my stomach doesn't have the chance to do jumping jacks.

There are a few different species of falcon living together in a giant netted enclosure: brown, grey, black, saker, and peregrine. "Which one is the peregrine?" She's facing me, still holding my wrist. I free myself from her grasp and point to the bird.

It's perched on a long branch, its blue-grey back to us, wings ready to carry it away.

She steps closer to me, following my finger with her eyes.

"They're the fastest animals in the world," I say, a little too close to her ear.

"They can dive for prey at over 200 miles per hour."

"I get why she's your favorite. She's beautiful." Her voice is hushed and thick with awe.

Oh boy.

"Yeah." I take a picture.

"There you are," Uncle calls to us. We turn and find him with a leaflet in his hand.

He thrusts it out to us. "There's an aerial demo and info session in fifteen minutes!"

He's too excited. He's not the one who just squeezed out loud, fool.

Tara examines me and cracks up.

"We'd better hurry to the arena if we want to get good seats."

On our way to the amphitheater, we find a concession stand; the line is growing exponentially. "Do either of you want a soda or something?" Uncle asks.

"I'll take Diet Coke. Ooh, and a soft pretzel, please, Daddy?" Tara's tone is saccharine, like a five-year-old who's begging for a new toy. Uncle melts over it—a chocolate bar forgotten in the sun.

"Anything for you, Vedika?"

"I'm good, thanks."

"Okay. You two, head over. I'll meet you there."

Once he's out of earshot, I say to Tara,

"You've got him wrapped around your finger."

"Always have." She winks.

THE small area is already swarming by the time we walk in. All the seats at the bottom of the bleachers are full. Tara puts her hand to her forehead, blocking the sun from her eyes, and scans around.

"Up there," she points. "We'll have a killer view, and the birds will fly in from back there, right over our heads."

Do not squeal again. "Sweet."

We clamber up to the very top row of the bleachers. Our backs are against the broad post of a tall wooden fence. I look around and check out the view for myself.

There, across the showground, I see a face I've prayed and prayed I'd never have to see again. I squint hard, hoping that my mind is misinterpreting the woman's aged features, morphing a complete stranger into my worst nightmare. But it's really her, still decked out in the same style of hideous floral muumuu she was so fond of. Nandini Goddamn..

I was with her for half a year. Those were the longest six months of my life. The thing I remember most about her house is the kitchen. It was so tiny. And it locked. I recall: the sound of the door being slammed and bolted behind me—thunk-cha-chink, hours and hours in the dark, bloody knuckles from pounding incessantly to be let out, the blue mop bucket I had to use as a toilet—the putrid fucking smell of it.

My heart is pounding so hard, so fast.

Thumpthumpthumpthump. How long can it keep that up before it gives out, even if it is healthy now?

Either my lungs have stopped working or every last molecule of oxygen in the atmosphere has been sucked away because I suddenly can't breathe.

Shit. ShitShitShit! What do I do? What the hell do-

"Are you okay?" Tara.

Gasping. No words, only gasping. God.

Oh, God. What is this?

"Vedika, look at me." Her hand was on my cheek. Now, her eyes So blue." Focus on my chest. Breathe with me. Deep and slow.

In… and out." Inhale. Exhale. I watch her chest as her lungs expand and contract. It rises and falls. Rises and falls. Measured and steady. With her. In and out. In and out.

Huff. Puff. “That’s it. Just like that. You’re doing great.” Her palm is in the middle of my back, rubbing. “You’re going to get through it. Deep breath in and out. In… and out.”

Is this going to last forever? Please, please, just let me die soon. I can’t—gasp—huff, puff. Hiccup. Inhale. Exhale. Tara, please stay with me.

“I’m right here. I’m not going anywhere.”

Did I say it out loud? The heat of her skin through my shirt... I shut my eyes.

Breathe. Breathe. Hiccup. I open them; she’s still with me.

My face is wet. Why is my face wet?

Tears. Wipe. Wipe. Breathe. Hiccup. Huff.

Puff. In and out.

Inhale. Exhale. Rinse and repeat.

My heartbeat is starting to slow down, and it’s becoming less difficult to take in air.

She is still touching me, her voice calming as whitecaps crash against the shore. “What do you need, Ved? Do you want to leave?”

Ved. That’s me. “Yes.”

She takes my hand. Leads me down the bleachers, step by step. Then, outside, beyond the wooden fence.

She steers me to a recessed nook.

There’s a boulder with a flat top. She sits me down on it and stands in front of me. So close I could... I rest my forehead against her abdomen. I’m sapped, no energy at all; it’s this or fall on my face. She strokes my hair again and again, gentle fingers combing through long strands. Feels nice. “It’s okay. You’re okay, now.” she murmurs.

"What's going on?" I hear Uncle ask.

Tara keeps doing what she's doing and doesn't move away—not a single inch. "I think she had a panic attack."

That's what it was?

"Vedika?" He sounds too close. I turn my head and find him with one knee in the dirt. The food and drinks are in a box on the ground beside him. And then I see the worry on his face. "Let's get you home."

Chapter 15

I'm in my bed. What the fuck? It comes back to me in pieces. The Jim Corbett Show The aviation show The amphitheater. Nandini Aunty. Tara. Her eyes. Her hands. She didn't leave me.

I remember the car ride back to the house, with Tara sitting next to me in the back seat. My temple against her shoulder, her arm around me, her hand rubbing the crown of my head And then Kavita Aunty brought me up to my room, tucking the covers tight around me.

The sunlight streaming through my windows tells me that it's early afternoon.

It was near sunset when we got home from the Jim Corbett Show. So friggin' parched. Need water.

I climb out from under the bedspread.

My feet are bare against the downy coral carpet. I'm wearing sweatpants and a muscle tee. When did that happen? Aunty helped you change. How humiliating.

I drag myself out of my room and down the stairs. The TV is on in the living room, volume turned down low. Tara is on the couch in a pair of pink plaid pajamas and her glasses. Those things are great. Please wear them all the time. She sees me and pushes herself upright. "How are you feeling?"

I gather some saliva and swallow it. "I imagine this is how it feels to get struck by lightning." I rub my forehead. "What time is it?"

She glances at the cable box and back at me. "12:27. On Monday."

"What? Crap, I slept through school! Hold on, why are you home?"

"My parents had to go to work, but we didn't want you to wake up to an empty house, so I took a sick day."

"You didn't have—"

"When are you going to realize that I don't do anything I don't want to do?" She motions for me to come sit beside her. I pad across the living room and collapse backwards onto the couch. "What happened? And please don't say 'nothing,' because one second you were fine, and the next you totally weren't. It's like something set you off."

Ah, balls. I was hoping I'd never have to tell this tale to anyone again.

But I don't have the mental prowess right now to make up a believable lie. And anyway, I don't want to lie to her. She was so compassionate throughout the whole mess that she has more than earned the truth.

I take a breath and steel my nerves. "Do you remember when you asked me at the Witch Museum if I was claustrophobic, and I told you I wasn't?"

"Uh huh."

"I lied. I am, kind of. And at the bird show, I saw Nandini Aunty, who's the reason why. Anytime I did anything she didn't like, she'd stick me in this horrible little kitchen and leave me in there for hours—an entire weekend, once." I sigh. "Sometimes I think it would've been better if she'd just hit me." Physical scars are nothing compared to mental ones.

"God, Vedika." She scoops my hands into hers. "That's messed up. I'm so sorry." There are tears welling in her eyes.

Please don't cry for me. "It's fine,"

"It's not fine! Of course you'd react that way to seeing her again. She traumatized you. It's called PTSD." She drops my hands and balls hers into fists. "I want to hunt her down and beat the shit out of her!"

"That's sweet in a twisted way. And the way you talked me through it was really sweet, too. I appreciate it."

"It's nothing."

It's everything. "How did you know what to do?"

"I learned it in Life Skills last year. I'm glad I did, too. The way you were breathing, I was afraid you were going to pass out."

I'm struck with guilt from out of nowhere. "Sorry, I ruined your day out with your dad."

"You didn't ruin anything. We were having fun, then something happened that was beyond your control. And hey, you got me a three-day weekend, so...

Ha. I fold my arms across my chest.

"If that's the case, the least you can do is make me lunch as a thank you. You're so rude."

"You skinny little wiseass." She giggles, then signals toward the kitchen. "You're on."

We raid the fridge and find gold—all the ingredients for the sandwich. We make two overstuffed sandwiches, sit at the table across from one another, and eat and talk about stuff I've never talked about with anyone.

"What do you want to do when you grow up?" she probes.

I was always too focused on surviving into adulthood to consider what I wanted to do once I got there. "I think I want to be a wildlife photographer—maybe for National Geographic or something." That's it.

That's what I want. "What about you?"

"Historical archivist."

I have never heard anyone ever answer that question with 'archivist!' "You want to spend your life in a musty basement somewhere doing research and collecting old stuff?"

"Yes, that sounds fabulous." She is 100 percent real. I admire the hell out of her for it.

"That's awesome. Do you know where you want to go to college for post-graduation yet?"

"Stanford University, US. It's my first, second, and third choice. They have an unbelievable history department and world-renowned faculty." She rolls her eyes. "And a 19 percent acceptance rate."

"You'll get in."

"You don't know that."

"Yes, I do."

The Lip Bite. What goes on in her head when she does that? I can't figure it out.

"Where do you want to go?"

"I don't know. I'll probably end up at the National Institute of Design."

She straight up crows. Why does she react that way all the time? Why do you like it so much? "You will not go to The National Institute of Design," she asserts. "You're too smart to waste your time at an Indian college."

"Too smart to, too poor not to." She kicks her chair back a little. "No.

No! I'm not tryna hear that. Where do you want to go, in your heart of hearts?"

"School of the Art Institute of Chicago." Huh? I guess so.

She smacks the tabletop. "Yes! That's your college. You're going to study photography at that, and then you're going to become a famous wildlife photographer, and the entire planet is going to fawn over your work."

"Stop."

"I will not stop. You're doing it. Pinky, promise me." She throws her fist up, pinky-out.

"If you promise me that you'll go to Stanford University like the undercover smarty-pants that you are,"

"Deal."

We pinky swear. Skin like cashmere. I don't want to let go, and she doesn't let go.

We sit there, fingers hooked together for, I don't know, how long. Right as my heart is about to burst through my ribcage, she moves. She picks up our plates and takes them to the sink.

I go over to her. "I can do that."

"I've got it." She's austere all of a sudden; her muscles are rigid. But then she checks herself and bites it back. "Seriously, it's already done. Why don't you go find us something to watch on Netflix?"

"Are you in the mood for anything in particular?"

"Something funny."

We're next to each other on the couch, deep into the first season of a show called Modern Family, and we've both been dying of laughter. "I love Claire. She's so funny."

"It's everyone," she says.

"What? No way."

"Yes!"

"What's going on here?" Uncle pokes his head into the living room.

"Hey, Dad. We're watching TV."

"I heard you guys laughing. It's good to see you're feeling better, Vedika."

"I am. Thanks."

"My wife is going to make a big deal over cooking for you tonight, so better get an idea of what you want," he says before disappearing upstairs.

Tara nods in agreement. "Mom's like that with food. If you're stressed, she cooks for you. If you're happy, she cooks for you. Grandma's North Indian; that's where she gets it from."

"Um, that's perfect. You know how I feel about food."

"Yeah, I do, Scrawny." She pokes her finger into my stomach, and I squeal like the Pillsbury Doughboy. Her eyes go wide.

"You're ticklish!" She attacks my sides. I writhe against her, bat at her hands, and grab ahold of them. She stares at me, smirking.

"You've thwarted me for the time being, but I know your weakness now. You are forever screwed."

I hate being tickled. I don't like being touched in general.

And I like both, as long as she's the one doing them. I am forever screwed.

Chapter 16

The photography club is in the computer lab again. Mr. Ravi informs us that Fall Gallery Night is next Wednesday, and he wants us to use today's meeting to choose and prepare the eight photos we're each allowed to display. He's loaded two of the badass mega-printers at the back of the room with glossy 8" x 10" photo paper.

Tara and I have cued up some of our pictures and are standing around waiting for them to appear from the ether, transformed into real-life pixels. I had to convince her to do it; it took some prodding, but she relented after I told her she didn't have to hand them in even though we were asked to. The Dead Trees photo is the first of hers to be printed. She snatches it from the tray.

I tap its top corner. "You should hand that one in."

"No."

The next picture to print is one I took of her—the one she caught me editing. My turn to snatch.

"Is that for the gallery?"

No way; this is mine. Okay, freak. I shake my head. "I wanted a hard copy to see how it looked on paper." She's relieved but doesn't say so. Bad enough, I snuck the dumb picture. "I should've asked you first before I snapped it."

"It would've been forced, then. This is authentic."

So, she's fine with me seeing her, the veiled her, as long as I keep it between us.

My pictures are starting to backlog the tray. She gathers them up and scans them over—a seascape and a landscape from Park, the Indian bald eagle,the peregrine falcon, and the series of the boy on the swing. "These are so good." Face reddening to commence in three, two, and one. "Thanks."

Another of her photos pops out onto the tray—a close-up shot of her friends dancing at a cricket game. Shreya is at the top of the lift, and Meera and Kritika make up the base. They're all fixated on the crowd, beaming. She misses it. I want to come out and ask her why she quit, but if she wanted me to know, she would've told me by now. Instead, I say, "That right there is a yearbook photo."

She inspects it. "You might be right."

"There's a game tomorrow night, isn't there?"

"Yeah. Away at the Race Course."

I don't care much for cricket. Still, I want to go. For her. "Are you going to take me, or what?"

Her eyebrows try to climb off her face, as if that were the most startling question anyone has ever asked her. Then she smiles. "Totally."

FRIDAY NIGHT We go to the game. The field is nicer than ours, in addition to their team being on a whole other level.

By the end of the second quarter, we're down 115–13 overs—shameful for everyone save the kicker—and the sun is gone from the sky. The stadium lights are wicked bright, but they do nothing to stop me from freezing my funbags off. Kavita Aunty said to wear something warmer than jeans and a hoodie, stubborn mule.

Tara, the paragon of foresight, brought a thick fleece blanket as backup to her long wool trench coat. She notices me shivering and strips the blanket off her shoulders. She scoots closer to me and wraps it around us both. Then my hands are in hers, and she's rubbing heat into them.

"What the hell is wrong with you? It's like you've never been to Dehradun in October before."

"It was humid earlier!"

"Again, it's Dehradun. In October."

"Alright, I get it; I'm a terrible Mass-hole."

She chortles. "You are." Now her eyes are on me as well as her hands, and my gut does that somersault thing. Damn it. It's so weird and so nice. Or, it would be nice, if it were caused by someone else.

DANCE MUSIC PUMPS through the sound system, and the crowd gets loud. I glance down at the field and see that both colleges' cheerleaders are on the fifty-yard line. Tara lets go of my hands and shifts her attention to the pitch. "Whoooo!" She adds a piercing whistle. I watch a rush of enthusiasm take hold of her as our college gets ready for the cheer-off.

I'd have loved to see her out there. Our squad has some sick moves, for sure, but I'd bet a fat stack on her being the best of them all. Hey, look, skirts! Really short ones.

If only I gave a single sh*t about any of those other girls.

THE CHEER-OFF IS OVER FASTER than it began, and the girls are already headed back to the sidelines. Tara stands up. I look at her, confused. "I'm going to say hi, and then we can leave."

"You don't want to stay for the rest of the game?"

"The best part about quitting the squad of dancing is that I can bounce whenever I want. I saw what I came here to see. Plus, we're losing, and you're cold." She motions for me to follow her down to field level, and I do.

Her friends are glad that she came, even Avani, who's always kind of bitchy.

Tara gives them a few glowing words on the performance and a round of high fives.

She shoots the shit with them for a while and looks over at me just in time to catch my teeth chattering. "Okay, ladies, I gotta get Vedika someplace warm before she turns into a sad, skinny meat popsicle." We say our goodbyes, and then we're out.

Chapter 17

Kavita Aunty is up earlier than usual for a weekend morning; I hear her bang into something downstairs in the living room and squeal.

"Crap!" She and Uncle are both the type that like to sleep in—sometimes to nine, if they can—and who could blame them? I would if I could, but my stupid body never makes it past seven o'clock, no matter how late I may go to bed or how tired I am when it happens. Except in the case of a panic attack. And that was the most terrifying experience ever; 10/10 would not recommend it.

Tea or coffee? Yes, coffee; that's what that aroma is, coffee; how astute. Get some immediately.

I shamble out to the hallway and meet Tara as she's exiting the bathroom—white tank top wrinkled, one leg of her bright pink-and-aqua tartan PJs scrunched up around her calf, hair looking like she had a heaping helping of electricity for breakfast—and she is still breath-taking. Forever screwed. Understatement.

"Morning," she says through a yawn.

"Good morning, birthday girl."

"Fuck." She smooths her hair.

"Did you forget?"

"About my birthday? No. About the party? Yes. I just want to sleep."

That's troubling. "Are you sick?"

"No, I feel fine." She pouts. "Can we say I'm sick? I'd love to skip it."

"After I threatened your friends with death to ensure that you get the best party ever? I don't think so."

"You're lucky I like you," she groans.

I'm not lucky. I like her. "We're going to have fun tonight, okay? I'll hire a clown to make balloon animals if that's what it takes."

"So cute," she says under her breath.

Her face goes rosy; I wasn't supposed to hear that.

What's cute, me or balloon animals?

Lol, 'me! ' Been huffing paint? "I need coffee."

"Mmm. Caffeine."

I'll let her go first and follow her down.

"BIRTHDAY HUUUGS!" Aunty clobbers her as she saunters into the kitchen. Tara's a good sport about it and hugs her back. "My little girl is all grown up! I can't believe it. It seems like only yesterday we brought you home from the hospital."

That's all Tara is willing to endure.

"Okay, Mom." She pats Aunty's head and pushes her out of her arms.

These precious moments between her and her parents make my heart swell. I don't know if she realizes how #Blessed she is. I really hope she does.

"How would you feel about doing a birthday brunch? Since you've got your party tonight, you won't let me make a big dinner because it 'takes too long." Tara gawps at me. "You see what I have to put up with?"

I know she's joking, but I want to be snarky about it anyway, like, Oh, your mom loves you and wants to celebrate your birth? The horror! Instead, I smile and say,

"Now, now."

"Yes, we can do brunch."

That was the right answer. Kavita Aunty is thrilled.

Tara pours herself a cup of coffee and one for me. She takes hers black, as always.

She ladles two spoonfuls of sugar into mine and adds a pinch of milk. When she hands the mug to me, she asks, "What?" What 'what'? Your stupid jaw is hanging open. "You know how I like my coffee?" Yew knyo mehmehmeh.

"I paid attention." Her phone rings in her pants pocket. She snatches it and looks at the screen; her face has joy written all over it.

She peeps at her mom and says, "It's Dad," then answers the call. Aunty and I can hear Uncle singing "Happy Birthday" into her ear as clearly as if he were on speakerphone. She's beaming throughout the whole song.

Tara CHOOSES a swanky gastropub downtown called Taro for brunch, a complete American-type breakfast. Their menu is chock full of ornate dishes: cinnamon apple bostock—I have no idea what that is—and fried egg with hazelnuts, chanterelles, blackberries, and green garlic. Avocado, egg, and bacon waffle sandwich. Honey and ricotta scone? Who eats this boujee crap?

The waiter has taken Tara and Aunty's order—an egg and cheese sandwich and strawberry-cream cheese crêpes, respectively—and I still haven't decided what I want. I should've asked for the damn kids' menu. "Um, can I get regular, plain waffles?"

The waiter regards me with mild contempt. "Plain waffles," he repeats. "Okay, miss."

Aunty taps his arm after he's written down my order and motions for him to come closer. He bends, and she mumbles something unintelligible into his ear. When he stands, he says, "Certainly," and then leaves us.

"And now..." Aunty reaches into her purse, removes a small, blue snap-lid box with a dainty white bow on top, and slides it across the table to Tara.

Tara pops the box open. Inside is a rose gold ring in the shape of a crown with clear diamonds embedded in each of its points, and a delicate chain-necklace is strewn through it. "Mom, this is-" Her breath hitches in her throat. She has tears pooling in her eyes.

"Happy birthday, sweetie," Aunty says.

There's sadness in her eyes, such a contrast to her smile. She reaches out to Tara, touching the back of her hand.

"Wear it close to your heart."

Tara dabs at her eyes, then removes the necklace from the box and turns to me. "Can you help me put it on?"

I nod, take the chain into my hands, and undo the clasp. She bunches her hair in her palm and swooshes it off her shoulders. I slide the necklace around her neck and redo the clasp. She lets her hair drop, then straightens the crown and rolls it between her fingers for a second. She respects her mother. "Thank you so much. I'll wear it every day."

"You're welcome."

THE MEAL CONCLUDES with the presentation of a piece of chocolate pastry and a tall, lit candle stuck in the middle of it. A small group of staff gathers around our table and sings an off-key rendition of their own birthday song. When they've finished, Tara looks at me. "Blow it out with me."

"You need help with one candle? You've got to quit smoking."

"No," she titters. "You weren't with us for your birthday, so we'll celebrate it now."

Aunty goes, "Aww."

Please don't let me blush. Please. No deal, hunny; here's your pink! I cleared the lump from my throat. "On three?"

"One, two, three." We extinguish the flame of existence together.

The staff gives us a round of applause, then disperses. Tara plucks the candle out of the cake, slides the plate between us, and hands me a dessert spoon. "Happy super belated birthday." She holds up her spoon for a cheer.

"Happy actual birthday." Clink!

Aunty watches us, grinning, as we delve into the sugary treat.

Chapter 18

Tara flies down the steps, taking them two at a time. It's nine thirty; we're half an hour late to her birthday party. Is she wearing jeans? Yes, skinny, shredded ones, and a pair of white and pale-blue Nike high tops. Well, I never... Her shirt is more what I'm used to seeing in baby blue, long-sleeved and off-the-shoulder, short enough for her midriff to peek out from below its hem.

Her hair is pin straight and up in a high ponytail, and her bangs are jagged. She usually wears it down and wavy. There's almost no makeup on her face. She doesn't need it anyway; she's prettier without it.

I've gone in the opposite direction, making way more effort than I ever do.

My hair is loose around my shoulders, with a'sexy mermaid' style crimp, rather than trapped in my preferred low, messy bun. I'm in a pair of tight black pants, a white button-down, and a fitted military jacket—also black. I've got dress shoes on my feet, bought special for the occasion.

I'm even wearing eyeliner and friggin' lip gloss! I feel like an imposter, a pod person.

But I must admit, I look good.

"I'm ready if you are." She takes her first solid glance at me of the evening. Her left eyebrow arches, and her mouth goes a tad agape. If she were someone else, I'd have a pretty good idea of what she's thinking, but because it's her, it isn't that.

She's surprised that I've gone through the trouble, is all.

"I've been ready."

"Good. Let's go."

Aunty says, "Be careful. If you need a ride home, call me. No matter how late." Her mouth contracts into a worried scrunch.

Why? I don't think Aunty's the type to get behind the wheel drunk.

"I will!" Tara grabs her car keys from the hook, and we're out the door.

Bhavy, Meera, Avani, and Kritika followed my recommendation to make this the best party ever; they've gone all out. There are some decorations—a giant rainbow Happy Birthday banner strung across the living room archway and a few bunches of balloons here and there, tasteful, not like at a child's party.

The kitchen counter is stocked with every variety of alcohol known to man, and there's a fat beer keg sitting in a big green bucket of ice on the floor. I wonder how they got it all. There's a stack of pizza boxes on the table, too, and some chips and dips in bowls.

The music is loud and thick, with heavy bass and smooth synths. The house lights are low, and they've set up string lights that flash in time to the beat of each song.

There must be a hundred people here, and it's only ten thirty. If this keeps up, there's no doubt the cops will show up within the hour. Maybe Tara would prefer to have this shindig broken up early. Get 911 on speed dial, then toolbag.

Nope.

"Tara, happy birthday! This party is lit." Her friend, I think his name is Kartik, slinks his arm around her and hugs her tight to his letterman jacket. "It's good to see you out again. You haven't been to a party since"

"Have you gotten a drink yet?" She yells over him and pats his shoulder. "There's a massive keg in the kitchen. Get your ass in there and tap it!" She gives him a shove in the right direction, then grabs my forearm and hauls me in the other.

People are congregating in the living room—some are dancing, others are sitting around talking, laughing, and drinking. Tara doesn't seem interested in doing any of it. Truthfully, she seems stressed out. I want to help her relax, but I can't do that if I don't know what the problem is.

"I need to get some air. It's too hot here. Wanna come outside with me?" She gives a curt nod. I take her hand, somehow don't freak about it, and tow her through the sea of kids to the back door.

There's no one outside. We've got the patio to ourselves for a little while, at any rate. There are plenty of places to sit, yet she chooses to park next to me on the small loveseat. The sky above us is clear; the moon and stars are so brilliant, they're the only light we need.

"Nice night."

She looks to the heavens. "It is."

"Your friends did a good job. This party really is lit."

"Yeah."

"Here." I pull out the small, flat package I've had buried in my front pocket for hours and hand it to her. "Happy birth-day."

"You got me a present?" Her appreciation is sincere. Her eyes are overflowing with it.

"It's not much." I don't have a lot to give. I'd have done more if I could've.

She knocks her shoulder into mine like she's heard my thoughts, then tears at the corners of the sparkly-green wrapping paper. When it falls away, she gasps.

"How did you know I needed these?" It's a pair of pink, wireless-charging knock-off brand AirPods—I could never afford the real ones on my stipend—but these are supposed to be of comparable quality.

"I heard you mention to your mom before your run the other day that your old ones weren't charging right."

"You notice everything, don't you? I mean, you're like, hyper-aware of your surroundings."

She picked up on that, huh? No use lying to her about it—not after she had to coddle me at Jim Corbett, definitely not after she heard one of the shittier parts of my life story. "This is going to sound messed up to you, but it's a survival skill. I've had to watch my step a lot."

She takes my hand, slips her fingers between mine. "You don't have to do that with us." She doesn't say we'll never hurt you, though that's what she means.

"I know." I honestly do.

The ranch sliders glide open, and a handful of tipsy kids spill out onto the patio. She drops my hand, jumps up fast, and shoves the earbuds into her jeans pocket. "I should head back inside. It doesn't look good if the guest of honor bails on her own party."

"You're right."

She cuts through the small group—all of whom slur out birthday wishes—and ducks into the house. She doesn't check to see if I'm behind her. What is her deal?

She's so hot and cold sometimes. You're one to talk.

"Do YOU WANT A DRINK?" I ask once I've caught up with her.

"No, thanks. I'm okay."

I amble to the kitchen alone. I'm not much for alcohol, though I opt to pour myself a beer. As I finish, I hear her shout so loudly that it trounces the music: "What are you doing here?" She's perturbed more than pissed, but definitely both.

She's not in my line of sight; I can't see who's on the receiving end, although I have a solid idea. I leave the beer on the counter and rush into the living room. She is face-to-face with Kanan.

Kanan's posture is tense and stiff as a board. His fists are clenched at his sides.

Tara's not much better, with her arms folded across her chest. "I asked you a question."

People are gawping at the spectacle as if they're expecting a physical fight. That's not what this is. What is it, exactly? I know they don't like each other, but this is beyond awkward.

Kanan's jaw slackens. "Jatin invited me."

Tara's eyes are glassy. Is she going to cry? "Can you leave?"

Kanan doubles down. "This might be your party, but it's his house. I'm not leaving unless he asks me to."

Tara scans around for Jatin. He's nowhere to be found.

Damn it. I have to squeeze through two muscular-ass football players to get to Kanan. "Hey, you." I flash him a smile and focus on him and only him. Everything's cool. "Come get a drink with me." It takes a tiny nudge to get him moving.

"Dope. I need a beer." He nails Tara with a look I can't quite place. "Happy birthday."

I steer him around Tara, and we disappear into the ocean of bodies.

Kanan hops up to sit on the counter. I have a'she came with me, she's leaving with me' policy when it comes to large gatherings, but I might have to break it this time. "Do you want to go?"

"Nah. She's being a bitch. Screw her," he says. He doesn't mean it. His expression tells me that he is hurt, not heated.

I reach around him to grab a cup, fill it with beer, and hand it to him, then pick up the one I left on the counter. "Drink."

We dance, song after song. I'm afraid to let him stop. As long as we're staying together, he is not looking for Tara. Neither am I. I haven't seen her in a while. I hope she's okay.

A new tune pumps through the speakers, older but so damn good—Zeds Dead "Lights Out." It has a slower, sexier sound than the previous track. The bass reverberates through my torso. The singer's voice gives me goosebumps.

Kanan puts her hands on my hips and pulls me closer to her. Please, don't. He does, bows his head to make up for the height difference between us, and plants his lips on mine. He gives himself a little taste of me with his tongue. One more try. I grant him entry into my mouth.

His lips are soft, and he is a good kisser.

Still, it's wrong.

I hate having to turn down. It's never easy, but it's better than stringing them along. Please don't let this ruin our friendship. I palm his shoulder and push him gently away. "Kanan."

"I had to shoot my shot." He smirks. "I think we're both tops."

We erupt into raucous laughter. By the start of the next song, we're right back to dancing.

"IT'S ALMOST MIDNIGHT. Turn the music off!" Avani yells to whoever's playing DJ for the evening. "Where's Tara?"

"Right here!" Tara stands up from the couch. Or she tries to stand. Her legs are wobbly and about to quit on her.

"Get over here, birthday girl!"

That's not going to happen. She's blown past buzzed and gone straight for crunk.

I'm about to leave Kanan and go to Tara when Karthik jumps to his feet. He slithers an arm around her waist and takes more than a little bit of her weight.

"Here we come!"

Kritika flicks off the lights. Meera and Bhavya present the cake, ablaze with enough candles to burn the place to the ground.

"Happy birthday to you." Everyone, including Kanan and me, joins the chorus.

It takes everything Tara has to blow out the candles. She turns a sickly green the instant the last flame dies.

Funny how your body functions when you're drunk; one minute you can barely stand on your own, the next you're able to run to the bathroom unaided. The bathroom is where she's hauling ass now.

Karthik is too embarrassed for her to follow.

and make sure she's alright.

I go over to him. "I've got this one."

"Cool," he says, relieved.

Tara's hair is still in its ponytail—I've secured her bangs behind her ears,so I don't have to hold it off her face. Instead,

I rub her back. The sound of her retching is bad. The smell of Jägerbombs and bile is worse.

She finishes vomiting her guts into the toilet. I hand her some TP so she can wipe her mouth. She sits, back propped against the ceramic sink basin, and gapes up at me. "You're soft in there." She smiles and points at my heart. "Reminds me of my sister."

HER WHAT? "I didn't know you had a sister."

A vexed snort leaches out of her. "Why would you? Not like anyone ever talks about Raina." She slurs her sister's name.

Raina! "I don't even have any pictures of her in the house. Guess it's easier to try to forget she ever existed than wrap your head around what happened."

"What happened?"

"She died two years ago."

Holy weeping Christ. That's why no one has ever mentioned her; it's too painful for them. "I'm sorry."

"Yeah, me, too."

"How." I shouldn't ask—it'll sting for her—but I need to know. "How did she die?"

Her head lolls back. She scrunches her eyes and swallows hard. "Not tonight. Not on my fuckin' birthday."

"Okay." My voice is so hushed, it's near a whisper. "Come on, I'm taking you home."

HER ARMS ARE WRAPPED around my torso, and I have my arm slung around her shoulder. She's leaning against me so hard that neither of us can walk in a straight line.

I have to get her home, but I don't want Aunty to see her like this. I wish you had a license now. Shit. I could call a cab, but I don't have any cash on me. Uber might be an option.

And then Kanan is with us.

"I hate to ask—"

She stops me. "No worries. I got you."

I POUR Tara into the backseat of Sweet Trixy, slide in next to her, and slam the door. Kanan turns over the engine and shoots us a look in the rearview mirror.

She's seen this spectacular shitshow of Tara's before, perhaps more than once.

The hell? Oh my God, Raina.

Tara's eyes are closed, and her head is resting on my shoulder. I smoothed her hair.

It's a long ride and a short one all at once.

"CAN YOU GET HER INSIDE?" Kanan questions from the driver's side window.

Tara's a tad more put together now after her micro-nap. "Yes. Thanks for the ride."

"No problem."

He idles at the curb until we're in the house, then I hear her drive away.

It's one in the morning. The house is silent. Aunty's asleep. We take the stairs slowly and quietly. She's got her arms around me again.

I flip the switch in her bedroom, and the overhead light flickers on. "Too bright," she growls. I lower her onto her bed, turn off the overhead, and switch on the desk lamp.

I grab the garbage pail from beneath her desk. "I'm leaving this here for you in case you need it." I show her the pail and exactly where I'm putting it.

"Mmm." She unbuttons her jeans.

Please let her be able to get undressed on her own. "Can you get me a shirt? In the… thingy…" She flaps her hand at her bureau.

I chose an oversized tee from the top shelf. By the time I turn around again, she's in her bra and panties. I look at the carpet and study its geometric patterns as I hand her the shirt. My work for the evening is done. Without another word, I leave, turning off the lamp and closing the door behind me.

Chapter 19

I'm startled awake by the sound of Tara's voice passing my door in the hall. It's not angry—necessarily more annoyed. "You can't just barge into my room! I've asked you a hundred times to knock. God, I'd kill for a door that locks."

Then comes Aunty's voice, collected.

"Your car wasn't in the driveway. I was making sure you were home."

Taea chokes back her exasperation. "I know. Sorry."

It's silent for a moment. I figure it's as good a time as any to intrude. I open my door and poke my head into the hallway.

"G'morning," I say, wiping the remainder of sleep from my eyes.

"Good morning," Aunty replies.

Tara says, "Hey!"

I step out and close the door behind me.

Aunty smiles at me. "I'm making breakfast. I hope you're hungry. I mixed too much batter; there'll be about a thousand pancakes."

My stomach rumbles at the mention of food. "I think I could eat a thousand pancakes on my own."

She perks up. Good answer. "So, you accept the mission! Excellent, excellent. See you down there." She bounds downstairs.

Tara's mascara has run amok. I want to reach out to her and wipe away the black streaks from under her eyes. "You look like shit." The words creep past my lips without permission. Such a charmer.

I anticipate indignation, but she chuckles, then winces. Her hand rockets up to her right temple, and she massages it. "I feel like shit."

"Wash your face and brush your teeth. It'll help."

She shuffles to the bathroom. "Thanks for everything last night, by the way."

"You should thank Kanan. He's the one who gave us a ride."

Her mouth curves into a frown.

I can't stop staring at either of them over breakfast—or even hours later, as the three of us laze on the couch in the living room watching TV.

Raina.

I've seen the incredible amount of love this family has for one another, and I have never felt so fortunate not to have a family of my own. I cannot imagine what it's like to have a piece of my heart torn away the way they have. I don't want to imagine it. Yet both Tara and Aunty—and Uncle, so cheery and positive all of the time—are so normal, carrying on with their lives as though they aren't suffering. Maybe they aren't suffering every minute of the day—not anymore, anyway; maybe two years have given them some time to heal. But still… A single second of that kind of heartache is enough for eternity.

All of a sudden, I feel unbelievably stupid. Blind. I never even noticed it.

No, that isn't true. I've caught glimpses of their sorrow—droplets that seeped through tiny fissures. But those crevices were always plastered over so quickly that I wasn't able to make sense of it. Now that I know, I wish I hadn't. I hate being aware of their burden. I hate that they have to bear it at all.

I hate that I know I'm living in Tara's dead sister's room, and that's why she was so freaked out about knocking on my door.

I hate how awful it must be for her, the loneliness she must feel, and how she'll never ever say it out loud.

I hate that I know Raina and Kanan were friends, and that's why Aunty was so surprised and happy to see him that day.

Because regardless of whatever happened between Tara and Kanan, Aunty still cares about her dead daughter's friend—she's the kind to nurture even guttersnipes like me.

What I hate most of all is how helpless I feel; there's nothing I can do to make it better for any of them. I'm a spectator observing the aftermath of their calamity, useless as a glass hammer.

"It's getting late, honey." Aunty pats Tara's thigh. "Why don't I drop you off at your car?"

"Okay." She turns her attention to me.

"Wanna come?"

"Yeah."

I NOTICE her messing with her ring-neck lace when we stopped at a red light on the way back from Jatin's. It's not the 'getting used to new jewelry' kind of absentminded fiddling; it's purposeful, introspective. I understand why—it isn't just another pretty bauble to add to her collection. I gesture to the miniscule crown.

"That belonged to your sister, huh?"

She's caught off guard by my insight.

She crumples her lips, determining what she wants to disclose. The light turns green. She puts her foot on the gas, then nods and says, "My parents gave it to her for her last birthday. It was the only piece of jewelry she ever wore." A subtle smirk.

"She wasn't into glitzy girlie stuff, unlike me. Sometimes I wondered where she came from; the two of us were such opposites."

"I've seen that between siblings before. I think it's common."

We take a turn, and she brings the car to a stop in front of Park.

She used to come here with Raina. They probably grew up playing here—countless hours on the swings or pretending to be Princess and Knight in the castle. It must be excruciating for her to be here now.

She looks at me. "Last night, you asked me how she died. Do you still want to know?"

"Yes, I do." And she wants to talk about it.

She turns the engine off and pulls the keys from the starter. "Take a walk with me."

We head for the playground. She's quiet the whole way, her hands jammed in her coat pockets. I'm glad the sun is setting. It's starting to get chilly; all the children have gone home. She jumps on a swing and kicks up mulch. "It's a long story."

I make myself comfortable on the swing next to hers. "I've got time."

"I've never told anybody before, not even my parents."

"I'm listening."

She takes the deepest breath and exhales hard. "Kanan and I... we killed her."

What the ever-loving fuck is she talking about? This girl has her secrets, and I'm sure Kanan does, too, but this would be too heavy for any two people to keep quiet. "Wait. That doesn't make sense. Start at the beginning."

She pinches her bottom lip between her thumb and forefinger, gives it a slight twist, and lets it go. "Raina was a little more than a year older than me, a grade ahead in school. And she was so cool. I was the typical baby sister who wanted to do everything she did. She got into a dance group, so I did, too. Ahh. Okay. " I don't know if you know this about Kanan yet, but he's really good at math. Like, so good, they put him in eighth grade algebra when he was in seventh grade. That's where he and Raina met. Raina sucked at math, and Kanan, being the nice person that he is, wanted to help her. They got along really well, and after a while, they were inseparable. Raina was an awesome big sister; she always included me in everything they did. We were a trio, the Three Amigos, you know? For a long time, it was great, up until the end of sophomore year."

She fidgets a bit and takes another breath.

"That's when things started to change between Kanan and me; they got physical. It started with a kiss on the cheek, and then the next thing I knew, we were sneaking away from Raina all the time to go make out. I told myself it was hormones or something, that I wasn't actually into him.

But I was into him. It was so confusing. We agreed to keep it low-key, and we managed to do that for a while. Until one night over summer vacation, there was a party.

"It's hazy, but this is what I remember:

We were both a little drunk—him more than me, I think—but it doesn't really matter.

The room was dark, except for the streetlights coming through the blinds. I could barely see him, but I felt him—he pushed me up against the wall, pressed himself against me, and we were kissing harder than we ever had before. His hands were up my shirt. I unbuttoned his jeans, so fast and so clumsy, because I wanted him.

I'd been waiting so long for it to happen, and finally it was going to.

"Then the bedroom door flew open.

The music from the party wasn't muffled anymore. The light from the hallway was so bright. Someone screamed his name.

It was Raina. She didn't even give us a chance to say anything; she just stomped out.

I chased her all the way down the street, begging her to talk to me. Eventually she turned around and yelled, 'You've been lying to my face, the two people in the world I trust the most!' The last words she ever said to me were, 'Find your own way home' before she got in the car and drove away."

She wipes tears from her cheeks. "The craziest thing is she wasn't even drinking that night. We did a coin toss, and she lost, so she was the DD. She must've taken a curve too fast. Her Jeep kind of tumbled off the road and wrapped around a tree.

Do you get it now? Kanan and I killed my sister."

Raina. Kanan. Tara. Finally, she's in full focus—sharper than she has ever been. Grey wasn't always one of her colors; she used to be pink, unadulterated. And then she lost too much.

"You did not!" I'm surprised at the sternness and loudness of my voice.

She edges her swing away from me.

Too firm. This is a delicate conversation.

I can't be so adamant." I've had a relative in Delhi who had two daughters—even a set of twins. Trust me, I have seen some arguments. The sisters fight all the time.

You had a misunderstanding with yours, and she stormed off—that's normal. She wasn't thinking clearly. She had an accident, and she died. It's horrible, and I'm sorry that she's gone, but it wasn't your fault." It wasn't Kanan's, either.

She sighs. "The worst part is that Raina probably would've been cool with it. Like, who cares if I'm with Kanan, right? I could marry Kanan tomorrow if I wanted to. I think it was the lying; she couldn't stand it. I'll never know for sure."

"It's not the easiest thing—realizing you're different and owning it. It can be scary. When you care about people, their opinions of you are important. You might think they're evolved and open-minded, but there's always a chance you're wrong."

"That's true. But I knew Raina; she loved me. I should've trusted her."

"You can't beat yourself up about it forever. You can't beat Kanan up about it forever, either." Poor Kanan

She rubs her forehead. "Things got way too fucked up between us to ever salvage.

It's best for both of us to stay away from each other."

"I understand."

"Now that you know what happened, I'd appreciate it if it could stay between us."

I have to tell Kanan that I know; otherwise, I'll always feel like I'm lying to him about this terrible, mountainous thing.

More importantly, I want him to know that this is a secret he doesn't have to keep anymore. Now, there are three people in it. There's a crowd. And one is the loneliest number. "I'm not going to say anything to anyone." Anyone who didn't live it

Aunty IS STILL CURLED up on the couch when we get home. Tara sits down beside her, and I drop onto the recliner. "You were gone awhile," Aunty says.

"I told her."

Aunty sees the look on her daughter's face; she doesn't have to ask what I was told.

"I am so sorry, aunty." It's inadequate, but it's all I have.

"Thank you," she says with a wounded smile.

Chapter 20

It is the strangest day. There's been a knot in my stomach since I woke up. I want to talk to Kanan about the knowledge Tara dropped on me, but at school... There are too many prying eyes and ears, and I don't know how he'll react, so privacy is best. I sent him a text between E and F Blocks asking if we could hang out after he was done with tennis, but he hasn't seen it yet.

Tara and I have an exam on *1984* in English tomorrow that's worth a third of our grade for the marking period. Mrs. Sunanda gave us an updated question guide this morning. We're having lunch together to get a jump on cramming. I don't know what made her think that studying in the cafeteria would be feasible. It isn't. It's too noisy. Her friends don't seem to understand the concept of studying either—they keep interrupting us after every other question.

"Yo, Ved, are you and Kanan a couple or just smashing?" Kritika asks.

Tara's head snaps up from her notecard. She gives Kritika the nastiest look I've seen her give anyone to date. The scowl makes Kritika wither, a flower at the mercy of a killing frost.

I'm thrown by the question, too.

"What?"

Kritika surveys Tara, asking, 'Permission to speak?' without words. Tara's lips are pursed, her brow raised. She's waiting for her cue to strike. Kritika goes, "Like, the entire school saw you guys making out at Tara's party, and you're always together." And? "Would you have a problem with it either way?"

She shakes her head. "It's your business, not mine."

"Then why the fuck did you ask her?"

Tara spits. "Because you have to stick your nose in everyone's business, right?" To me, she says, "You don't have to answer that."

I let myself touch her shoulder the way I've seen my uncle do sometimes, hoping it would pacify her and giving little thought to what it'd do to me. "It's okay; I don't mind." I glare at Kritika. "Kanan and I are just friends."

"Uh huh," Kritika retorts, then looks down at her food tray and stabs her fork into the pile of potatoes.

Why bother? The zipped pocket of my messenger bag vibrates. I open it and grab my iPhone.

Kanan: Yeah. Come 2 practice?

That's something jocks ask their girlfriends to do. Come watch them practice.

Boring. But this is my chance to talk to him.

I skim my eyes around the café and see him at our regular table, phone in hand.

Will do.

I turn to Tara and notice her leering at my phone before she can flick her eyes away from the screen.

Got ya. "I'm gonna stay after school. I'll catch a ride to the house later."

""Kay." She holds a flash card close to her face. "Winston commits thoughtcrime by writing what in his diary?"

"Down with Big Brother"."

I watch students' football practice from the middle section of the bleachers. Kanan and his coaches run it like they're equals, dividing up groups for passing drills and, later, a mini-scrimmage. He is impressive and really knows the game and his teammates' individual skills. I wouldn't be surprised if he went professional someday.

I got to catch one of his matches. I like tennis.

It's one of the few sports I understand.

The coaches call it a day, and Kanan heads for his bag on the sideline bench.

He signals for me to join him on the field as he's toweling the sweat from his neck.

"Suh?" He throws the cloth at me.

I shriek like a total priss and lob it back at him. "Gross."

He chuckles and stuffs it in his gym bag.

"Ready?"

"Mmhmm."

"Did you have an idea where you wanted to go or..." He asks.

"Someplace quiet so we can talk."

He wasn't ready for that response. It concerns him. "Uh, okay. I know a place."

He pulls his car into D Block Park, right up to the deserted baseball field. He gets out of the car, and I follow him to the diamond, where he glides onto the bench in the home dugout. "This work?"

I peep around. There's no one in sight.

"Yep." I slide in next to him.

"Man, you're so serious right now.

What's goin' on?"

I don't know how to start. There's no delicate way to phrase it. It's a band-aid.

covering a bullet hole. Rip that bitch right off. "Tara told me about Raina, about how she died, and everything that led up to it."

He folds his hands together, brings the sides of his knuckles to his lips, and lets a puffpuffpuff out against them to warm them. Then he drops them into his lap and concentrates on me. "Everything?"

"Everything." Not a detail was spared.

He lets out a disbelieving snigger. "I wasn't sure she'd ever have the balls for that."

"Well, surprise."

"I'm relieved. Not being able to talk about it has sucked for me."

"We can talk about it, if you want." He smacks his lips together. "What's there to say? My best friend died, and my first girlfriend ever pushed me away because she blamed it on our relationship. I loved them both, then, just like that." He snaps his fingers—"I didn't have either of them anymore." He lets out a breath. "My run-in with Tara at the party?

That was the first time we'd spoken in almost two years. Everyone figured we drifted apart without Raina around, like she was the only connection we had, and I couldn't say any different because outing her would've made me an asshole. It was a clusterfuck." He tries to stop himself from tearing up but fails—falls into a deep, silent, body-shaking kind of sobbing.

It breaks me.

I don't hesitate; I wrap my arms around his neck and tug him into the tightest embrace. His hands climb my back, grasping swaths of my hoodie. "You can let it go now," I whisper into his ear. "Let it all go." I held him for the longest time as he quietly cries.

HIS EYES ARE STILL BLOODSHOT when he drops me off at home, he seems lighter in every sense. "Remember that thing I said about you being a politician when you grow up?" He asks as I'm about to hop onto the curb.

"What about it?" Take it back. You should be a therapist. You even got Tara to open up to you."

"I didn't do anything. I just listened."

"It's more than that. Something about you made her want to talk. Same with me.

I guess what I'm trying to say is, "Thanks." That makes me smile. "Anytime."

I missed dinner and forgot to let anyone know I'd be out. Aunty is cool about it, though. She meets me in the hallway outside the living room, takes one look at me, and asks, "Are you feeling alright?"

"Yeah, sorry. I lost track of time!"

"It's okay. There are leftovers in the fridge."

"Thanks. I'm gonna go study. Big test tomorrow."

As I head up, I run into Tara on the second-floor landing. I know there's something off about me, and I can't hide it because she squints at me and wonders,

"What's with you?"

I hardly have enough room for all of my own baggage, so dealing with other people takes a lot out of me. Sometimes when they get really emotional, it makes me feel like I'm drowning—a symptom of empathy, I suppose. The last two days I've been hit with wave after wave and... "I'm so tired."

She does something so unexpected that I can't do anything but capitulate: She hugs me. My arms snake around her waist, and suddenly we're holding each other.

It's funny how a single reflexive motion can turn a hug into a hold.

Her citrusy scent inundated my consciousness. Every part of my body feels warm, and all of my muscles slack. I could get used to feeling like this. Safe. Safe in her arms. I tear myself away from her. "I know we were supposed to work on those test questions for tomorrow, but I need to go to bed."

"It's not a problem. Get some sleep."

"G'night."

Chapter 21

Raina's premature departure from the world is something that we all know about now—nothing more than that. Neither Tara nor Kanan seem to want to talk about it any further. I haven't heard her name at all in the last two days. It's fine—better than having heard it to begin with.

Amit Uncle got back from Japan around midnight last night—I heard the security alarm beep when he came in. He knows that I know what happened to his eldest daughter; I overheard Kavita tell him as much before I walked into the kitchen for breakfast. He doesn't do it to me.

He hands me a package wrapped in washi paper. "Souvenir." He grins. "Next time, we're all going. Family trip."

Family trip… I know better than to question him, so I opt to gulp down my disappointment and open the package. There's folded cloth inside. I unfurl it. It's stunning. "It's beautiful. I love it."

He winks. "I thought you might."

"Dad!" Tara bounds into the kitchen and leaps onto her father's back.

Uncle goes, "Oof!" Then he scoops her into a bear hug. "Hey, Kiddo!" He kisses her forehead and produces another package from the back pocket of his jeans. "For you." He smirks as he hands it to her.

She opens it, pulls out a cream-colored card stamped with Japanese characters, and below those: "Kan-za-shi,' she reads. She plucks the present from the box. It's a traditional Japanese hairstick with a strand of white-pink faux cherry blossoms attached to the end and gold filigree on each leaf. "This is gorgeous!"

"Two for two." He pumps a triumphant fist.

Tara takes a gander at my tapestry.

"Oh, cool!"

Aunty's at the stove making omelets, which is insane. I don't know how she manages to cook breakfast every morning and forget when she has to spend her day in court. I know when she's going to be in front of a judge, her outfits are smarter than when she's headed to her office: suits, dark blues, and grays, rather than colorful business-casual dresses. "And where's my present?"

"You'll get yours later." Uncle gives her a naughty eyebrow wiggle.

Gag!

Tara goes, "Eurgh!"

Aunty chuckles and plates the eggs.

"Let's eat!"

I'm not hungry anymore, but I make myself scarf my omelet anyway.

MIDWAY TO SCHOOL, Tara says, "So, Gallery Night. Are you excited?"

No, I'm petrified. Mr. Ravi told me that my photos were "really lovely," but that's his job—to encourage us. No one else has to say nice things. They could call my work straight trash, and I'd have no choice but to swallow it. "More like nervous."

She shoots me a glare that lets me know it's the dumbest thing she's ever heard. "Don't be. I told you your stuff is good, and tonight everyone else will see that, too."

"Mmm. Maybe."

"Not maybe. Definitely."

Damn it. Sometimes I can't stand it when she's kind. It makes me like her more. "Okay, definitely."

"Better." I catch her beaming.

I ACED THE ENGLISH TEST. The only thing left to dread is Gallery Night, which starts in thirty minutes. The photography club arrives early to the auditorium to finish last-minute prep. The place is set up to look like a real art gallery. There's a section for paintings, one for sculpture, one for performance art pieces, and one for photography. Tara and I are sitting at a table in the photography section, mounting photos on gray mat boards that Mr. Ravi gave us—he said it would be more professional if they were displayed that way, and I decided to take his word for it.

I've numbered each of my eight pictures to show that they should be viewed in order from left to right. The first two—the eagle and falcon—are cool-toned and natural; the next four—the series of the boy on the swing—grow gradually warmer; and the last two of Salem willows are overwhelmingly vivid, their red-orange tones and saturation tuned up high. It's a theme, to be sure: Beauty comes in many forms. I wish I could've shown a picture of Tara. She's got all the forms covered.

Mr. Ravi calls to me as I finish mounting the last picture. Tara and I both look up. He's approaching the table with a tall woman who looks like she time-jumped out of the seventies—flowing brown skirt, beige music tunic top, curly brown hair down to her waist. Everything but a crown of flowers "Vedika, Tara, this is my friend Sara. She's a professor of photography at the School of the Art Institute of Chicago."

"Hello." She shakes our hands.

"Hi," Tara says.

"Professor." I nod.

"Sara," she corrects me. "Do you have a moment to discuss your work?"

I peek at Tara. Her eyebrows are raised, and she's sporting a simper.

"Sure." I pull out the folding chair next to my mind, and Sara sits. She picks up each photo and is quiet as she examines them.

"The gradation of color is very striking. Can you tell me a little bit about your reasoning behind grouping these shots together, and why in this particular order?"

"Uh, yeah." "I motion to the left side of the table. "These are raw; there is no editing at all; this is exactly how I captured them. And as we move to the right, the photos become more and more heavily tweaked—light and shadow, color intensity, blurring, or crispness. I was trying to highlight the difference between real and manufactured and how both can be alluring in their own ways."

"And Mr. Ravi told me that all of our photos were taken with a basic point-and-shoot camera. Is that right?"

He talked about my stuff with her.

Duh, simpleton, why else do you think she'd be wasting her time with you? "All I had to work with was a Canon PowerShot, so yes."

She covers her mouth with her fingers and scours over each picture again. "These are fantastic. I'd love to see what you could do with more advanced equipment. You have an eye for the truth of things, the stuff that exists beneath the surface, and that's a rare gift. I hope you continue to nurture it."

"I'm going to try. My plan is to major in photography next year."

"Glad to hear it." She reaches into her clutch, pulls out a business card, and hands it to me. "If you need advice on putting together your portfolio—say, for an application to the School of the Art Institute of Chicago in the fall—I'd be happy to help."

I'm gobsmacked. "That would be great. Thank you."

"You're welcome." She stands. "Keep taking pictures. Tara, it was nice to meet you." She goes to rejoin Mr. Ravi, who's setting up the refreshments table.

Tara's rubbernecking me. "A photography professor just critiqued your work, called it fantastic, and wants to help you get into college. How are you not flipping out right now?"

"I am. On the inside."

"You can do it on the outside; you know, you should."

I'm too practiced at keeping heartfelt joy to myself—I never know how fleeting it might be, and I like to hold onto it for as long as I can. If no one else knows about it, no one else can wreck it for me. She's seen my worst, though, so that has to entitle her to my best, too. "Okay, okay, that was so cool!" I throw my head back and squeal into my hands.

"There you go," she says through her laughter.

I'VE BEEN POSTED UP near my photos and haven't heard any negative comments on any of them from anyone so far—baffling, since kids can be cruel. I've had a bunch of strangers talk to me about them, ask where I took them, and ask what software I used to edit them. I've gotten a ton of "Wow," "Pretty," and "Nice." Even the art teachers have expressed their appreciation. It's beginning to get overwhelming with all these compliments. I was never good at taking them.

The auditorium is getting wickedly full. Loads of parents are piling in to view their kid's artwork, as if this were a professional exhibit—their son or daughter's big break. It's bittersweet for me. I'm happy that so many of my peers have parents who care enough to show up for them, and I'm sad that I don't.

"Yo, Ved, these are sick AF."

Bhavya? And Mani, and Himanshi, and, of course, Kanan. Good thing Tara's off checking out the sculptures. "I can't believe you guys came."

Kanan screws up his features. "You were stoked enough about this to invite us. We know it was important." He throws his arm around my shoulder and makes me stand in front of my display. It's the hundredth time tonight, but this time feels special.

"The ones of the little boy are so cute."

Himanshi comments.

Mani adds, "The color's nice, too. Crazy blue."

Bhavya moves her face closer to the picture of the peregrine. "Eh, yo, what kind of bird is this? A hawk?"

"It's a falcon."

"Bruh, what's the difference?"

I let out a puff and launched into a mini-anatomy lesson on raptorial birds. The five of us chat for a bit, until Kanan spies Tara approaching. She elbows Mani. "Let's go look at the sculptures, guys."

"Aight," Bhavya responds, "deuces." She daps me.

"Nice work," Himanshi says, and he gives me a high five.

Mani nods at me. "Good shit." It's the most polite thing she's ever said to me.

Kanan puts his arm up for a hug. "Thanks for inviting us. It was very cool."

The dam's been broken. Hugging is going to be the way it is for us now, and I'm good with that. "Thanks for coming."

When they've gone, Tara sidles upside me. "Guess who's here?"

"Who?"

She pointed to the rear of the auditorium. There, coming through the propped open doors, care Uncle and Aunty. "You invited your parents? You didn't even submit any photos."

"They're here for you, dummy."

Oh. Wow. That's something else. There's a heat rising from my chest, splashing out all over me. I know this feeling. No crying!

Uncle spots us first and points us out to Aunty. Both of their faces light up once they realize I've seen them. The edge over to us through the crowd. "Hi, girls!" Uncle says. Aunty waves, then goes straight for my pictures. Uncle joins her.

I don't want to stand too close to them. I still haven't gotten rid of the lump in my throat, and if I overhear their hushed words to each other—especially if they're praising—it won't bode well for my No Crying mandate.

After a while, Aunty seeks me out. Her eyes are bright and soft. "These are wonderful, just gorgeous." She clasps my hand, gives it a little squeeze, and lets it go without any urgency.

Uncle echoes the sentiment: "You did a great job, kiddo! I'm proud of you." He pats my shoulder. Proud of me? Don't you dare tear up! "I'm glad you like them. Um, excuse me for a minute."

I head out of the auditorium as fast as my feet will carry me without breaking into a jog. The bathroom across the lobby is empty—a mercy. I turn on one of the taps and splash some cold water on my face. Drip. Drip. I stare at my reflection in the mirror until I'm certain the threatening torrent has dissipated.

Uncle AND Aunty stayed the entire evening. The four of us stroll around, taking in the artwork. Uncle gets really into a performance piece called Shadowplay, which is self-explanatory: colorful paper screens, a spotlight, and the shadows of gyrating bodies. Neither Tara nor I understand the appeal, but different types of people like different types of art.

At nine o'clock, the head of the art department closes the night with a speech thanking all the visitors and asking for a round of applause for all the student artists. Uncle, Aunty, and Tara make a show of clapping for me, and I can feel my cheeks flushing. Afterward, I take my photos down from the canvas, and then Tara and I walk her parents to Aunty's car.

"Thank you for coming tonight, guys," I say. But it falls flat. They showed up for me in a way no one else ever has; the least I can do is give them each a hug. And I want to, so I go for it—Aunty first, who's so gentle about it, and then Uncle, who gives me what must be the best version of a dad hug in existence, little "rawr' included, just like with Tara this morning.

As they drive away, I decide that I wouldn't mind if mom-and-dad hugs were to become a more regular occurrence in my life. Within reason.

TARA KEEPS SHIFTING her attention between the road and me on the drive to the house—harried glimpses stolen when she thinks I'm not looking. Is she going to say something or not?

"My parents really like you. Dad said you're 'a good girl' and I was like, 'Okay, Boomer,' because who even says that anymore?'

I chuckle. It's exactly what I needed. "I like them, too."

"Yeah, they're alright."

No, they're extraordinary.

"I love the picture of the boy jumping off the swing—the shadowy one where he's blocking the sun. Can I have it?" She asks as we're entering the house. I'm carrying all of my photos in my hands, piled on top of each other.

"I'll trade you."

"For what?"

"You have to let me take your picture with legit, full knowledge and permission.

"What, like, right now?"

"Whenever you want. We'll do a photoshoot in the park."

She does her lip-bite thing and mulls over the proposition. "If you promise to make me look as beautiful as you did the first time,"

"I told you that wasn't me. It's all you." Whew, ballsy. Where'd that even come from? And there's the trill in my goddamn stomach again.

She pushes her hair behind her ear and drops her gaze to the floor. "Okay, it's a deal."

I flip through the photos, pull out the picture she requested, and hand it to her. "Advanced payment for services to be rendered"

She goes tsss. "You'll never make any money with a bartering system."

I shrug. Who needs it, anyway?

Chapter 22

All anyone can talk about at school on Thursday and Friday is something called a Pep party that's going down tonight. The concept of this particular social gathering is completely foreign to me: all the senior athletes across every sport from every season get together to throw this huge celebration of their jockdom, as if that's the only interesting quality any of them possess. Big yawn. It's semi-sponsored by school, meaning that coaches and other affiliated adults are welcome, but I've heard that some kids sneak in alcohol right under their noses, which is the most high school thing ever—tactless and excessive. There are enough unsupervised house parties for underage alcohol consumption; they could stand to give it a rest around their coaches.

Bhavya is psyched about going. Kanan is not. He seems uneasy over it. The bell signaling the end of lunch block rings, and, as we're herding out of the caf, I ask about it. "You want to skip the Pep Party? We could do something instead."

"I'm a captain. Captains can't swerve it."

Oh, I see. This school has its own tradition, like the Fall Ball in November instead of a Homecoming dance at the start of the autumn sports season. I guess it's to make everyone feel included, not just the people who've earned letter-jeckets. "I can see you're thrilled about it."

He lowers his voice. "I don't know if Tara's going to be there. She quit cheerleading, but..."

For fuck's sake, can't these two parley long enough to honor something they both think is monumental? I was hoping that now that they've each gotten it off their chests, things would be a bit better—at least semi-tolerable. "I could try to get her not to go." How, ask her out to dinner and a movie? like she'd say yes. Bisexuality doesn't mean 'attracted to every individual on earth.'

"No. She has as much right to be there as I do. I'll give her the sidestep."

"I'd offer to come with, but I'm not even jock-adjacent."

He stares at me like I'm a genius. "You can come."

I shake my head. "I'd feel like I'm crashing.

"If she asked, you'd go?"

Shit. "I doubt she'll ask." Even if she did, I couldn't accept it now. It'd be too unfair to Kanan. I refuse to choose sides or play favorites, despite the ridiculous crush I have on Tara.

Tara's ready to leave for the party around seven. She's wearing a black and orange St. Mary College cheer T-shirt. Sparkly megaphone, duly noted. "Are uniforms the required dress code for this get-together?" I wonder from my spot on the recliner—my official favorite seat in the house.

"Traditionally, yes, for the fall sports. Since I don't have mine anymore, this will have to do."

"Give 'em hell."

She splutters. I think that's the end of it, but she reverses course and walks into the living room. "You wouldn't want to come, would you? I'm just putting in a cameo." She makes a half-hearted attempt to hide her hopefulness.

Parties seriously aren't her thing. Not since Raina died. "I really wouldn't." Damn her and her dejected eyes.

I hear the ding-dong of the doorbell from my room and look at my desk clock—seven forty-five.

"Vedika!" Uncle hollers. "You have a visitor."

Footsteps pound up the stairs. There's a knock on my door. I open it to find Kanan, long auburn locks loose and flowing over his football jersey that's half tucked into his jeans. "Hi? Come in."

He takes a hesitant step through the threshold and peeks around. "It's weird being in here again. The furniture's different."

I want to tell him that Tara can't stand it, either. "So... What's happening?"

He slips his hands into her back pockets. "You weren't at the party.

"Tara didn't invite me."

He folds his arm across his chest. "I call bullshit."

"Okay, fine. I didn't feel like going."

"Why not?"

"I don't want to get stuck taking care of her again if she gets plastered." It's only half untrue. Her birthday was a disaster, and I honestly didn't like seeing her that way, but I'd be alright with taking care of her if she needed me to. The whole truth is, I don't want to be a shield for either of them; I want them to hash it out. They can't go on egg-shelling indefinitely.

"I'm not built like that."

"No, you aren't." He relaxes and smirks. "We'll take it as it comes. Let's go, get dressed."

He wants me to be there badly enough to have left the damn party to come get me. How can I say no to him? Try, 'If I can't go in my pajamas, then I can't go.' Sigh. "Give me a sec." He doesn't move. "You know you have to get out for me to get changed, alright?"

"Bashful?"

"You're incorrigible."

"So I've been told."

I give him a joking elbow, and he shuffles out to the hall.

He tells me that the Pep Party is being held at Karthik's house—his dad is the assistant coach of the boys' basketball team—and he lives on the other side of town, the less-rich part. We turn down a road that edges up against Club, and it becomes clear to me that there is, in fact, no 'less-rich' part of this town.

The road transforms from paved to unpaved, and the tree line on either side of it gets thicker. "You're not taking me into the woods to murder me. Are you?"

"Nah, I like you; wanna keep you around."

We pull up to an expansive stone ranch house. The gravel driveway is overflowing, with cars spilling onto the manicured grass. Kanan doesn't care anymore than anyone else; he parks on a patch of green stuff.

A few spots ahead of sweet Trixy is Tara's BMW. We saunter past it, and Kanan's entire body goes rigid. He's already seen her once tonight, so why? It's hard for him too—every single time. "You are way too tense. Want to hear a dirty joke?"

"Please?"

"What do Chinese food and pussy have in common?"

He's already snickering. "What?"

"An hour after you've eaten, you're hungry for more."

He guffaws. "That was dirty to you? You should hear my brothers."

"I haven't had the luxury of brothers, so that's the best I can do."

"It was good." He palms the doorknob, and we enter the party. It's basically Tara's birthday 2.0, except everyone's in costume, er, jerseys, and there are grown-ups—not the legit kind, the overly-friendly-with-teenagers, desperately clinging to their lost youth kind.

Kanan says a few hellos to athletes from other sports, mostly cricket.

They're all in full uniform; they must've come from a game. How do they, like, jump or whatever, without those things bunching into their assholes?

We find his teammates. There are six of them gathered around the billiards table, shooting pool and chatting. I've only ever talked about him and Bhavya, so I'm out of my depth. Still, I can fake comfort pretty well in group settings. He introduces me to everyone. I mingle, smile, and laugh along with them.

"What do you think?" a girl named Isha asks me.

"I've gotta tap out on this one."

Bhavya says, "An ass is an ass; it doesn't matter who it's attached to."

"Uh, Big Papi?"

That answer earns me a round of giggles.

"Oh, farm, you are full homo, hundo p!"

"I said I wanted to tap out."

"Great song," Kanan interjects. I strain to hear it over the din of voices. "Get Lucky" by Draft punk

"Oh yeah." I tug him onto the makeshift dance floor.

He knows all the lyrics and sings along as we dance. He has a nice voice, right on key. It's the most laid-back he's been all night. I like it; it's the best version of him—the way he should always be, with no stress or sadness weighing him down.

And then I see Tara. Meera and Avani are working the bar, doling out sodas or beers to the adults and, no doubt, spiked juice cocktails to the kids, and she's hanging around with them.

The song changes, and I stop dancing so abruptly that it knocks Kanan off his groove. "Sup?"

"I want a drink. You?"

"Yes." His mouth curls into a frown as he spots the drink station.

No more goddamn eggshells! "Cowboy up, Kanan!" I take his hand and drag him to the bar.

Tara sees us coming and tosses a glare at Kanan. I hear her say, "I'm gonna dip,' to her friends, and she's off.

"Cowboy up," Kanan stammers a touch above audibility. He grabs Tara's wrist as she's passing us and yanks her to a halt. Tara tries to snatch his arm away; Kanan won't let her go. They lock eyes, and I see the pain on Kanan's fence—bare, inescapable. "I miss Raina, too, you know. She was my best friend. And I miss you."

Tara's gaze darts over to me. Yes, we discussed it. Then it's back on Kanan, and her jaw drops open.

Kanan knows about what she's thinking and adds in a hurry: "You know what I mean, how tight we were before all that. I wish we could go back to the way it was."

"Not gonna happen!" Tara barks. Then, quieter, "Every time I look at you..."

I know that she's not just angry; she's choking on guilt and grief, but all I can seem to concentrate on is her anger. And it makes me angry. Because the two of them had something rare and beautiful before everything went to hell: sincere friendship.

For once, I don't censor myself. I don't even care that there are people around us. "You're an idiot, Tara!"

Her eyes are ready to pop out of her skull. "Excuse me?"

"You're an idiot," I repeat, lower this time, and take a step closer to her. "You can't accept that accidents happen, and you're either too blind or too stupid to see how much Kanan cares about you. I would burn the whole world to the ground for a friend like him. Honestly, do you think your sister would want to see you two like this? 'Cuz I don't."

"What do—"

I throw my hand in the air. "I don't want to hear it." Then I'm pulling on Kanan's arm. "Get me out of here." He looks startled but leads me away in spite of himself.

"Go fuck yourself, Vedika!" Tara yells at my back.

I don't turn around.

INDIGNATION, righteous or not, isn't something I'm used to emoting. It's too frank and too dangerous. I'm drained, leaning against Sweet Trixy's trunk. Kanan is wearing a guise of utter astonishment, scarcely visible in the dimness of the landscape lighting. "I can't believe you said that to her. Nobody talks to Tara Nanda that way."

"She's not the fucking Queen of England."

"She knows that now. I think everyone does."

"I did get loud for a second, didn't I?"

"Uh huh."

"Well, you're both my friends, and I don't like that you can't even be in the same room with one another because of something that wasn't anyone's fault. There's no blame to place here."

"I know that."

"And I really don't like that there's nothing I can do to make her feel better."

"No, that's on her."

I huff. I want to help her get there, but she has to want to get there herself.

"Thanks for sticking up for me."

"That's what friends do, isn't it?" Isn't it?

He grins. "Yeah."

Chapter 23

I manage to avoid Tara on Saturday by holing up in my room, only leaving for the occasional foraging trip to the kitchen. I even skip dinner—sitting at the table with her is a nonstarter. I tell Amit uncle and Kavita aunty that I'm feeling unwell when they come to check on me, which technically isn't a lie, although it's my emotional wellness that's suffering. Kavita Aunty's maternal instinct shines its brightest. She even goes so far as to take my temperature. She's relieved when the thermometer flashes 98.6. I hope it doesn't make her suspicious. "It's probably allergies. Mold," I say. This is true, but we've had a mild autumn so far with very little rainfall.

Amit uncle runs to the store for medicine.

When he returns, he has a glass of water ready. He undoes the child-safety cap and breaks the aluminum seal, then pours a pill into his palm and presents it and the water to me. "Down the hatch." He really does think I'm a child in need of a father. You are.

It's so heartwarming, I can't take it. I do as I'm told and swallow everything.

Once they're gone, I pop in a Blu-ray, one of a handful that I own, of the classic sci-fi horror They Live, and fall asleep.

BY LATE SUNDAY AFTERNOON, it has become intolerable. And we still have another day off. Our first—with a bit of luck, our last—argument had to happen on a three-day weekend. I wouldn't have expected it to go down any other way; fate was always going to make sure I'd have a remarkable amount of time on my hands to brood over it.

Tara's BEEN out for a while. When I ask Kavita Aunty about it, she tells me she's at the mall with Avani and Shreya.

Her absence is advantageous. I can let my guard down while I plant my ass in the recliner and figure out the best way to remedy the shituation.

Groveling for forgiveness won't work; that would annoy her. A simple apology won't be enough. Why the hell did I act without considering the consequences first?

I could cry? That's some weak shit. The only acceptable time for tears is during a panic attack, when my logical brain goes into hibernation and my primordial lizard brain takes over.

I could write her a note? Do you want her to forgive you or laugh in your face?

I could buy her flowers? Lol, wut? No, that's weird. Total wifey move.

The front door opens and closes. I shut my eyes. Please be Amit, uncle. I open them again and see that Tara is standing in the hallway with about fifteen bags in her hands.

Retail therapy.

I scamper to my feet. "Hey."

"Hi."

"You need some help with those?"

She holds out her left hand. I bundle the handles and take the bags from her.

"Come upstairs with me?" she asks.

We head to her room. She closes the door. I place the bags on the floor, then turn around and squirm under her gaze.

She puts the rest of the bags down on her desk. "We should talk." She motions to the bed. "Sit down."

Not her puppet. Or her dog. I sit. Her mattress is the same as mine: comfortable and shape-conforming. She takes a seat beside me. "Look, I wanted to apologize. I shouldn't have told you to go fuck yourself. That was out of line."

"I deserved it. I wasn't the most gracious version of myself, either. I'm sorry, too."

"I know I can be a bitch sometimes, all the time when Kanan is involved."

She groans, "I hate it that I can't just, like, chill out when he's around. I even switched my gym elective last year because I couldn't handle being in class with him for 45 minutes."

"It's the same for him." That's not my truth to share, but she needs to hear it.

"I know. I broke his heart."

That's another thing he can't forgive himself for. "Broken hearts mend. What he can't stand is that his presence hurts you."

She rolls some of her wavy tresses around her finger. "I can't wait to graduate."

Graduation. The only thing I have ever looked forward to is my first step toward freedom—getting to decide what's best for me, living on my own, never having to fear being screamed at, slapped, or locked in a goddamn pantry ever again. Now, I'm wishing it would never come. What happens to us when we're not forced to be together under the same roof at the same school? I couldn't bear it if our relationship were temporary. Regardless of anything else, I care about her. I want her in my life.

"Anyway, I got you something." She leans forward and plucks a paper shopping bag from the desk. She digs inside, pulls out a medium-sized box wrapped in white paper with a rainbow ribbon tied around it, and hands it to me.

I stare at it—at her. "What's this for?"

Compensation for guilt.

"Do you need a reason?" She shrugs. "I saw it and thought of you. Open it." She scoots a little closer to me. I feel her body heat.

I yank at the ribbon, and it comes un-done. I then glide my finger beneath the taped flaps, careful not to rip the paper.

Unwrapped, the box reads Nikon D7500,

18-55 VR Kit. It's a DSLR camera—a very expensive one. My breath catches in my windpipe. "This is too much. I can't accept it." And I can't look at her. Her eyes are all over me, though; I can feel them as if they were her hands.

"Yes, you can. You need a good camera, not that shitty one Mr. Ravi lets you use. Besides, I owe you a photoshoot, and it sure as hell isn't going to be with a PowerShot."

I don't know if it's because of the sudden influx of honesty or the absolute deluge of emotion, but I lose my damn mind and forget who the hell I am. I kiss her… on the lips.

When I move away, she lets out a tiny breath—the ghost of a breath.

Fuck me dead. "I am so sorry! I—"

She smile "And you called me an idiot."

"What?"

She can see that she's going to have to explain it to me like I'm five. "Kanan showing up to my party wasn't the worst part of the night for me. The worst part was when I saw you kissing him. I don't know, I just didn't feel that right".

"Oh." After that thing in the café with Kritika, I thought she might be jealous, but of me, not of Kanan.

“Come ‘ere…” She wraps her hand around my neck and tugs me in for another kiss. Her tongue slips into my mouth. No, I let her slip her tongue into my mouth.

What the fuck are we doing, and why does it feel so right? And then I slip mine into hers. She tastes sweet, like strawberries. I crave more of her.

My arms encircle her waist; she more than allows it; she’s eager for it. She lies down and wrenches me on top of her. Her fingers slide into my hair. My hands are on her hips. Our legs were entangled.

God, I could kiss her forever.

Yep, full on making out with your friends who stay in the same house. Shit! I push myself away from her and sit up, breathless. “Wait, Tara, I don’t think this is right.”

She sits up, too. “But it feels right to me.” She reaches for me again. I caught her wrist.

“No.” There’s a difference between something feeling right and being right.

Her mouth twists into a pout. Disappointment? Frustration? An amalgam of both. “I alrea

dy have friends. I don’t need or want another one. What I want from you is this. You understand me, and there is some different energy when I’m around you.”

This thing between us has never been that way. We both understand that much, maybe even from the very beginning.

“Your parents…people” I was just starting to get comfortable in their house and with them. That’s tanked.

“I get that you’re scared this could screw things up with them and your living situation. Honestly, right now, I’m not even ready to tell them that I'm bisexual, let alone that I like you. So, if you like me too, can we try? You and me, no one else has to know until we're both ready."

We could keep the same secret for different reasons. What is her reason?

'Who cares if I'm bi or whatever, right?' She knows who she is, but if she says she isn't ready, then she isn't ready—the 'why' is what matters. She still blames that part of herself for Raina and doesn't feel like she has the right to be happy. Her motive for keeping it a secret isn't about me; her eyes are imploring me to say yes. She does want this.

What do I want? I want to not have to agonize over the possibility of her parents finding out, hating me, and kicking me out onto the street. And her. You want her.

God, do I. "I don't know."

She sighs, launches off the bed, pads over to her door, and opens it. "Let me know when you've figured it out."

I swallow my heart and stand up. There's nothing left to say, so I leave. She closes the door on me.

Chapter 24

The Silent Treatment, day one—it's not the first time I've ever been on the receiving end. I've never minded it before, but because I'm getting it from her, it kills.

She's the one who holes up in her room today. She doesn't come down for breakfast, lunch, or anything else. I spend hours loitering around downstairs, waiting for my chance to say anything. Every time I think we might end up in the same room, I'm wrong. It's as if she's checking around corners with a mirror, making sure I'm nowhere in sight before walking through the door.

After a while of simmering, I text Kanan. He's at a state training camp in Rishikesh, so he can't hang out. Bhavya's there, too. Himanshi is working on a research paper. I still haven't gotten around to getting Mani's number.

I take a walk to the park and watch some kids play. It doesn't help.

I try the little pond. Sitting on the bench, my mind is flooded with thoughts of Tara. I destroyed everything with a kiss.

How could I have done something so asinine? So thoughtless. It isn't like me at all. I've always been so careful when cultivating my connections with people. Since moving here, I've changed. Kanan, Tara, Amit uncle, and Kavita aunty—they've overwhelmed my barricades. My ammunition is depleted, and I have no cover from them. This is going to be the battle that causes me to lose the war.

Perhaps it was only a matter of time, but I think it's just them, who they are as individuals, the best of humanity—sad and sensitive and imperfect, yet still warm and thoughtful and accepting. I wasn't prepared for any of it. It's terrifying and wonderful, and even if I've ruined it, I wouldn't trade it.

Tara. Damn it.

Aunty doesn't allow her to miss dinner.

We sit across the table from each other in our usual places. She avoids looking at me as much as possible.

I am a street scamp begging for scraps.

I want her gaze. I want her to smile. I don't care if it's to call me a 'motherfucking-rat-bastard-cowardly-piece-of-shit,' I want her silky voice saying whatever words she's willing to say.

I thought I'd take an actual bullet before I met a girl who hit me like one. I

I think I'd have preferred the bullet. So dramatic. Accurate, though.

THE SILENT TREATMENT, day two—she leaves for school without me. She told her parents she had to go in early for extra help with an English assignment, which may or may not have been the truth. My money's on not.

Amit Uncle isn't about giving me a ride. It's the first time I've been inside his black BMW SUV, and the newness of it gives me something else to concentrate on for a while: the tan leather interior, the chrome dashboard accents, and the huge touch screen recessed in the console. There are lots of knobs to turn and buttons to mash. I press a button and accidentally open the sunroof. Amit uncle doesn't mind. He grins and says, "Enjoy the weather while it lasts. It'll be raining soon."

Rain. School cancellations. Twenty-four hours trapped inside, with Tara hiding from me like I'm death personified.

Winter is gonna be awful.

I lean back in the seat and shut my eyes.

It's been a day and a half, and I don't know how much more of it I can take.

English class. She's been sitting at the desk beside mine since my first day. This morning, she sits on the opposite side of the room, way up in the front. The boy who usually takes that spot is confused.

He asks her to move. I hear her say, "Sorry. I'm waiting for a new box of contacts. Do you mind if we switch for a while?"

The kid's so elated that Tara's even talking to him; all he can do is nod. Feel ya, bro. He ambles to the back of the room, glides into the seat next to mine, and goes,

"Hello."

Yeah, sure, whatever. "Hi."

I don't know if she's going to leave me to my own devices this afternoon, but it's better to be proactive. At lunch, I ask Himanshi if she can give me a ride home after school. She's surprised. "Tara has a doctor's appointment." I'm so good at lying; it's such a shitty character trait.

Tara's not bad at it, either. Are all people good liars, or is it only the people who are broken?

"Yeah, no problem," she responds.

"Thanks." She's great at this friend thing. They all are. I think I could've asked Mani for a ride, and she would've said yes, too. I need to work on becoming a better friend to them. And to Tara. If I keep telling myself that all I'm interested in is her friendship, can I convince myself that it's true?

Can you teach a fish to fly?

I ARRIVE at the house to find the Nikon on the floor in front of my bedroom door.

There's a bright orange, heart-shaped sticky note attached to it. You FORGOT THIS. —A

Oh, you fucked up so badly. I'm still fucking up. How do I stop? Giving her what she wants—what I want—is the worst idea in the history of ideas. But will this ever end?

if I don't? It might not. Do I deserve for it to end? My idiocy knows no bounds.

I've BEEN persona non grata for ninety-six hours. Somehow, Amit uncle and Kavita aunty haven't noticed it. Or if they have, they've decided to let us settle our problems on our own. If I weren't already aware of it, this would be their tell that they raised two daughters for sixteen years. I'm thankful for their parenting style; it would be awkward if they insisted on getting involved.

What could I tell them: I have a painful crush on your daughter? What could Tara tell them: I want to bang the girl you brought into our home? Holy crap, this is bad.

On the subject of bad, the car ride to school this morning. Tara waited for me, and it would've been better if she hadn't. She put the radio on. It was louder in her car than it had ever been, but for all the wrong reasons—no banter, no laughter, none of the stuff I've come to enjoy.

I don't know where to begin to fix this.

When you upset and humiliate someone, you can't take it back with, "Whoops, my bad!" It's exceptionally hard to make things right when you hurt someone like her, someone who's so careful with their emotions that they guard them like they're vile, perilous things. Oh, so, someone like you? Yes. Except she has never done anything to hurt me. To the contrary, all she has shown me is kindness.

I wish it had never happened—not just this awkwardness I've caused with my in-decision, but the kiss, too. How is it possible that it was the best and worst kiss of my life?

The entire situation blows a big donkey dick, going all the way back to the start.

If I had met her under different circumstances, I would be 100 percent all about her. What complete moron wouldn't be?

It's so unfair that she has to be the daughter of the most decent, friendly—no, genuinely caring—people I've ever had.

They've been good to me in ways I didn't even realize people could be. They go out of their way to include me in everything.

They're there for me. They want me to be comfortable in their home. More than that, they want me to feel like their home is my home.

Thanks so much, fate! You could've at least kissed me before you bent me over and fucked me.

What I'm feeling right now—it's real. I don't have the vocabulary to describe it, but I'm aware of its existence, and that's plenty.

"Ay, Ved, you good?" Bhavya interrupts my silent contemplation with a stone tossed into a pond. Raging rapids, more like.

"I'm good." I grab my water from the lunch table and take a sip. Should be thanking her, sappy fool.

"Aight. Yo, so, Kanan, I was reading football stats. They're 9-1-0 this season. They got a First Team All-Starter on their roster, too, their goalie."

Kanan huffs. "Of course, they're good this year. I'm the captain; they have to go and make things hard for me."

"I don't see the issue," Mani comments. "And aren't you guys 10-0?"

"Barely. Last week, Marblehead put one in early, then held us scoreless until the sixty-third minute." She nods at Bhavya.

"You saved our asses that day, man; you got the ball rolling, literally."

Bhavya shoots her a grin. "I do what I can, sis."

"Wait, is this game your last one?" I should probably already know the answer to that. Welp, you've def established yourself as a garbage friend.

"No, but it's our rivalry match, and it's away, and as far as I can tell, they're the only real threat left to our perfect season." She rubs her eyes with her thumb and forefinger. "I hate it."

I don't get college rivalries.

They're so minor in the grand scheme of things, yet jocks treat them like they're this huge deal. I suppose most kids don't have bigger things to worry about. It must be nice.

"You should come to the game," Himanshi says to me. "We could use another voice cheering for Kanan."

"People yelling your name, that doesn't throw you off?" I ask Kanan.

"I do better under pressure."

"Okay, I'll be there." I force a smile.

The conversation veers off in a direction I can't follow.

Tara. Tara. Tara.

NIGHT, day five. We almost collide in the hallway as I'm exiting the bathroom. At first she looks alarmed, the result of a near miss, then her mien morphs into sadness. It's the closest we've been, physically, since...

I cannot continue to live like this. I'd rather be shoved into a pantry. "This obviously isn't going to work for either of us anymore. I'm gonna call my uncle and aunty in Delhi."

"Don't." She glowers at me. "My parents won't understand why you want to leave. They'll think it was something they did and feel like assholes over nothing for eternity."

That's where she gets it from—the upshot of having a big heart. "I can't-"

"Not here."

Right. Amit uncle and Kavita aunty have gone to bed; having this discussion outside their door is not advisable. I don't want to have it in her bedroom or her space, either. I know my room is out of the question for her, though. "Let's go to your room."

She flinches at the suggestion but relents. I follow her. The door creaks as I close it behind me.

She sits on her bed. I opt for the rolling chair and notice the photo of the boy on the swing pinned to the wall above the desk.

We stare at each other in silence until it gets too uncomfortable for both of us.

Talk, you invertebrate. "I know this is my fault, and maybe we'll never be the same again, but I miss spending time with you. And it's only been what, five days?"

"I miss it too. I don't…" She gulps. "I don't think I can be alone with you. It's too hard when all I want to do is—"

"I get it." I really, really get it. Her eyes are on me, all soft and longing. I wish she wouldn't look at me like that. I can't take.

Then, from nowhere, I'm hit with the smartest, stupidest proposal ever. "I have an idea, and I need you to hear me out before you respond."

"Okay?"

"I want to go to Kanan's football game tomorrow night. It's the biggest match of the season, and it's away at the golf course. They're our arch enemies or whatever, right?"

"Uh huh. If you want to go, go. You've never asked my permission to hang out with him before."

"Firstly, you're not doing an awesome job of hearing me out. Secondly, I'm not asking your permission; I'm asking you to come with me."

"Seriously, this is the solution you came to me with?"

"Sometimes you have to force yourself to chill in difficult situations. It'll suck way less than feeling like garbage every time she walks into a room."

"Yeah, but—"

"Do you know what it took for me to talk to you after days of nada? A hell of a lot."

"That's different. Football is his thing, like his arena. You should go with your friends."

Bhavya's on the team. Himanshi and Mani plan on going, and I could go with them.

"I don't want to. I want to go with you. It's in public; there'll be lots of people there, so you won't get any ideas." I waggle my eyebrows at her. Please laugh.

She does. There she is! It's the best gift the universe could've given me.

The tenseness between us begins to waft away. I amp up what little charm I have to eleven and smile real wide. "Come on, you were a cheerleader; you're supposed to have school spirit. Show me how it's done."

"I'll consider it if..." She lets her words hang in the air.

"If?"

"If you kiss me. Right now. Like you mean it, not a lame peck on the cheek."

Clever. A round of tit-for-tat. Except I'm playing checkers while she's playing chess. It's not a game for her. It's a prompt:

Remember that I'm still here, waiting for you to choose me over fear. I'm willing to do the same. I don't need a reminder of how amazing it felt to kiss her; that's not something I could forget. "I'm pretty sure this is blackmail."

"You came up with the barter system, not me." She shrugs her shoulders. "It's a big ask, so that's the trade; take it or leave it."

It is a big ask, and I very much want to kiss her, but I shouldn't—not two seconds after I've made progress. Not ever. If I don't do it, things will just go back to being horrible. To hell with it.

I scoot the chair closer and reach out to her. She closes her eyes as I take her face into my hands. I press my mouth against hers, and my heart goes crazy. Her lips are warm and smooth. She still tastes like strawberries. I feel the tip of her tongue brush against my lips. Too much restraint is waning. I break the contact.

She opens her eyes and exhales. "I'll come with you."

Chapter 25

Xavier High School is older than ours, Bertram. Their stadium is bigger, however, and it is packed—St. Mary fans on one side of the field, Xavier supporters on the other, a divided sea of school colors, orange and black, and scarlet, white and black, respectively. Panthers vs. Lions.

It takes some perusing, but I find Mani, Himanshi, and Nitin in the stands. Tara and I go to join them. "Hey, guys," I greet them as we take our seats. "You all know Tara."

"Hi," she says, without any shyness.

Mani's taken aback by her presence, but she covers it quickly. "Yo."

"Hey." Himanshi gives her a smile and a wave. She's so mature. How many girls our age would be so chill around their boyfriend's ex?

Nitin takes Himanshi's hand, a show of reassurance. "Sup, Tara."

I check for a reaction from her. Nothing but a nod in his direction. Unruffled. She must have loved Kanan, although I don't think she would admit it if I asked. I wonder if they'd still be together had things not happened the way they did. Maybe she'd be out with her family and friends.

Maybe she'd be happy. I think eventually love gets too big to contain, and you have to share it with the world or you'll erupt like a volcano.

Pangs of jealousy hit me. Unjustifiable.

They'll never be together again, and we'll never be together at all. I puff them away through clenched teeth.

The whistle blows, and the match is underway.

Tara gets wicked into it, yelling and cheering, even shouting the occasional word of encouragement to Kanan. Her school spirit trumps everything. She was an incredible cheerleader, I'm sure of it.

Damn it, why does she have to be so stunning? And magnetic. And lovely.

And... watch the friggin' game!

The match is rough, bordering on dirty. The ref is worthless, calling almost nothing a foul. Kanan has been getting knocked around more than his fair share. Xavier has come prepared. They know he's the captain and want to keep him off the ball by any means necessary. Somehow, he's maintaining his collectedness, waiting for the perfect moment to get even. His every move is calculated and deliberate—every pass is immaculate, even the ones that fly clear across the field. I can see, in real time, how good he is at math. This sport is very much about geometry, and he's nailing it.

EIGHTY-SIX MINUTES into a ninety-minute contest, neither side has scored a goal. St. Mary came close twice, but Xavier's goalie is too good. Just as I'm starting to think this thing might end in a draw, Kanan sees his opportunity; he slide-tackles the legs right out from under Xavier's attacking striker. It's legal; no whistle. He comes up with the ball in his possession. And then he takes off down the field. He has support from Ishank on his right flank. But he has no intention of giving up control. This is his house now.

The dogged determination in him is palpable to everyone watching. The whole crowd is on its feet. Xavier's fans are shouting, "Get on 22! Stop him, stop him!" Our fans are shouting, "Go, go! Come on, Kanan!"

Xavier's midfielders can't catch up to him; he's a rocket. He splits the defense and jukes the sweeper. It's between him and the goalie, matched for talent. Nope, not even close. He flicks the ball from his right foot to his left and launches a missile right over the keeper's head and into the net.

The sideline official sounds his whistle.

It's a goal.

"Yes! Yes!" I squeal, fist in the air.

"Woo! Yeah, Kanan!" Tara shrieks.

She's clapping like mad.

Every St. Mary College player near Kanan leaps on top of him, whooping and hollering. They're patting his head and his back. Bhavya sprints all the way from the backfield to give him a hug. He's about to be the hero of this game.

Celebration over, the players start jogging back to their positions. Xavier's goalie kicks the ball into play; his team is too deflated to mount any kind of comeback.

A minute or so later, the referee checks his watch. He puts his whistle up to his lips and blows out three bursts. It's over.

One game closer to his perfect senior season.

And I'm so close to tears; it's preposterous.

This is what it's like to feel proud of someone? It's wonderful!

Tara is in my arms. I'm in hers. We're smiling and jumping. If this were another place and she was another person, I'd be kissing her right now. Stop.

THE TEAM IS MAKING their way off the field. We descend the bleachers and head toward them. We meet Bhavya first, extend congratulations, a "good game" from Tara, and a "You were awesome" from me.

Kanan is lagging a bit behind. I turn to Tara. It's enough that she's here; I'm not going to make her speak to her. "I'm gonna talk to Kanan. Meet you at the car?"

She gives me a headshake. "He obviously won the game for us. I can choke back my shit for a quick congrats."

Is she taking my advice? Weird.

Kanan sees Tara. Tara sees Kanan.

Neither of them look to be on the verge of crying. I hug Kanan with no reluctance. "Great game! You were incredible."

"Thanks."

"Nice goal," Tara says.

Kanan smiles and nods in appreciation.

The moment is interrupted by a commotion behind us. Someone yells, "Hey, 22!" We all spin around. The Xavier striker Kanan tackled is stomping toward us.

"What was that dirty-ass tackle?"

"Flawless is what."

He's in Kanan's face now. "Fucking dyke."

"What'd you call me?"

I've never been in a fight, but I know what the start of one looks like—the split second before someone pops off. This boy is teetering on the edge. He shoves Kanan. "You heard me!"

Kanan isn't going to let it go. Aw, hell.

I'm about to jump between Kanan and the boy. Tara beats me to it. She's got her arms up, hands waving. "Calm down."

"Move, asshole." The Xavier player smacks her right across the face.

Tara is shocked, her mouth hanging open and her hand on her cheek.

Oh, someone is going to die tonight.

I snap. Without warning, my knees are in the grass, and I've got the boy pinned beneath me, my left forearm pressed against his throat. He's gurgling, struggling against my weight. He must have twenty pounds of pure muscle on me. He's gonna need the strength of an army! My knuckles collide with his face, making a wet thud noise. There are people all around us screaming, "Oh my God!" "Whoa, whoa!"

"Stop!"

Someone grabs the collar of my jacket and yanks me off of him. Once I'm on my feet, I see that it's Kanan, with blue bangs dangling in his face. "Let's go, let's go," he spits as he hauls me away.

In the distance, there's an adult, a coach, helping the boy off the ground.

There's blood dribbling from his lip.

That's what she gets for hitting my girl.

My girl… "Where's Tara?" I bark at no one in particular.

"I'm here." She steps to me and presses her palms against my sternum. Her forehead is resting against mine. Her eyes are so bright, glistening with unshed tears. Concern, fear, or pain? There's a reddish mark on her face where she was slapped. I run my thumb over it. She winces.

"Are you okay?"

"I'm fine." She puts some space between us. "Are you?"

"If anyone ever puts their hands on you, I'll fucking kill them." I know the words come from my mouth, but I don't recognize my voice.

"Alright." Her tone is soft.

"Take her home," Kanan says to her, tense. "Right now."

We shuffle to the car, Tara's arms around my waist the entire way.

We're at the kitchen table; she's sitting next to me, holding an ice pack to my battered knuckles; they're already swollen. The mark on her face has faded. I'm thankful that Kavita Aunty and Amit Uncle are having a date night. "I don't know what happened; I blacked out."

"What happened was that bitch hit me, and you stepped in. That's it."

"Did I scare you?" I've witnessed enough people turn violent to know that it can be horrifying for a bystander. I don't ever want to be that violent person, and I don't ever want Tara to be afraid of me.

I wanted to protect her, and I did. But that doesn't make it okay.

"I wasn't scared of you; I was scared for you." She smirks. "Who knew you were such a badass?"

"I'm not." Only for her. She leans in and kisses me—a reward for my rash behavior that she's taken for gallantry. I don't merit it, but I pucker into it anyhow. Kissing her does feel right, more so every time. This is the last time. It has to be. I'm getting too indulgent.

The front door opens. Kavita, Aunty Hollers,

"We're home!" Tara stands up quickly, takes the ice pack, and tosses it in the freezer. She spins around and presses her back to the fridge just as Amit uncle walks into the kitchen, doggie bag in hand. "How was the game?"

"Good," she replies, glancing at me. "We won."

OVER THE WEEKEND, THINGS ARE BETTER BETWEEN US. All it took was nearly killing someone. It isn't back to how it was before—not as effortless—but if this is our new normal, I'll have to take it, even if it's not enough. What would be enough wouldn't be right.

When you feel this way about someone, is it ever really wrong? We're not blood. A few months ago, we were strangers. Perhaps once we're out on our own, away from her parents and their house, I can consider it. What is it, eight months?

No time at all, given any significant life span. The future isn't a given for anyone, though. I'm sure Raina thought she had thousands of tomorrows ahead of her. Not doing yourself any favors with that line of thought. No, I'm just making myself feel like I'm wasting time trying to escape the inescapable.

Chapter 26

Bhavya, Mani, and Himanshi have a study group in the library for their chemistry exam. Nitin takes advantage of the girlfriend's reprieve and has lunch with some of his friends. That leaves Kanan and me on our own.

I thought about texting him an apology over the weekend; it warranted a face-to-face conversation. Also, I'm chicken-shit and wanted to give him time to cool off in case he was pissed at me.

The day is unseasonably warm. We decided to eat at the Grand Cafe, grab our trays, and take them out to the courtyard. It's quiet enough around us to have a discussion without garnering undue attention to my brutal attack, which is the last thing I'd want. It was bad enough that a couple of guys brought it up to me in Life Skills this morning. I joked that street fighting was something I wouldn't have to learn in class. It wasn't funny, but they thought it was. That was the only time it's been mentioned to me. "About the crap I pulled at the game," I start. "I hijacked your big moment. I'm really sorry."

He takes a bite of his sandwich, chews, and swallows. "Don't apologize; you didn't start it. I was a hot second from swinging on him myself. I can take a lot, but... You did me a favor. Coach would've given me detention until graduation." Yeah, I'm stunned that there were no ramifications for me. I expected to get hit with a suspension first thing this morning. I guess it's a good thing I'm the new kid in town and nobody knows who the hell I am. "So, we're okay, then?"

"For sure."

We continue with our meal in a tranquil setting. He keeps looking at me like he has something else to say. It gets unnerving fast. "What's… up?"

"Nothing." He uncaps his tea and swigs it.

"Bull."

"Are you two together now?"

Losers say 'what?' "What? Who?" He deadpans. "Which am I, too blind or too stupid?"

"What are you talking about?"

He lowers her volume. "You and Tara."

"Er, I—"

"Bro, I know her. The way she was with you after the fight was all handsy. Either you're already a thing or you're going to be one soon."

I'm done. My mask has crumbled. It's so easy to read, it might as well be a library book.

"You can tell me, I'll keep it QT."

He never told anyone about what happened between him and Tara. The boy can hold a secret like a vice. "We're not a thing. But there are... sentiments? On both ends."

"Gasp! Shocker. I knew she was bisexual." He rolls his eyes.

"What's stopping you?"

"Come on."

"No, really."

"Uh, for starters, I'm living under her parents' roof. This is India; have you ever seen comments on social media about this kind of love?"

"Way I see it, living under the same roof, that's a bonus." My turn for an eye roll. "You don't think it's, I don't know, kind of incestuous? She's my friend, and I don't wanna ruin it."

"You're not actually related. It's not like you grew up together or anything.

You might as well be roommates, and if I understand porn right, roommates smash all the time."

That makes me laugh. "You're crude."

"Yeah, yeah," he chuckles. "Your situation might be 'unconventional,' but I don't think there's anything wrong with it. You like who you like. It's obvious that you like each other."

There's something else I haven't considered. I can't believe it took me so long.

To think of it, dating your friend's ex is against the Friendship Code; even a garbage friend like me knows that. What's the lesbian equivalent of Pals Before Gals? I could not stand hurting one more person with my stupid, irrational feelings—that goes twofold for Kanan.

"Would you be okay with it if we got together?"

"Our ship left the harbor a long time ago. It turns out it was the Titanic. And about the bisexual thing, I already knew about Tara." The faraway look in his eyes He's not in love with Tara anymore, but he's always going to love her. I've heard that can happen, particularly with your first.

"You should go for it. She's worth it."

"Maybe someday."

"Don't wait too long. Someone else will scoop her up."

He's 100 percent correct about that. Girls like Tara can have their choice. of anyone they want. I still don't know why she'd choose me.

I'm not sure when it happened, but we're all gathered around the dining room table, engrossed in our own work.

Amit uncle's next to me on his laptop, coding something. Kavita Aunty is scanning over files, comparing what she finds with the words of an open book—the ABA Guide to Family Law. I'm pretending to be studying my Consumer Mathematics notes, but really I'm replaying my conversation with Kanan from earlier, over and over. *You should go for it.* It means a lot coming from him; more than encouragement, he's given his blessing. I didn't realize how important that was to me until now.

I keep stealing glances at Tara from across the table. She's not doing anything special—twirling a pencil as she pores over an equation—nevertheless, she looks beautiful.

Right, she's beautiful. I've determined that as a stone-cold fact. I want to swim in the aqua pools of her eyes, play with her long milk-chocolate hair, and kiss her perfect lips, cute nose, and high cheekbones until humanity's extinction yadda yadda.

What do I like about her?

I like... That she laughs at the most awkward, inappropriate things. I like it when she smiles, because that means she's giving herself a break from her guilt. I like that she's soft-hearted, even though she tries to hide it, and that she says exactly what she means with a little too much acid or otherwise doesn't say much of anything at all. I like that she's smart and funny and ambitious and supportive of my ambitions. I like that she makes me want to be better—more open and honest. I like that I want her to be happy and safe.

Whoo boy, you've got it bad for this one. Then I can't let her slip away, can I?

"Tara."

"Hmm?" She looks up from her text book.

I take too long to respond. She drops her pencil and stares at me. I shoot out of my chair as if someone lit a firecracker under my ass. Amit uncle and Kavita aunty gawk at me like I'm nuts, but it's brief. "I have to show you something."

She trails me into the hallway. Once I'm sure we're out of her parents' line of vision, I take her by the hand and drag her all the way up to her room. I shove us both inside and slam the door behind me.

She's got her hands up, palms facing the ceiling, like, What the hell is happening right now?

Do it if you're gonna. I grab her hips and kiss her hard. When I pull away, she's relieved. Relieved that I kissed her or that it's over? Ask her, dumbass. "What's that look?"

"I was starting to think you weren't—" That won't do. "I am so into you. I can't control it, and it's bugging me out a little." Bugged out? Frightened.

Her mouth is agog. I've stunned her.

Stunned yourself. "I know what you mean." Her parents. Their house. I can't dwell on it anymore. I have only ever felt 'right' about one person in my whole life, and it's her. "I want to be with you."

She smiles, seizes the collar of my hoodie, and presses her lips to mine—once, twice, three times. "Took you long enough."

I never stood a chance against this girl. Now, the question is, "How do we do this? Is guerrilla-style dating a thing?" It's so absurd, I can't help but laugh. She laughs, too.

No, for real, though. The concept of having to be on the DL is new to me. That's one of the good things about not having parents—no one to potentially be upset with my sexual orientation or choice of partners. I've gotten lucky so far—none of my uncle-aunties cared—but I've heard horror stories.

"It can be fun if you think of it like a game. Have you ever played Manhunt?"

She reaches for the drawstrings of my hood and gives them a few twirls.

"It's like a mashup of Tag and Hide and Seek, right?"

"Mmhmm. The objective is to be as sneaky as possible." She's wrapping the cords around her fingers. My hood is getting tighter around my neck. And she's pulling me closer. I watch her lick her lips. I can't tear my eyes away.

"That does sound like fun."

I assume she's going for my mouth and ready myself. She swerves at the last second and kisses my cheek. "See, I'm good at sneaky." She grins.

"Yes, you are."

Chapter 27

There are two things about Manhunt dating that are insufferable. One: the fact that I'm allowed to touch Tara now, but seventy-five percent of the time—when we're at school, when we're with our friends or her parents—I friggin' can't. And two: the straight edginess I carry in the pit of my stomach around Amit uncle and Kavita aunty.

It's like I've backslid to how I was when I first moved in—shy and reserved, unsure of how to behave. It's not an awesome sensation to lie to them. Not that I've ever felt good about lying; it's just something that was a necessity sometimes. I've never had to do it all the time, though; that takes adjusting.

Some evenings, dinner is a nightmare.

Yesterday, Tara had the audacity to play footsie with me under the table. We had to have a talk about it afterwards. I told her that it's great at lunch, or at Starbucks, or literally anywhere else, but I can't handle it while having a meal with her parents.

She was cool about it—in a sincere way, not that feigned indifference she's so good at.

It's BEEN A WEEK, and it has already become obvious to me that she is a seasoned pro at sneaking around. She's been amazing with me. She can sense when I'm getting overwhelmed—it's always in the house when there's little else to concentrate on but our proximity to each other and her parents. In those moments, she signals at the stairs, then climbs them. I wait a minute or two, then follow her up.

When we're alone, she cups my face or presses her pointer finger to the tip of my nose, reassurance that she understands and that she thinks we're worth all the trouble the cosmos is throwing at us.

It will be seven and a half months until I can move out of their house. Things will be easier then. Thinking long-term. It's dangerous, I know, and premature, but I've permitted myself to envision a future with her. I'm afraid of it yet wishful for it, and the disparity is something I haven't quite reckoned with. If things work out the way I hope, I'll have a long time to get acclimated to it.

I'VE BEEN TRYING to divide my time between Tara and Kanan as fairly as possible, so I decided to have lunch three days a week with Kanan and The Squad and the other two days with Tara and The Dazzel Brigade. When I floated the idea to Tara, I said, "I don't want to be one of those girls who gets with someone and drops their friends."

He replied, "Good. I can't stand those types of people."

So far, it's been going well.

"YOU WENT FOR IT," Kanan says as we're queuing up to pay for our chicken roll.

Just as well, I don't have to tell him; my new balancing act is all it takes for him to come to the conclusion.

"Yep."

"Good for you."

He said she'd be okay with it, but that doesn't mean he is. A person can change their mind about anything at any time.

I inspect his features for a semblance of affront and find none. "Thanks."

"I have to say, it's pretty dope that you're not ditching us for her, unlike this dude." He pitches a thumb at Nitin, who's riveted by whatever Himanshi is saying and whose friends are on the other side of the cafeteria.

"I told you from the start there's enough of me to go around."

"Then, are you up for a driving lesson Sunday? You're getting good; you might even be ready to take the test soon."

I pull Tara and laugh. "Yes to the lesson. Hell no to the test."

Chapter 28

"Our next project is going to be all about portraiture," Mr. Ravi says.

Oh, crap! I blanked. I snatch the Power Shot from my bag and raise my hand.

"Yes, Vedika?"

"Sorry. I wanted to return this before I spaced it." My new Nikon is in its branded case on my desk. Mr. Ravi and a handful of kids glance at it and at me. That's right, I robbed a bank a few days ago, and this is the fruit of my labor.

He motions for me to come up to the front of the class. I pop the camera onto his desk, then mosey back to my seat.

Tara's giving me a shit-eating grin.

"I never did give you a proper thank you," I murmur.

"Mmm, I think you did."

Her smugness sets off my stomach thing. I can let myself appreciate it all of a sudden. Nice.

"We're going to take some photos outside today," says Mr. Ravi. "Find yourself a partner for test shots."

"You and me?" I don't know why I need to ask.

"Always."

I'm the first test subject, sitting on a bench in the fading sunlight. "Don't look at the camera," she directs.

"What should I do?"

"Like, anything else."

I shift my attention to the dead trees and am overcome with gloom. They're as pathetic in real life as they are in Tara's photo of them—strange, scraggly things.

I hear her press the camera shutter, click, click, click. "Perfect." She sits next to me and looks at the screen. "You're a knock-out."

A knockout? "No, I'm not."

She leans in close to me. "Excuse me, I have impeccable taste."

"So do I."

Lip bite. "We're crazy hot together."

We're in public; I cannot kiss her. I spring to my feet. "I've been dying to use this." I unzip the camera case, pluck out the Nikon, and attach the lens to its body.

"Ready for that photoshoot?"

She runs her fingers through her hair.

"Yup."

THE NATURAL LIGHT IS GORGEOUS. Correction: Tara haloed by the natural light is gorgeous. She's leaning against a young oak tree, one knee bent, foot propped on its trunk. The grass is littered with orange and crimson leaves, a stark contrast to her light denim skirt and lavender sweater.

Snap, snap. Zoom. Snap. Snap. These portraits aren't going to need any editing—not even a spot touch-up.

Those big blue eyes Also, the look she's giving me—smoldering, seductive. Wit-woo. My lens is liable to catch fire at any moment. I stop, assess the pictures. "Um, can you come here for a second?"

She kicks off the tree and saunters over. I scroll through the photos for her. "Notice anything?"

"The colors."

That and… "You're giving me 'fuck me eyes' in every single picture," I mumble.

She goes red. "I am not!"

I roll through them again.

She concentrates hard. "I didn't even realize I was doing it."

Not that I'm complaining. "I think I'm going to have to use my friends as models for this project."

"That's a good idea," she snickers, then flashes into seriousness. "If any of them give you 'fuck me eyes,' they're dead." I know who she means by "any of them," and that's not something that'll happen. I have to tell her that Kanan knows we're together. I've been dodging it. Again, I'm chicken-shit. I resolve to do it as soon as we're alone.

In the meantime, I'm enjoying how adorable she is when she's grappling with the green-eyed monster, even if it is unfounded. "You don't have to worry about that."

She forgets that we're outside the school, surrounded by classmates. I watch her stifle the impulse to touch me. She pouts, and then it's gone. "I don't know; I don't trust that Avani girl."

I fall to pieces, chuckling. "She does have incredible hair."

She gives my arm a playful slap. "Okay, yeah, she does."

AFTER CLUB, We hop into her BMW. She jams the key in the ignition, and I stop her from turning it. She studies me with curious eyes.

Say it, you gutless wonder. Shit. I prepared myself to receive livid words, hide my hands in the sleeves of my hoodie, and crumple the cuffs into my fists. "Kanan knows about us. I didn't tell him; he guessed."

She taps the steering wheel.

"I gathered. He's not dumb."

And they used to know each other so well. "He promised to keep it to himself."

"He will."

Even after everything that's happened, all the hurt, and all the time that has passed, she still trusts him. Will she ever trust me that way? I have to prove my worth.

"Let's go home." She starts the car.

I marvel at her coolness, the earnestness of it, and the entire drive.

Chapter 29

For this week's date night, Kavita Aunty and Amit Uncle are going to see a movie. It's definitely Kavita Aunty's choice. The most sophisticated stuff I've heard Amit uncle listen to is about old movies only. But it's poles apart from Kavita aunty's taste in music.

Amit's uncle appears in the hallway outside of the living room, decked out in a neat charcoal grey suit and a dark blue necktie. My first thought is that he looks like a kid who's been coerced into dressing up for a wedding on Sunday. It's bizarre—he's a jeans and t-shirt kind of dude, the occasional polo if he's feeling fancy. Tara whistles at him from beside me on the couch.

"I clean up nice, huh?" He straightens his tie.

"Very handsome," I say. "You might need a haircut soon, though."

He smooths his graying sideburns. "I need 'em all cut."

Snort. Dad jokes! So corny, yet so delightful. Who knew?

"I'm ready." Kavita Aunty strolls into the hall.

She's in a flowing, floor-length chiffon and lace saree—stormy blue—sporting more makeup than she wears to work, yet still understated and classy, as with everything she does. Tara is the perfect combination of her parents—the best of both of them. It's kind of crazy. I wonder what Raina looked like. I wish Tara would talk about her. Ask her. No, not tonight.

"Dang, Mom! You're gorge."

"She's right."

Kavita Aunty tilts her head at us and smiles.

Amit uncle helps her into a navy double-breasted pea coat. "Thanks, hun."

"You girls have fun." She said

Oh, we're going to. We've got our own date night planned with Netflix. The 'N' Chill' part is up to Tara. I've been letting her set the tempo. My comfort zone for physical stuff is broad when I'm with someone, all things considered, so it's best left to her to decide what she's good with and when.

"Bye, girls," Amit uncle says. They leave, and we're alone.

It's my turn to pick the movie, a horror film called The Happening. As much as for my own enjoyment, I used to choose horror movies for the jump scares and the squeezes they'd earn me. Tara has carbon fiber nerves where films are concerned, so my cunning falls flat. I like it; it means she

chooses to touch me, rather than does it involuntarily.

I press play, and the opening credits roll. She scoots close to me and takes my hand.

It's nice sitting together on the couch, holding hands. It's not often we get to be this touchy-feely outside of her bedroom.

She leans over and pecks me on the cheek.

That's nice, too.

Thirty seconds later, she climbs onto my lap, cowgirl-style. Whoa. "Um, what—" She wraps her arms around my neck, dips her head, and kisses me, a first for the living room. Living room! I peel my lips from hers. "Do you realize where we are?"

"Uh huh." She kisses me again. "My parents will be gone for hours. I want to make the most of it while we can." I let out a deep breath. She squinches her eyes at me, brushes her fingers through her ringlets, and swoops them to the side. "Unless you're not feeling it." She moves to dismount me.

I'm feeling this and more. I grab her waist and make her stay. "Who said I wasn't?"

She flashes a mischievous grin, then frames my face with her hands. This time, I crane my neck and kiss her. I glide my tongue into her mouth. She makes a surprised 'mmm' sound. It's a good surprise; her tongue responds to mine.

She is the best. Kisser. Ever. It's like she's been kissing girls her entire life; none of that gross stuff teenage boys train girls to expect. No poking around for my tonsils, and zero slobber.

Then she does this thing she hasn't done before—sucks in my bottom lip and gives it a tiny bite. My entire body shudders. I moan into her mouth and grip her hips a bit tighter. She pulls back, eyes full of awe. "You liked that?"

She doesn't wait for my answer; she just moves her kisses to my neck. I feel the gentle pressure of my skin being drawn into her mouth, her teeth nibbling. Yes, I liked it.

A bit too much. I'm liking this a bit too much, too. "Are you trying to give me a hickey?"

She pauses and looks at me. "Yes. Marking my territory." Another series of nips.

Whew, damn. "And how am I supposed to explain it to people?"

"Tell them you're having a torrid affair with a sexy younger woman," she whispers into my ear. More sucking.

I slink my hands under her shirt, up her spine, and relish her lithe physique.

The front door whooshes open, then slams closed. Tara tries to clamber off of me, but ends up ass-on-the-rug with a muted thump.

Amit uncle rushes into the kitchen and backs out again. He sticks his head into the living room and shoots a questioning look at his daughter. She has scrambled into a split and is stretching sideways, grabbing her ankles. Awks.

Sexy. Her ass should be declared the eighth wonder of the world. "Forgot the tickets?" She frowns at him.

He nods at her. "Don't pull a muscle watching that movie." He scampers out of the house.

My heart is thrashing against my ribcage. I've thrown my hands over my mouth like I've witnessed a kitten wander onto a highway, and she's silently laughing so hard that tears are streaming down her cheeks. "That was close!"

"No more fooling around on the couch!" I bend down, give her my hand, and pull her up.

"Yeah, no." She composes herself beside me. "Is it okay if we cuddle, though?" I've got a girl who'll bite my lip and, in the next breath, wants to cuddle with me.

Multifaceted. Another thing I like about her. "That we can do."

I put my arm around her, and she rests her head on my shoulder.

We watch the rest of the movie snuggled together. It's even better than making out.

As WE'RE HEADING to bed, she stops in front of my room. "I wish I could stay with you tonight." Her eyes bulge, and a blush inches up her neck. She's not ready for that, and neither am I. "I mean, I wish I could sleep in your arms."

Her parents aren't home yet. I could hold her until she falls asleep, then tiptoe to my bedroom. It would be risky.

Fuck, I hate these hormones! I press my lips against her forehead. “Someday.”

“You promise?” Her eyes.

I swear. “I promise.”

Chapter 30

Tara is pacing the floors. Amit uncle, Kavita aunty, and I gawk at each other across the living room.

From their expressions, it's obvious we're all thinking the same thing—she's acting weird. I've never seen her antsy before, and they haven't seen it in a while. That makes me worry. I hope it isn't because of me, although it's entirely possible. She may have been an All-Star with Kanan, but they didn't live in the same house; their bedrooms weren't separated by a paltry slab of sheetrock and some paint. And last night was... sexually frustrating. She should've rubbed one out, too.

"Honey, what's with the one-woman waltz?" Amit uncle asks.

Lol.

Tara folds her arms across her chest.

"I don't know. I'm bored."

"See, this is why I didn't want you to quit cheerleading. All your friends are at the football game, and you don't know what to do with yourself."

Ooh. That's the most Mom Thing Kavita aunty's said since I've lived here. Hardline nag. I want to defend Tara and tell Kavita Aunty that the only reason we're not at the game is because it's forty degrees out and raining. Hell, Tara still wanted to go. I told her it wasn't going to happen because, three days from now, she'd drop dead of pneumonia. Yes, it was a total mom thing to say, but when it comes from someone other than your mother, apparently it's cute. That's what she called me, anyway. Cute. I'll take it.

OKAY, so I fix things. It's who I am. I am about to hammer this nail. The first idea that pops into my head is: Let's go to the mall.

I hate the mall; there are so many people and so much stuff, and everything's oppressively bright and expensive. And why are there so many goddamn different perfume smells everywhere? Ugh. It's sensory overload. Tara likes it, though. Why couldn't she prefer Amazon shopping sprees like every other Zoomer? It doesn't matter. I am so down to go anywhere with her; it's ludicrous. I'd figure out how to get us to the moon if she wanted to pay it a visit.

"Tara, will you take me to the mall?" Could've done with more enthusiasm.

If she were a kindergartener and I were Santa Claus, she couldn't be smiling any wider. "Lemme get dressed."

"Um, you're already dressed?"

"Yeah, like a slob."

She's in yoga pants and a long-sleeved St. Mary's Cheer tee, appropriate attire for a shopping trip, but whatever. Dat ass doe. "Alright, weirdo, go change. I'll be here."

She jets up to her room.

Amit uncle and Kavita aunty are both scoping me.

Why? "Thanks for being such a good friend to our little pain-in-the-butt," Amit uncle says.

I am slapped with shame for masturbating to thoughts of his daughter not even twelve hours ago. Oh, Amit uncle, you dear, sweet man, I owe you so many apologies.

"It's no big deal."

TAN KNEE-HIGH HEELS. Sunburnt-orange mini dress. Off-white knitted cardigan.

Full face of makeup. She does not slack off. Me? Vans. Black hip-hugger jeans with holes in the knees. Black Pink Floyd hoodie. Backward Red Sox cap No makeup—save for a little concealer over my hickey. I am wearing my hair down, though, so that's something. What a mismatched pair! How is she not embarrassed to be seen with me? I'm embarrassed for her.

The sheer size of Pacific Mall is intimidating. As I gape at the directory, I do a count: 147 retailers. Overkill. Who needs to go into that many stores? I shop at Myntra for crying out loud. It suits me fine.

Walking through the place, I can't begin to tell the difference between H&M, Gap, and Lifestyle. The clothes displayed in each of their windows are identical.

Tara does not share my point of view—she bypasses all of them. "Can we go to H&M?"

"Whatever you want."

"Whatever I want? You asked me to—Oh." There it is, the look of understanding. And something else: she wants to kiss me. She won't, not when we're out in the world. Make her promise to, someday. Touché. "You're so thoughtful," she says instead.

"I try."

"There's seriously nowhere you want to hit up."

"The food court. After you've dropped mad stacks at thirty-two stores, that is."

She titters. "You got it."

We roamed around for about a decade—for real, I've got gray hair now.

The only thing she purchases is a 2000 rupee Balenci-blah-blah leather tote that looks like someone graffitied all over it. I was googling apartments the other day and found a few hovels for twelve hundred a month, and she swiped her mom's Amex for that exact amount without a blink.

What the hell does she see in me? Is she into slumming it? ' Because that's going to get old for her real quick.

"Hungry yet?" she asks as we're exiting the store.

"Perpetually."

WE'RE DIGGING into food court Chinese—the best kind there is. I'm slurping my last noodle, and she's eating her Chinese platter. Am I one of those noisy eaters? I hope not; that's disgusting.

"Do you ever miss your parents?"

That was random. There's no logic to missing people I've never known, and yet... "Sometimes. It would have been if they witnessed me going to college, at least."

Her features slip into a guise of total animosity. "Who the fuck was the person who hit them?"

Me being sick might've been the reason they gave me up. I'll always wonder.

"I don't know; I never saw him." "He paid some money to all the police officers to hide his identity."

Damn, that's bleak.

She rubs her forehead.

I want to change the subject and talk about something less dreary. I still want to know more about Raina. Tara must have good memories of their childhood. Amit Uncle and Kavita Aunty are too incredible not to have given them hundreds. I can go for it if I handle it with kid gloves. "I wish I'd had a sibling or two. I think it would've been fun.".

Her expression goes from startled to joyous in an instant. “It is like having a built-in best friend. I was never lonely, that’s for sure.”

“I bet. And you and Raina were so close in age.”

“Yeah, my parents slayed the timing. But two babies at once? No, thank you.”

No joke. “What was she like? You said her style was different from yours, but... She leans back in her chair. “She was serious, a thinker. She’d get lost in her head all the time. I had to try so hard to make her laugh, but it was hilarious when she would—huge and loud, from her belly, you know?”

“Same as yours.”

“Ha! It is.”

I love that she’s talking about Raina so freely. I want to hear more. “Cheerleading doesn’t seem like a sport for serious people. It’s too... cheery.”

“She switched from dancing when I got to middle school. She was great like that; she knew I wanted to get into it and gave me the push I needed. She was super competitive—always had to be the best at everything she did.”

“Was she the best dancer?”

She giggles. “She couldn’t dance to save her life. There is absolutely no rhythm. But she could yell and had real jock muscles, so that made up for it.”

“I’m sorry, I’ll never get the chance to meet her,” I let slip, and I smothered a grimace as I waited for her reaction. She’s alright; I’m glad to be talking about her. I wouldn’t be surprised if this is the most she’s talked about since she died.

“She would’ve liked you.”

"You think?"

"I like you, so yes."

Would she have told Raina about us? Is her affection for me unwavering enough?

Why it exists at all is beyond comprehension.

"I'm sure I would've liked her, too."

She grins and reaches for my tray. "Finished?" I nod. "Good. I want to take you to Thrash. Their clothes are rocker chic, more your flavor."

I'm not sure my pockets are deep enough for shopping in a high-end mall like this one. But it's not the moon; I can make myself swing it. "You couldn't have told me that before I stuffed my face." I pat my stomach. "No way I'll fit in anything now."

"Oh, shut up, Scrawny!"

If Scrawny is my nickname, what's hers, Busty? She does have nice—hold it right there. "Okay, take me."

I COULD GO BROKE in this store on the band tees alone. I manage to rein myself in, but I do decide to spend fifty bucks on a BABYMETAL hoodie—the novelty is too good to ignore. Tara tries to swipe Kavita Aunty's Amex at check-out. I prod my fingers into her side, and she squeaks. "It looks like I'm not the only one who's ticklish." I press my card into the card reader.

"What a dirty trick!"

"All my tricks are dirty." It sounds more salacious than I intended. She notices, averts her eyes to the floor, purses her lips, and goes pink. Right. "Pray you never get to see me hip-check anyone."

That gets me a chortle.

I CAN'T STOP LOOKING at her as we're walking to the car. Being with her in this oasis of capitalism, our differences have become that much more blatant. I don't want her to see me as some kind of foray into living on the wrong side of the tracks, a leave of absence from the affluence she has known all her life. That would be an experiment. I've got big feelings for her, and it'll hurt too much when it comes to an end.

The car ride is quiet until I find the nerve to speak. It's a question I've been mulling over for far too long. Sooner or later, it's going to get in the way if I can't

get past it. She's def flipped your honesty switch. "I've been wondering about something."

"Mmhmm. What?"

Deep breath. "Why do you like me?"

She doesn't laugh for a change. She takes her eyes off the road and frowns at me.

"Are you serious?"

"Deadly."

Back to the road. "Because you're easy to talk to. You're funny, intelligent, and so sweet that you make my teeth hurt. Not to mention you have the cutest ass I've ever seen."

Wow. "Did you practice that answer? Because it was incredible."

"I've had a lot of time to think about it." The lip-bite thing "When would you say our anniversary would be, like, hypothetically?"

It's the way of the future. She's thinking long-term, too. "Umm."

“Because our first kiss was on October 11th, and then all that stupid crap happened. I just... I want every second to count.”

That is literally the most romantic thing anyone has ever said to me. Thank God I kissed her, accidentally or not.

“Then it would be October eleventh.”

She smiles.

Chapter 31

Sunday morning, I find her in the bathroom, door wide open, wearing a hot pink Nike sports bra and black leggings. Dear Universe, my sincere gratitude for the invention of Spandex Her body is bangin'—years of training for the more gymnastic cheerleading routines. In contrast, I'm bones and sinew; I'd probably break a hip if I did any sort of exercise beyond walking everywhere. Scrawny is right. How you have B-cups is a miracle. She seems to like my build, though; it's all good.

Holy crap, she has a tattoo! Tasteful Roman numerals on her right side, a touch below her bra line: VII. XV. MMIII. I didn't notice it that night after her party. It isn't fresh; she's had it for a while. I do the math in my head. It has to be her sister's birthday.

She's pulling her hair into a high pony when she sees my reflection in the mirror.

"Good morning."

"Morning." I glance around the hallway, making sure her parents aren't in hearing range. "That outfit. I can die happy."

Her smirk is diabolical. "I'm going for a run. Care to join?"

"By 'running,' do you mean 'strolling at a leisurely pace'?"

"Not even a little bit."

"Better if I stay here, then. Kanan is coming to pick me up for a driving lesson soon anyway."

She scrunches her mouth to the side, releases it, and shrugs. "Okay." I'm almost certain she means it. "Too bad you're going to miss me glowing with sweat."

No worries, gorgeous; we'll get around to that soon enough. Ba-dum-tss. "I'll catch it next time."

Kanan tells me that he's outside at ten o'clock on the dot, as we discussed. He's already sitting on the passenger side, window down. "Yo."

"Yo, yourself." I slide into the driver's seat and start Sweet Trixy down the road.

As I reach the stop sign at the top of the block, I fixate on how he is always on time. I guess that comes with being a disciplined person. I'm kind of envious of him for it. I dislike being late, not because I'm particular about being there for the start of something, but because I don't like to be the center of attention by showing up in the middle of things and interrupting.

Outside of school, I'm not the best at being punctual, which definitely has something to do with the wonderful commitment issues I have—my tardiness is generally due to getting caught in a heated debate with myself over whether or not to go at all.

I'll never forget how mad one of my friends was that I arrived for dinner with her parents at seven thirty, when I was supposed to be there at seven. She made me a new asshole for it. Meeting her parents wasn't something I was inclined to do. I thought about skipping it altogether, even as I was jumping off the train at the station a block from her house and right up until I rang her doorbell. Needless to say, I wasn't dumbfounded—or heartsick—when she dumped me two days later.

Kanan says, "Bang the right onto the highway."

"The highway?"

"Put your big girl's clothes on and do it."

Even if I wanted to argue, I would lose, irrespective of the fact that I'm behind the wheel. "Okay, okay."

ROUTE 10 ISN'T CLUSTERED. I'm relieved. If it were a weeknight, there'd be a ton of traffic, and I'd be frazzled. We're headed south, out of Garhi Cantt, toward "Do you have a destination in mind?"

"Nah."

"You're going to have to tell me where to go; otherwise, we'll end up nowhere."

"You want to go to THE DAFFODILS HOTEL & RESTAURANT? We can."

He's insane. I don't even have my permit—this is definitely illegal—yet he'd be perfectly fine with me driving eighty miles and crossing state lines. "How are you so chill with letting me drive all the damn time?"

"I feel calm when I'm with you. I dunno why."

He does that for me, too. At first, it was jarring. Now that I've gotten used to it, it's

nice. We can just be—no pretense is necessary.

"I have to know... How is it living with Tara since you hooked up?"

"It's friggin' torture!"

She sniggers. "Thought so. You've got bigger balls than me. I couldn't have survived."

It's weird talking about Tara with her ex. Don't think of him as Tara's ex; he's your friend.

"Yeah, either I have a pair of brass ones on me or I'm out of my mind."

"It could be a little of both."

"You're probably right."

We don't end up at THE DAFFODILS HOTEL & RESTAURANT, but we do continue on our journey. It takes every ounce of courage I have to keep us on the road; the switch from a two-lane mini-highway to a six-lane, sixty-five miles per hour dystopian hellscape is almost enough to make me piss myself off.

Kanan coos support the entire way.

"You got this." And, "You're doing great."

We pull off into Market Shopping Center to make a U-turn, and I think he's my best friend. It sounds so steadfast and stable, the opposite of everything I'm used to, yet I don't panic over it. It feels natural and easy—something that simply is, like it was destined to happen. Maybe it was. The thing I'm learning about fate is that resisting it is pointless—it has the upper hand of inevitability and will win in the end.

My stomach grumbles. As with everything else, life-changing realizations make me hungry. "Let's stop for something to eat."

He goes, pssh. "Dude, your appetite is ridiculous!"

"You ain't kiddin?"

Kanan drops me back at the house around one. I've got my hand on the front door, about to twist the knob, when I hear Tara shout, "Go put it in her fucking room yourself!"

It's disconcerting. She can be sharp-tongued sometimes, but she doesn't yell at her parents; that's a line she won't cross.

I enter the house very quietly and am relieved to find she's not in my line of sight. The divider wall separating the entryway from the living room affords me some cover; I haven't been spotted. It's not that I'm trying to eavesdrop; it's that whatever's happening here sounds heavy—there is no way in hell I'm going to let my presence interfere.

"You do not get to speak to your father that way, girl," Kavita Aunty says, her tone harsher than I've ever heard it. "And I don't understand why you're so angry. It's only laundry."

Then came Amit's uncle's voice. "Right. What's going on?"

"What's going on is that I hate that room!

I hate that it isn't Raina's anymore! You just gave it away, like... Tara huffs away her rage. "You can't replace her, okay? It doesn't make a difference how many people you help or how well we may get along; none of them will ever be my sister."

How long has she been holding that in? Have I helped her or made it worse by coaxing her pain to the surface?

"Is that what you think we're trying to do—replace Raina?" Kavita aunty asks.

"Isn't it? There's a hole in our lives now, and—" Her voice trembles and cracks. It's the sound of someone being overcome by tears. "And you're trying to shove someone into it, but it's shaped like Raina. No one else will ever fit."

"You're right, there is a hole, and it can't be filled." Kavita Aunty's voice breaks, too. "You and your sister made my life complete. I love you both so much, and I miss her every day. But even when she was here, there was enough love and space in this house for someone else."

"Tara, honey," Amit uncle starts, his tenor cool and soothing as a salve. "Don't you remember we talked to you and Raina about us wanting to invite Vedika to stay with us?

It was hard for us too. And the only reason we put anyone in Raina's bedroom is because it's so much bigger and nicer than the office.

We wanted whoever we brought into our home to feel like they had their own private, safe space."

This is the moment I choose to make my presence known. I step over the threshold between the hall and living room. Tara's eyes are on me, horrified.

She knows I've heard everything. Then her gaze drops to the floor. She wipes her tears away with the back of her hand.

"Shit. You did tell us. But then nothing ever happened, and—you're right, Raina's room is much better than the office. I'm sorry, I've been stewing about it all this time."

Kavita Aunty looks at her daughter with such sympathy that she's fit to burst. "I wish you'd said something sooner. You can talk to us about anything." Her attention flutters over to me. "That goes for you, too." Not anything. Not the most important thing.

Tara sucks in a deep lungful of air. "I want the pictures of her and all of us together to go up again. I miss seeing her face."

"Oh, sweetheart," Kavita Aunty says, "we took them down because we thought seeing them every day might upset you."

She shakes her head. "Taking them down upsets me."

"Okay," Amit's uncle cuts in. He throws his hand up and motions for her to follow him. "Come on, let's do it right now."

I pick up a framed picture of Raina from its new—old? Renewed—spot on the fireplace mantle. It's a school photo; the wavy blue backdrop is universal. She looks about sixteen. Her hair is darker than Tara's—nearly black—and she has Kavita Aunty's brown eyes. "She was really pretty," I tell Tara. "She took after your mom. You look more like your dad."

"Hmm." She beams at the photo. "Oh my God, she hated posing for pictures. She was such a pain in the ass that day.

Mom asked her the night before to wear something nice, and that morning she rocked up into the living room in a T-shirt and sweatpants, as usual."

Yes, please, talk about her until you've run out of air! Show me all your feelings, good, bad, and in between. "What'd your mom say?"

'No, ma'am! You march right back up those stairs and change," she twitters.

"Raina tried to argue her way out of it, but eventually gave up. She knew Mom wasn't going to budge." Her grin vanishes. "You know this had nothing to do with you, right? I'm happy you're here. She's been on my mind a lot lately, that's all."

"Yeah, I know." I touch her arm to send it home. "I know."

"Good." She looks at me and fidgets, apprehensive of whatever thought has popped into her mind. "Do you think- um, forget it."

"Do I think what?" Hit me with your worst; I want it, as long as it's real.

"Will you come with us to the cemetery the next time we go? My parents can't handle being there for very long. They always head back to the car before I'm ready, and it would be nice not to be alone."

I throw my arms around her neck and pull her into a hug, not worrying about whether or not we'll get caught being too intimate. It's a huge deal, her wanting me to stand beside her as she grieves over her sister's grave, trusting me enough to let me see her at her most vulnerable. "Of course, I will," I whisper.

She tightens her grip on me.

In my periphery, I see Kavita Aunty walk into the living room. She smiles at the scene she's stumbled upon. It's an innocent hug.

It's fine. No, it's not fine. I care so much about her daughter, but in a very different way from what she's thinking. I'm sorry, Kavita Aunty. I tried to fight it; it was too strong.

I let go of Tara. Kavita Aunty comes over to us.

"This place looks much better now."

Tara takes in all the pictures, finally in their rightful places again. "It really does."

I'm about to turn in for the night, reaching to switch off my desk lamp, when there's a faint rapping at the door. My bedside clock lets me know that it's after midnight, too late for it to be either of the adults in the house. They've long been asleep.

I'm right. Tara's on the other side, head bowed and staring at her bare feet.

What is she doing, testing her mettle?

I hold out my hand. She snatches onto it. It isn't enough—she can't conquer the inertia on her own. I guide her, inch by inch, inside. I try to leave the door open in case she decides to dash out again. She wants it closed.

I roll the chair away from the desk and motion for her to take a seat. She prefers to stand. She's digging her toes into the carpet, jogging her muscle memory. It's been more than two years since she's stepped foot in this room, as if it were a canyon cordoned off after an avalanche, and it's taken that long for the packed snow to melt away.

I watch her glance around at everything—the walls, the ceiling, the rug, the bureau, the bed. Her eyelids are fluttering so fast that they rival hummingbird wings.

And then she's crying—or rather, weeping—trembling as the salty water splashes down her face.

She's in my arms; I don't give her the option not to be. Her quivering shakes my soul. I kiss her forehead and her sodden cheeks. She staggers out of my embrace and leads me to the bed.

We lie down together. Her head is resting half on a pillow and half on the inside of my elbow. She presses her face against my chest, and the spot where my T-shirt meets her eyes gets soaked through. We're holding onto one another so tightly that I can't tell where my body ends and hers begins.

I skim my fingers through her ringlets.

Soon, the sounds of sobbing transform into the soft, steady breathing of slumber.

I don't want to wake her. I don't want us to get caught, either. She wished for this, and, albeit under far more somber conditions, happenstance has granted the request.

Who am I to argue? The solution to the conundrum is this: I keep her close to me all night, not daring to fall asleep myself.

AT FIVE FORTY-FIVE, the burgeoning pink-orange sky peeks through the blinds, and I whisper into her ear, "Tara, it's time to get up."

She stirs, sniffles, wipes at her eyes, and looks at me. "You let me sleep here." She shows me a tired smirk.

I swish her bangs away from her eyes.

"Well, you were very sleepy. And I promised you someday, didn't I?"

She gives me the gentlest kiss before pushing herself off the mattress.

She opens the door just wide enough to peer into the hall. The coast is clear. "Thank you," she turns around and mouths to me, then heads to her own bedroom.

There's an hour and fifteen minutes before I have to get ready for school. The wakeful night was worth it if it brought Tara some measure of absolution. I climb under the covers and shut my eyes, hopeful that her wounds might, at last, begin to heal.

Chapter 32

My Bio midterm is tomorrow, and I am mid-freak out over it. Regular tests get me stressed; tests worth so much of my overall grade are about ten times worse.

I had planned to start cramming yesterday when I got home from school, but instead I crashed hard—that early morning nap barely got me through the day. Still, I don't regret the sleepless night. Tara's been different since—brighter, more at home in her home.

We're studying together in the living room, a joint decision we came to after we both bombed a quiz in English last week.

All homework is to be done in the common areas. Neither of us can concentrate for very long in her room. We always end up talking, laughing, and making out—not at all conducive to learning.

I'm going over one of the more confusing parts of bio: dominant and recessive genes. My notes look like this:

BB = brown eyes, dominant.

bb = blue eyes, recessive.

Offspring with a BB + a BB parent can have BB—brown, bb—blue, or bb-green or hazel eyes.

Succinct for such a complex topic.

I'm smacked with a familiar ache, which seems to have ramped itself up over the last little while—that conversation with Tara at the mall and all the huge, complicated feelings about Raina that the uncle and aunty have finally let out. It's not my favorite subject, my parents, but I can't stop myself from wondering what color irises they have. I've always pictured my father with brown eyes, for some reason. I doubt either of them have black eyes, mine being such a peculiar shade of brown.

"You look like you're on another planet.

What's happening up there?" Tara reaches out to me and gives my temple a tap.

"I've been thinking a lot about my parents. I might try to find that driver now that I'm eighteen." That bastard did not get his punishment. It is already enough that I do not have any family now, but he is living his life peacefully.

She tilts her head and regards me, processing the idea. "You should."

"My Delhi's uncle doesn't have much information about him, and the police protect his privacy, so he couldn't give it to me anyway. I'm pretty sure I have to go to court to get my records unsealed, which means I'd need a lawyer, and I don't have that kind of cash."

"Really?" She deadpans me. "My mother is a licensed, practicing family lawyer; hello."

"How did I not even think about that?" I feign a stupid face. I did think of it, but no matter how close I may get with them, I'll always hate asking Amit uncle and Kavita aunty for favors.

She drops her pen, stands up, takes my hand, and pulls me to my feet. "Let's go talk to her about it. She'll know where to start." Kavita Aunty is upstairs in the office. The door is slightly ajar. We can hear that she's on the phone and is peeved at the person on the other end. Tara posts up against the wall and folds her arms across her chest. Patiently impatient. That's her to a T.

After a while, it gets quiet. Tara knocks on the doorframe.

"Yep?" Kavita Aunty says: We both sidle in.

It's my first time being here. I'm glad that they chose to give me Raina's room.

This one is a third the size, and the walls are lined with floating, unfinished wood shelves; it too closely resembles a large closet. I would never have been able to get any sleep. Hooray for PTSD, the gift that keeps on giving!

Tara relays my quandary to her mother.

Kavita Aunty taps her fingers on the desk. "Let's see. If I can get some information from my friends in Delhi, I have some friends in Delhi Police as well, and we will require a lot of proof to make a strong case against that man. " She clicks her tongue. Another series of desk taps "If a judge wants to try my patience, I'll claim I need access to the files of their case, and that'll stuff 'em right up."

Wow. 'We' and 'I.' She's jumping right in. "You must be very good at your job."

"I am." She smiles. "Don't worry, I'll take care of it."

No doubt she's an amazing lawyer, but being a mom is the job she's best at. I stumble toward her, bend over, and wrap my arms around her shoulders. "Thanks, aunty."

She gives me a tender squeeze. "My pleasure."

"SEE HOW EASY THAT WAS?" Tara wonders as we're plodding back to the living room.

"Yeah. I just don't like asking."

She grabs my elbow and spins me toward her. "We get one shot at life, Vedika. We have to go for the things we really want, even if we need a little help to get them."

What I want right now is to kiss her in broad daylight, here in the middle of the hallway. Of course, I am not that dim-witted. "I'll work on that."

"Good." She grins.

Chapter 33

I think I did pretty well on my Bio midterm, but by lunch I'm so fried from fretting over it that I need an extra-large coffee to perk me up.

Over the lid of my paper cup, I watch a guy I've never seen before shuffle up to our table. He's having a terrible time trying to hide his nervousness—he's sort of twitchy, and his light black eyes aren't sure what to concentrate on. I comb over his letterman jacket. His sport is football. His name is Manik, and he's a junior. "Sup, Tara?" He rubs his neck.

I take another sip of my coffee. Sup,

Tara? Bleugh.

"Hi, Manik." She drops the French fry she was about to chomp on and flicks the salt from her fingers. "What's going on?"

"I was thinking, if you don't already have a date for the Diwali party, will you go with me?"

I almost spit out my drink, but I manage to swallow it before it dribbles out of my mouth. Right, that dumb bootleg-homecoming dance is soon. It shouldn't come as a shock that someone's asking her; nobody's aware that she changed her status from 'Single' to 'In a Relationship.' 'It's Complicated,' at best, you turd.

Tara is chill as can be. "Wow, I'm so flattered, you asked. Thank you," she says, her tone sugary. She gestures to her friends. "We're doing a group thing, you understand. But I'll definitely save a dance for you." She gives him the most natural smile she can muster. No one other than me recognizes how bogus it is.

Man, she is crazy adept at turning guys down. No, duh, she's hotter than a five-alarm fire. She's probs had a hundred boys ask her out.

He's dejected, but gulps it down. "Oh, cool, it's all good."

That's that. He sulks back to his friends, who jeer him. "Loser!" "Told ya, fool."

Sorry, not sorry.

"Why'd you curve him?" Shreya asks.

Kritika adds, "Word. I'm shipping it." Tara peeks at me, contrite. It's a split-second breakdown of her veneer. She twists her lips at Shreya. "He's not my type." I don't suspect he would be, even if I weren't in the picture. She likes her guys tall, dark, and handsome, like Nitin and Kanan. I'm not quite sure how she likes girls.

Maybe with girls, it's more about personality?

That can't be it; you're a tool. decent-looking enough, however. No, she doesn't just want to get in my pants—our link isn't driven by carnal attraction only. We've connected on a deeper level; it's like we understand each other without really having to try. Now that I've experienced this, I don't know why I ever bothered with dating before. I mean, Aman was cool. Prior to him, Mohit I liked him, and it was almost right, but something never quite fit, like a puzzle piece that was slightly misshapen.

I guess I've been going along with it because being with someone is better than being alone. I've never wanted to give anyone all of me, or have all of anyonc, until Tara.

EVEN AFTER THE last bell rings, I'm still dazed by how much I wanted to tell off that Manik guy. It's odd. I don't consider myself a possessive person—I've hardly ever had anything to possess—and Tara isn't an object anyway; she doesn't belong to me. Girls aren't chattel for their partners, parents, or anyone else. The political incorrectness of it doesn't stop me from simmering over the fact that someone who wasn't me asked her to the dance.

She's chosen me, at least for now. Isn't it okay for me to want to bask in the incredible improbability of that?

I slammed my locker closed with too much ferocity. The door vibrates on its hinges.

"That's a mood," Kanan says. "Something up?"

I take a gander around, making sure there's no one else in earshot. "This guy asked Tara to the Fall Ball today. Right in front of me."

His eyes bug. "What'd she say? What'd you say?"

"She told him that she wanted to go with her friends. What the hell could I say?"

"Have you asked her?"

I glower at him like he's dense. "Are you out of your mind? We can't be together in front of people. It's India, that too, Dehradun; it's not America, okay?"

"You know you have to ask her now, yeah? Otherwise, she might think you don't want to go with her."

I hadn't considered that. I want to go with her, but what's the point of proposing it? She'll just shoot me down. "I can't."

"Shit. I forgot how much being on the downlow stinks."

"It does, but the last thing I need is for her parents to know I'm hooking up with their daughter. As for her coming out, you know how personal that decision is.

She'll do it when she's ready."

"What if she's never ready?"

What if she isn't? "Doesn't make a difference. You were right, she's worth it."

"I never thought she would tell anyone that we were a thing. I wasn't even sure whether she was into girls or just me, but she told you, and then you guys got together. Ask her to the dance. She might surprise you."

There is a difference between being out to the people you love and being out to random people. She's the queen of The Dazzel Brigade, so it's doubtful her friends would give her shit over it. "You're not going to shut up about it, are you?"

"Nah."

"If I ask her and she says no, I'm going to come crying to you. Relentlessly, until the end of time."

"What are friends for?"

A question hits me like a rockslide.

How is it that Kanan doesn't have, like, a harem of girls vying for his attention?

Forget his looks; he's such a good friend, he's bound to be a great boyfriend. "Are you going to ask anyone?"

"I'll have more fun with the squad... And Nitin," he chortles. "If you do end up going with her, make sure you pencil us in for a few dances."

"You bet your ass I will."

"ABOUT THE DIWALI PARTY," Tara says as she's gunning onto Sainik Road. "Are you going with your friends?"

I don't know if I actually want to go at all. I've never gone to a dance before, and I don't see any reason I should start now. She's a great reason. This would be the perfect moment- "School dances are wicked far outside my wheelhouse. I'd rather skip it." Anddd I blew it. What the fuck am I so scared of? She likes me. I like her.

Cue her inappropriate laughter. "Like I'd let that happen. If you're not going with them, you're coming with me and my friends."

Then technically, we would be going together, but it doesn't feel like it counts.

Although it's preferable to sitting alone in my bedroom brooding, "If my presence means that much to you, fine."

She smirks at the road.

Chapter 34

It turns out, in fact, that no one is ever too old to get excited about Diwali party. Shreya, Meera, and Kritika were stoked on the idea of going when Tara brought it up to them at lunch last week, and Avani showed some interest, too. They didn't bother to consult Tara on the dresses; they knew she'd opt for something better, more traditionally. They're more accepting of her quirks—these little things that set her apart from them—than I initially thought they'd be. It further solidifies the idea that they wouldn't give a shit if they knew she's into girls or that we're seeing each other. Pushing the issue is not something I'm prepared to do, though. I don't want to cause friction. It wouldn't be fair to either of us. I'm not eager to tell Kavita Aunty and Amit Uncle about us anytime soon either.

The sun's gone down, and we're both getting ready for the night's revelries. I opted for a beautifully simple yet striking outfit for the Diwali party. I wore a floor-length, sleeveless A-line gown in a deep indigo blue. The gown was crafted from sumptuous silk fabric and featured a subtle, intricate pattern of silver zari embroidery along the neckline and hem, adding a touch of shimmer and elegance to her look.

Tara's in the bathroom in front of the mirror, applying the finishing touches to her makeup, and I'm propped against the doorframe, ogling her, my mask dangling around my throat. She is looking awesome as always. She scurried around her cozy room, adorned with twinkling fairy lights and fragrant marigold garlands, preparing for the grand Diwali party. Her attire for the evening was carefully chosen: a resplendent silk saree in shades of deep crimson and gold, adorned with intricate embroidery that sparkled in the soft glow of the diyas. With a sense of anticipation and a touch of nervousness, she applied henna designs to her hands, intricate patterns symbolizing happiness and good fortune. I step inside, close the door behind me, then slink over to her. I encircle her and rest my chin on her shoulder.

"Careful," she warns.

"Gotcha." I kiss her neck and watch for her reaction in the mirror. It's a smile.

Here we go. "How would you feel if Kanan met up with us?"

"I was really hoping to have some silly fun tonight." She glares at my reflection.

"You already invited him, didn't you?"

She got yo' ass. It was selfish of me, I know. I wanted to celebrate my first Diwali in a decade with both of them." We talked it over. I told him that I'd have to get the okay from you and get back to him."

"You can't un-invite him; you're not douchey like that. And I'm trying to be less douchey, so I'm not going to ask you to." She's not douchey; she's sensitive—a massive distinction. "You sure?"

She nods. "I can't promise you that I'll be all smiles, but I'll do my best."

"Thank you."

"Uh huh. Now get out so I can finish.

You're distracting me."

"You're sexy when you're bossy." I place a kiss on another cosmetics-free part of her neck and bounce out of the room.

SHE BORROWS her dad's SUV, and we pick up The Dazzel Brigade at Shreya's house—it's on the way. We take the backroads to avoid the tourist traffic on the highway.

If parking was difficult on a normal Saturday afternoon in October, tonight it is downright nightmarish. After circling the surface roads for fifteen minutes, Tara gives up and pays for a valet. The cobblestone pathways are overcrowded, and we're forced to walk in pairs—Avani and Meera, Shreya and Kritika, Tara and me. It gets me wondering if her friends are oblivious to everything besides their own tits. We're together all of the time now; how could they not know we're dating? Then again, outside of Kanan, who only twigged because he's been there, The Squad hasn't figured it out either.

Most girls are too wrapped up in their own stuff to notice other people's.

I'd love to be more like that, but once it's ingrained, alertness is hard to shake. As with a feral animal, vigilance has always been key to my continued safety.

My phone chimes, dislodging the thought from my head.

Kanan: I'm outside Wicked Ink.

I remember where that was from the last time. We're a block away. I write back to him.

Be there soon.

"Kanan is here."

"You started hanging out with him again?" Kritika shoots at Tara. She's taken aback, though not judging. When Tara was part of The Three Amigos, was she not friends with The Brigade—no overlap?

There are still things about their situation. I don't know, and it isn't my place to ask.

It's not like it makes a difference. What matters is if and how they can move forward.

"Vedika wanted her to come. Tonight, we're all hanging out with her."

"I think she's cool," Meera adds, shrugging. As she says it, I decide that, out of all of Tara's friends, I like her the most.

No one else has anything to say about it. If they do, they won't voice it after Tara's declaration. To have that kind of sway over people... It's like her superpower.

We find Kanan standing with his back against the building's brick façade.

He donned a finely tailored, royal blue sherwani, richly embellished with intricate gold embroidery that glittered under the warm, inviting glow of the decorative diyas. The silk fabric of his attire had a luxurious sheen, exuding elegance and charm. Kanan's ensemble was completed with a matching churidar, which added a touch of traditional sophistication to his outfit. Tara nails me with a scowl that makes my freaking rectum prolapse. It's much scarier than the last time she let her jealousy show, yet in a weird way, I'm happy about it. She wants to be the only girl I look at. I can't imagine how she doesn't realize that she is.

"Thanks. Hey!" Kanan says to the group: Then, to Tara, "Dope, get up."

"You, too," he replies coolly.

"Let's do a lap; see what's good." Kritika

We head for the party hall.

I'm glad I brought my Nikon—it's strapped around my neck but isn't getting much rest. Every few seconds, there's something else to photograph.

I snap, snap, snap.

The Diwali party decoration was nothing short of enchanting, casting a spell of warmth and festivity throughout the venue. The entire space was aglow with a mesmerizing display of twinkling lights and radiant diyas. Strings of marigold flowers adorned every nook and cranny, their vibrant orange and yellow hues adding a burst of color to the surroundings. Rangoli patterns graced the entrance, intricately designed with colorful powders and flower petals, offering a delightful welcome to the guests. The centerpiece of the decor was an elaborate diya arrangement, a breathtaking amalgamation of candles and lamps in various sizes, creating a mesmerizing dance of light and shadows. The tables were elegantly set with glittering gold and silver accents, and the fragrance of fresh flowers and incense filled the air, adding a layer of enchantment to the festivities. The Diwali party decoration truly captured the essence of the festival of lights, creating a magical atmosphere that left everyone in awe. Every picture I've taken tonight is being submitted for my Photography Club portraiture project. I'll hear no objections from Tara or anyone else.

Kanan is friendly enough with the other girls, Meera in particular, since she's so receptive, but she mostly sticks with me.

I've been hyper-focused on balancing my attention between him and Tara. Based on Tara's displeasure at my reaction to Head Charge, if I don't get it right, there's a good chance the night will go to hell. I'm managing it well so far.

The atmosphere around us is helpful; it's so light and jovial that Tara and Kanan engage in short bursts of unflustered conversation about all the ingeniously costumed carousers we encounter. I fall a step behind them and observe with a satisfied heart as they stroll side by side.

I don't get to bask in it for long. Tara notices that I'm no longer keeping stride and looks over her shoulder to find me.

She slides her arm behind her back and wiggles her fingers. I brush my fingertips against hers, and she captures my hand.

She tugs me in between her and Kanan, then lets me go.

"Yo, let's go to the bar!" Avani yells to us from the front of the pack.

Tara gives her the go-ahead with a nod.

The dance stage at the Diwali party was a captivating focal point that set the mood for an evening of lively celebration. Positioned at one end of the venue, it was a platform adorned with opulent decorations and striking lighting. A backdrop of rich, velvet drapes in deep jewel tones served as the canvas for a splendid display of shimmering LED fairy lights and cascading strings of golden and silver tinsel. These lights created a mesmerizing, starry backdrop that complemented the festivities beautifully.

In the center of the stage, a polished wooden floor beckoned guests to dance, its surface reflecting the vibrant hues of the multicolored LED dance floor lights. Surrounding the dance area, tall candelabras with flickering candles exuded an air of old-world charm, while decorative pillars were wrapped in fragrant marigold garlands and strings of delicate jasmine flowers.

By the fourth song—a punjabi song' "Miracle"—we've all gotten very into the music. Kanan is to my right, and Tara is to my left. Both of them are singing, moving to the rhythm. It occurs to me that these two are my favorite people on Earth, and considering they've put their painful history aside to be with me tonight, I might be one of theirs, too.

How TF did I get so blessed?

"What's that goofy grin about?" Tara asks.

"I'm having a wicked good time, that's all."

I understand her expression. Despite itching to wrap her arms around me, she won't let herself. She doesn't do anything she doesn't want to do, but she doesn't do everything she wants to do, either.

Kanan nudges me with his elbow.

He's oggling a beautiful girl dressed in a saree who has a drink in her hand.

"I'd murder for a beer right now, wouldn't you?" he shouts.

"I don't actually like beer. It's better than spirits, and I'll drink it if it's there, but... Without a word, Tara takes off for the bar. I'm so stunned, I wonder aloud, "Where the hell is she going?"

Kanan does this half-snicker, half-out-breath thing: "She must still have her fake ID."

I can feel my eyebrows climbing my skull. "Her, what now?" Naturally, she has a fake ID. The entire Brigade probably has fake IDs. They're the Cool Girls, and that's such a quintessential Cool Girl thing.

The universe must've malfunctioned and sent me to an alternate dimension, because I never imagined I'd end up with a popular cheerleader type; they don't date girls. Not openly. There's a catch. And so, her happiness remains elusive, buried beneath her guilt. And mine, captive within the walls of her parents' home. Someday we'll be free; we just have to hang on.

Kanan smirks. "It's a really good fake, too, scans and everything. Never fails." He nods at Tara, who's already gotten past the burly bouncer. My gaze is on her as she gives one of the bartenders her order and then pays.

She strolls back to us with a beer in each hand, all unruffled confidence, boasting a simper at everyone she passes—including two cops. It's astonishing how she

can be so audacious at times, yet so timid at others. And it's astonishing how much I like both sides—every side—of her.

"Here." She hands one of the blue plastic cups to Kanan and takes a sip of the other. Kanan digs into the top of his kurta and pulls out a bundle of folded bills. Neat trick. Tara scoffs at the money. "Don't insult me." She doesn't wait for Kanan to thank her before joining her friends, who've separated from us a bit.

Kanan swills his beer. "She hasn't changed at all."

She has changed. A lot. The shiny Tara that Kanan knew is locked away inside of her. Still, there are pieces of the girl she used to be shimmering through the darkness; I'll keep prying them into the light for as long as it takes. She will be happy again. What she did just now—that's significant progress.

We watch a few more bands, and Tara imbibes a couple more beers before everyone agrees that we need food.

We take off for the center of downtown. There are long lines to get into every place we pass, but we jump on one outside a restaurant called The Village, Tara insists that the food is phenomenal and that I would die over their fried chicken.

Standing in front of us is a mixed group of guys and girls around our age, some in plain clothes, others dressed up, and one boy keeps looking at me. I'm not sure if I know him; he may know me from somewhere.

"Sick camera," he says, smiling and pointing to my Nikon. Okay, he doesn't know me. So, what's with the learning? "Where'd you get it?"

"Thanks. Uh, I'm not sure. It was a gift."

"Chroma..." Tara chimes in.

I snap, "Right, it's from there."

"Oh, cool." He disregards Tara and concentrates on me. "Are you from Dehradun?" Nope. "Yeah." I squinted at him. His irises are brown, and his pupils are vertical like a cat's.

"Those are some wild contacts."

He giggles, "Like them?"

"I do."

Tara announces to our friends, "I gotta pee."

"Me, too," I say. "You guys?" A collective head shake no. I spy a row of green chemical toilets a little way down.

There's not too long to wait to use them.

"Tara..." I point them out to her.

She gives me a headshake. "We'll be back."

WE'RE QUEUING for the toilets, and she turns to me, arms folded. "That guy was flirting with you, and you were flirting back."

"What? No! We were just talking."

"He was creeping' on you the whole time we were in line!" She twitters. "You're so bad at recognizing when someone's feeling you."

"Because I don't get what it is they could possibly be feeling," I admit.

"I wish you could see yourself through my eyes for even a minute, then maybe nothing that ridiculous would come out of your beautiful mouth ever again."

Ah, shit. If I don't change the subject this instant, I'm going to lose control of myself and kiss her in front of a hundred thousand people. "Hey, uh, that was cool of you to get Kanan a beer."

"It wasn't the first time."

"Will it be the last?"

"I don't know. Maybe not. It's starting to hurt less."

"That's something."

"Yeah."

A stall becomes vacant, and she signals that I should go first. I stepped in. As I'm about to close the door, she scurries in after me.

It's cramped, and it stinks of piss, but that doesn't affect her; she grabs me by my waist and jerks me to her. She plants her lips on mine and shoves her tongue into my mouth.

My surprise doesn't keep me from savoring her. I run my hand up the nape of her neck and into her hair.

It's different from all of our other make-out sessions—hurried and more needful, as though she has something to prove—I don't know if it's because of the beer, that boy flirting with me, or even my stupid whistle at Kanan earlier. Is it alright not to care about the reason?

She pulls back and flashes a sly grin. "I didn't actually have to pee. I wanted to see if I could get you alone."

Again with the mind-reading! "Same." She smashes her lips into mine once more and gives me a bite. She unzips my hoodie and slides her hand under my shirt, below my bra. Her warm fingers were rubbing and pinching. She sure as shit knows how to turn me on.

She takes my right wrist with her free hand, presses my palm to her inner thigh, guides me up her skirt. My fingers move on their own accord, and I slip the crotch of her lace pants to the side.

No!

I yanked my hand away. “Hold up.” Sex is the one thing I let myself be impulsive about, because it’s mind-blowing and I know I’m good at it, but I am not going to allow this to happen with her in a fucking porta-potty. And definitely not when there could be so many negative motives behind her wanting it. She shrinks away from me, embarrassed and slighted. I have to fix this.

“Tara.” I step to her and cup her cheeks.

“You deserve a bed and, like, candles and flowers. I want to do it right, when you’re sure.”

Her eyes are softer than I have ever seen them. “I—”

A loud banging kills the mood; the shoddy plastic door rattles beneath an angry fist. “Fucking hell, get a room!” a woman shouts.

We disintegrate into laughter. She unlocks the door, takes my hand, and pulls me into the busy world. The Banging Woman glows at us. Tara spits, “Fuck off,” and leads me back toward the restaurant.

Our fingers are still intertwined, and I’m dazed. It could be she’s feeling bold because her costume gives her a measure of anonymity, or maybe it’s the fact that there are so many other spectacular things going on around us that it’s unlikely anyone would pay attention to something as banal as two girls holding hands.

When we get closer to our friends, she does try to let go of me. I hang onto her a millisecond longer than I should. She looks at me with remorseful eyes. "I'll get there soon."

I can see how much she means it and how much she wishes she were already there. "I know, Babygirl." Babygirl! Damn, near fingered her in a porta-john, and you're freaking out about giving her a cutesy pet name? "Um, I, not—"

"Babygirl is good. I like it." She smiles.

I smile, too.

THE FOOD IS GREAT. The conversation is better. We chuckle a lot about stupid stuff, bad fashion trends, and dumb shit kids have done at college—getting caught vaping in the bathroom, pulling fire alarms to get out of tests, streaking at the last year—and it's the most ordinary yet sensational occurrence, just being a normal young person. I didn't realize it was supposed to be this way—a celebratory, carefree period in a person's life. They've inspired me. I'm going to try to enjoy the remainder of my college career as much as I can.

Throughout, Tara holds my hand under the table. It's a good place to start.

I like the sensation of her skin on mine. I don't much care how or where it happens, as long as it does.

We overstay our welcome—an hour and a half on the busiest day of the year—until Kritika goes, "Shit, it's eleven thirty.

My parents are going to flip."

"Time flies," Kanan says, and he hails the waitress for our check.

The server places the bill presenter in the center of the table, and Shreya grabs it. She's the math whiz of The Brigade, though I suspect she's not as good at it as Kanan. I have cash at the ready. Tara slides a hundo note from her phone case.

"I've got this," she says to me.

Uh, no. I slapped seventy bucks on the table. "Not tonight, you don't." My face must give away that I'm not going to sway on this one because she doesn't try to argue. In my mind, I've taken her to dinner, which means I pay; I won't have it any other way.

"You can be stubborn when you want to be." Once in a while. About etiquette, always. It's something Vipul, one of the friendlier people at the school in Delhi, taught all the boys—how to be a gentleman.

I remember he started including me in his lessons after I came out to him. He was the first adult I told, and that was his reaction: "Then you have to learn how to treat a lady, too." Simple, easy. He was a nice guy.

Shreya stuffs the collected cash into the check presenter. "Alright, we're out." And with that, the evening's merrymaking comes to a close.

WE WALK Kanan to the parking lot. He says goodbye to the Brigade first, then turns to Tara. "Thanks for letting me hang out with you guys tonight. It was fun."

"Yeah, it was."

Kanan and I are both aware that Tara's gaze is on him. Regardless, he throws a loose arm around my shoulders.

"I'll see you at lunch tomorrow."

"Yep. Text me when you get home, okay?"

“Okay,” he says, sliding into Sweet Trixy.

My eyes are all over Tara as Sweet Trixy disappears down the road. She notices. “Why are you looking at me like that?”

“Like what?”

“Like… that!”

This warmth is in my chest, in my stomach, and in every part of me. This is me proving the theory; I’m in lo—whoa, calm your feelings! It’s been, like, a few weeks. No, it’s been since the second I saw her—that very first moment our eyes met as she was jostling down the porch steps. I didn’t believe coup de foudre existed, then it happened to me, faster than a heartbeat. Everything that’s taken place since then has only made me more certain of it. Unless you’re trying to get dumped, let her say it first. If she feels the same, “Because you’re awesome.”

She does her signature lip bite. “You, too.”

“Guys, come on! It’s cold,” Meera calls to us from the sidewalk.

She loops her arm through mine, something I’ve seen her do countless times with Kritika, Shreya, or whoever else—acceptable contact. “Let’s go.”

Chapter 35

Kavita aunty's car is in the driveway, and Amit uncle's is not—odd for a Thursday afternoon.

Amit uncle usually ends the week working from home. He was here when Tara and I left for school this morning. Kavita Aunty headed out around the same time we did, but we didn't stick around to watch her drive away in her Mercedes. Amit uncle could have driven her to work, although I have no idea why he would. Tara is as confused as I am. She calls into the kitchen, "Mom?" No reply. She saunters to the staircase landing and hollers up the steps, "Yo, parental units!" Nothing. "Weird."

"Did they have something scheduled?"

"Not that I know of."

This could be bad. Something with her grandparents? "They would've let us know if there was an emergency, right?"

"Have you met my parents? One of them would've picked us up from school."

"True." Everything's fine; there's nothing to worry about. I open my messenger bag, grab *A Tale of Two Cities*, and park my ass on the recliner.

Tara tosses her backpack onto the floor near the coffee table. "Straight to homework. Such a diligent student."

"Gotta keep my grades up. I need as much scholarship money as I can get for university."I flip to the first chapter and start reading.

"Hey." She slips her hand under my chin, bends over, and kisses me—a reckless violation of the ground rules.

I kissed her back, though. "What brought that on?"

She falls onto the couch. "I'm happy you're taking our pact so seriously."

"Aren't you?"

She decides to dive into *Two Cities*, as well. "I've already started my application for an early decision. It's due December first." That's also my university's early action deadline. Today is the first of November; time is running out. Time is such a weird concept. It has always felt arbitrary; long stretches of it go by without any change until, bam, the universe throws everything into chaotic upheaval. "I should get on top of that, too."

"Yes, you should."

"I will this weekend. I promise."

I'm halfway through the third chapter when I glance over at Tara. She's lounging on her stomach, and her feet are doing little kicks in the air. How can someone be so cute while reading? I could spend the rest of my life watching her read. Minutes, hours, days, forever

Tara's words reverberate in my brain: We have to go for the things we really want. Taking her to the dance is what I really want.

I have to make myself clear about it. Quit dicking around and ask her.

"Will you go to the farewell party with me?" It comes out sounding like one word. Idiot.

She places the book on the arm of the couch like a little paper tent. "Was that not the plan?"

"I meant with me as my date. We could still go in a group with your friends, and we could sit out the slow songs." Baby steps.

"Can I think about it?" Ouch. It's better than a flat-out rejection, but I can't keep my features from betraying my disappointment.

"No, listen." She pushes herself up into a seated position, reaches out, and caresses my cheek. I nestled into it. For the second time today, we break the first commandment of Manhunt dating. The kiss is soft and sweet. "It's not that I don't want to. I just need to let the idea marinate, and I don't think it will be a great idea until we complete our graduation. My parents will freak out, and people are not that much open minded."

"I get that. It's okay if it's too much. I wanted to ask you, that's all."

"I won't leave you hanging; you are my favorite person on this earth."

"Okay."

"GIRLS, WE'RE HOME!" Kavita Aunty says this as the front door opens. I smell the pizza before I see it. She and Amit's uncle come into the living room.

"Where have you two been?" Tara goes into Adult Mode, crossing her arms and shooting daggers at her parents. It's adorable and a tad intimidating.

Amit uncle sets the pizza box on the coffee table and raises his hands as if he were being mugged. "Peace offering." He and Kavita Aunty sit together on the loveseat.

Kavita Aunty focuses on me. "We had an appointment with your lawyer for Delhi court."

A what? Why? Pizza.

"Did I do something wrong?" So many things.

"Not at all, kiddo," Amit uncle says.

Kavita Aunty's mouth droops open. "Don't be silly. You're a great kid, and we're glad to have you with us."

"Then what's happening?" Tara's defense. She's on the edge of her seat. Her furrowed brow, tight lips...

Tara posed the question, but Kavita Aunty directed her response to me. "I needed her to sign off on your records request. I didn't want to fax or e-mail it to her; Lord knows how long it would've taken her to get it back to me."

Whew. "I'm sorry. You shouldn't have gone out of your way."

"Nonsense."

Amit uncle thumbs up at his wife. "She's had to hire private investigators to find that guy. This was a cinch."

Kavita Aunty agrees. "Everything's sorted. I've spoken to a friend who knows someone who works at the police station and sent him the paperwork; he's going to expedite your parents' case. Once they receive information or any proof, we can request the court to reopen the case."

She's putting in so much effort for me without expecting anything in return. I don't know what to say. There is no expression in any language to convey the magnitude of my gratitude.

"That's great. Thank you so much."

"You're very welcome. Now, the two of you dig into that pizza before it gets cold."

"Don't we need plates?" Tara examines her mother.

Amit uncle shoos the issue away. "Take a walk on the wild side."

Chapter 36

"Vedika, is there something bothering you?" Kavita Aunty asks from the couch, putting down the Manila file folder she's been reading.

I made a mistake; I couldn't keep my face neutral while mooning over Tara's. Can I think about it? from last night. I honestly do understand where she's coming from—going to the dance with me, lowkey or not, is a grand gesture—but that doesn't change the fact that it stung. I want to do couple-y things with her, even if we keep them confidential. Isn't that what we are—a couple? "No, I'm cool. Kinda bored." I hold up the cable remote. "There's nothing on TV." I can't concentrate on reading.

The Squad is going to The 99 restaurant for dinner, but I'm not in the mood for a kiki or whatever-the-frig Bhavya called it.

Tara's in her room. She said she needed silence to write her entrance essay. It's a good thing; she shouldn't have to witness me moping like a spoiled brat, and that's the sight she'd get if she were here. It's useless to pretend otherwise; she knows I'm bummed.

"I was going to get dinner started.

Would you like to help me cook?"

It's Friday. "Aren't you and Amit uncle going out tonight?"

"Date night this week has been pushed to tomorrow. We have tickets for the movie in the afternoon. I asked Tara if the two of you would like to come, but she said you had other plans."

We do? "Ah, right. I blanked for a sec. Sorry."

"How about giving me a hand in the kitchen?"

I like cooking. It's something I've gotten good at over the years. I've had a lot of practice. Being able to prepare meals for yourself is essential for kids like me; sometimes it was the only way I got to eat.

"Why not?"

MAKING dinner with Kavita Aunty is fun. I didn't expect it to be, but she has the radio blasting, and she's singing along with the songs.

I get a bit carried away and foot it to the beat of one or two myself. We stuffed the last potato with crushed paneer, garlic, Indian herbs, and salt, and then she fried those potatoes to make dum aloo. "Nice job." She wipes her hand on her apron and holds it up for a high five. I'm happy to oblige her. "Can you do me a favor?"

I nod.

"Please go tell my daughter that dinner will be ready in forty-five, and she needs to get her butt down here to set the table."

"Will do."

I'M A SECOND AWAY from knocking on Tara's door when the sound of her voice stops me. "Like, what should I do?"

And then I hear Kanan, kind of crackly, as though they're FaceTiming. "If you don't take that girl to the dance, I swear to God I'm going to."

"You will not!" Tara brays.

"I will, too! Sorry, but she's hot."

"She is hot. That's not even what it's about. She's so endearing."

I should not be listening in on a private conversation she's having in the sanctuary of her bedroom. Forget that; they're talking about me.

"You said it. So then, what's your malfunction?"

"I'm a candy-ass little bitch," Tara sighs. "It's a lot, going from Netflix and Chill to full on the PDA."

"What PDA? You're going to eat dinner and shake your ass to some music. Don't fingerblast her on the dance floor, and you'll be golden."

More laughter from Tara.

"For real, though, she shouldn't be your dirty secret. I was, and I only ended up getting hurt. And you did, too. So, if you like her—and I think you more than like her because you called me to talk about her—don't screw it up, okay?"

Ah, enough. Knock, knock. "Tara?"

"I have to run. Thanks for the pep talk."

"You're welcome. Bye."

"Come in." I open the door. She sits up and scoots to the edge of her bed. "What's up?" Be cool. "Sorry. Were you on the phone?" I sit down beside her.

"Uh huh. With Kanan, actually. I gave him the super overdue apology I owed him."

"That's great. I was hoping you guys would reconnect."

"Nooo." She grins.

"What changed your mind?"

"You did, obviously. You became friends with him, which forced him back into my life. Then you yelled at me and kept pushing. It helped me see that I was being really unfair to him. He wasn't responsible for what happened to Raina."

"Now all you have to do is stop blaming yourself for something that wasn't your fault, either."

"I'm trying. Besides, I needed girlfriend advice, and since no one else knows I'm bi yet, she was option A through Z." Did she just say… "Girlfriend?" Her brows arch. "Too soon?"

It's not that it's too soon; it's that I like the sound of it too much. I don't know that anyone's ever made such a straightforward declaration of it. I am Tara Nanda's girlfriend, and she is mine. Unreal! "I am totally your girlfriend."

"Then, can I get a kiss from my girlfriend?"

I peck her on the forehead.

"Not the kind of kiss I was looking for, but I'll accept it. Oh, my bad, I got sidetracked. Did you need something?"

"Your mom told me to tell you to get your cute butt downstairs and set the table. She didn't say 'cute,' that was me."

Pfft. "Fine."

"By the way, what are we doing tomorrow afternoon?"

"Huh?"

"Kavita Aunty mentioned the movie and—"

"I made something up to get out of it. I wasn't interested in a double date with my parents, and I didn't think you would be either. Was I wrong?"

A double date with—Gross. I hadn't thought about the implications of our relationship for family outings. They seem impossible now. The whole dynamic is messed up, but it's too late to go back. I wouldn't even if I could. "You were not wrong."

"Do you even like this type of movie?"

"I can't follow it. Do you?"

"No. Getting two hours of a science movie isn't my idea of fun."

"We can go to the football game; that way, if your parents ask, we'll have something to report." I've told her how much I can't stand football; she's aware I'll only go because she wants to.

"Or we can watch the India vs. Pakistan match. It's the semi-final, right?" Okay, they're getting along better, but Tara is volunteering to be around Kanan for an extended period?

She crows at my awe. "I've got a handle on reading you, Scrawny, you know that?" Yes, I do. I haven't been trying to hide my feelings from her as much as of late. I want her to know me. I want her to love me, even the least endearing parts.

"Cool. You still have to set the table." I stand up.

"Ugh!"

"Come on, I'll help you." I heaved her off the mattress. She drapes her arms around my neck and rubs her nose against mine.

I've heard this called a 'kunik'; they were never my favorite thing, but she has me rethinking that position.

WE meet Mani and Himanshi on our way to the screening arena for the match and decide to sit together.

Once again, Ground is overflowing, which is to be expected for this game:

Pakistan dominates India in the first half, taking three wickets. In the second half, India played well. We are good when it comes to chasing a score in cricket.

There's an impromptu party at Isha's house. Kanan invites us. Tara is sincere in his congratulations; however, she isn't in the headspace to attend another bash with him. Parties in general won't ever be in her bag again. "Thanks, I'm gonna pass." She tugs at my sleeve. "You should go, though."

Really? "Are you—"

"Yes. Celebrate with your friends."

"Bitch, yas!" Bhavya says.

"I'll give you a ride home after," Himanshi adds. "It's close to my place, anyway."

"Seriously. I want you to go and have fun." Tara's smile. She means it.

"Okay, I will."

"Don't worry, sis, we'll take good care of her." Bhavya winks at Tara as we drop her off at her BMW.

"Don't get too drunk," she says to me with a smirk.

She knows full well that won't happen.

Losing control of myself isn't my style.

And anyway, Isha's parents will be there, so there probably won't be any booze.

"Harhar. I'll see you later," I reply.

"Bye, guys. Congrats, again."

The rest of us continue onto Himanshi's car, and I realize she's studying me.

"You guys have gotten pretty close, huh?" Finally, someone's noticed! "We have."

"It must be strange for her after, you know, losing her sister. It's probably nice, too, to have that kind of relationship with someone again."

Eww, no. "It's really not like that with us." I watch Kanan smiling and uncomfortable because he's the only member of The Squad who's clued in.

"Well, you're getting along. That's what's important, right?"

"Right." I have to remind myself that secrets aren't the same as lies.

Chapter 37

I promised Tara I would start working on my college application this weekend. It's already Sunday afternoon. I get comfortable in my desk chair and plunge headlong into it. I've visited the university website before, and it is everything I anticipated from a fine arts school—bright hues, bold fonts, dramatic video intros on every page. On this visit, I clicked the Apply link.

Postgraduate. There are fifty-two friggin' sub-links below it: Applicant Types, Deadlines, Standards, Financial Aid, and Portfolio Tips I know the deadlines. My grades meet the standards. Financial aid comes later. Portfolio tips are what I'm here for—I decided against e-mailing Sara Roscoe.

It felt wrong to ask her for advice when I had no intention of applying. If I'm not accepted to this university, I'll stick with my original, typical Indian college.

The portfolio requirement is fifteen to twenty pieces that demonstrate my 'strength and uniqueness as an artist!' They want me to show them the world from my perspective. Hahaha. How do I see this place mankind calls home? It can be ugly—violent, unfair, and unforgiving—which makes the beauty in it stand out so ferociously, like streaks of color in an achromatic mural. What makes it beautiful? Happiness, Sadness, Tenacity, and Vulnerability, Kindness. Friendship. Love. Tara.

I have to include photos of her in my collection. She's transformed my point of view. My favorite color isn't gray anymore. It's like she has become my new home; she feels like home and safe. I feel I belong to someone.

I have two new ones: the blue topaz of her irises and the soft pink of her aura when she smiles.

Very soon, it's going to become very difficult for me to keep myself from dropping the L word first, in spite of how terrified I am to be feeling it at all. Why wouldn't I be terrified? The people who were supposed to love me never did, so how could I begin to know how to do it properly? Love really is a volcano, and lava destroys everything it touches. I couldn't stomach it if I destroyed this.

Focus. Application form. Click. Here we go.

Tara corners me in the bathroom as I'm in the middle of my post-dinner teeth-cleaning routine. She observed me in silence for the longest time.

I hold the toothbrush in my left cheek and chomp down on the bristles. "What?"

"Did you finish your application?"

"Nrp. Pics ned wik."

"Okay. Another thing."

"Hmm?"

"The party"

It's been three freaking days since I asked... My anxiety over it hasn't been killing me or anything. How sneaky of her to bring it up now. I can't reply with a mouthful of toothpaste and saliva. "Urn-hurh?"

She lets out a gusty breath. "We're going."

I don't care that she'll see me being gross; I remove the toothbrush from my gob and spit the foamy mess into the sink.

"Duh." Spell it out for me, like I've only got two living brain cells. I need to hear it in no uncertain terms.

"We're going together."

"I see. You mean like on a date?"

"Omg." She rolls her eyes and wipes a bit of gunk from the side of my mouth.

"Yes, like on a date, but I can't tell my parents about it. And I think I won't be able to accept it in front of them." Her vibe changes in an instant. "It's okay. We can go together as friends." She's shamefaced. She shouldn't be.

Tara's struggling to come out as bisexual. In India, it is a deeply emotional and complex experience, shaped by cultural norms, societal expectations, and personal fears.

She might experience a profound fear of rejection from her family and peers due to the prevailing conservative values in India. The fear of being disowned, ostracized, or alienated from loved ones can be overwhelming.

"It's okay; I don't like the idea of slow dancing, anyway." Not that you've ever tried it. I will.

In the future. Possibly. When she's open to it.

"I shouldn't have made you wait so long. I was being selfish, pretending that I didn't understand why it mattered whether or not it was an official date. I know it's special—your first dance. It's natural that you'd want to go with your girlfriend. I'm sorry, I'm such a shitty one."

"You are not a shitty girlfriend; you've got stuff. Complex emotional stuff. I don't mind being in the closet so much. It's not bad here, as long as you're with me."

"God, I really… mmm." She wraps her arms around my torso and kisses me. Her lips are plump with tenderness and some other unnamable thing. Whatever it is, I like it a lot. It's an extra bit of warmth—another log on the fire we're stoking. She follows it up with a broad smile.

I push her bangs behind her ears.

"While you're in such a good mood, I should tell you that I plan to use some of the photos I took of you for my college submission."

"The ones in the park?" She looks okay with it—natural. It's not a strained attempt at stoicism. She was wrong the other day—neither one of us has a handle on reading the other; both of our walls are coming down, brick by brick. There are still a few layers left to dismantle.

"Yes. Is that alright with you?"

"Will they help you get in?"

I was already in love with her then—the camera knew before I did and captured the truth without my consent. The sheer candor of those portraits They'll be the reason I get in. "I think they will."

"Well then, you had better use them."

She strokes my cheek.

"Yes, ma'am."

Chapter 38

"It's mad cute. He jumps up and does karate moves whenever Michelangelo is on screen," Bhavya tells us between bites of her sandwich. Her eight-year-old brother, Mohit, has formed an obsession with the Teenage Mutant Ninja Turtles; the orange-masked character is his favorite due to their shared name. "He knows every word of the theme song and sings it all the time. He's driving my parents insane."

"The 'heroes in a half shell' line is weird," I blurt. "That's not unique to fictional mutant turtles; real turtles have half shells. Also, they're not turtles; they're tortoises—they're always on land."

Mani goes, "Umm? Arguable. They live in a sewer. Lots of water around."

"There's that, too! Neither turtles nor tortoises inhabit the underground like rats do—it's only a logical home for Splinter."

"Should they rent an apartment?"

Himanshi's entertained by the back-and-forth. Bhavya's chortling. Kanan smacks his lips together. "You're debating the realism of a cartoon about giant talking reptiles who were raised by a giant talking rodent and are experts in martial arts. Are you guys high?" He giggles.

"I may have toked up before class this morning," Mani replies, straight-faced.

"Gimme a break. I want to be a wildlife photographer, okay? I'm clearly very into animals."

"Quick question, ladies," Nitin interjects. He's got his phone in his hand. "How many stops must the driver make?" Are we all going to meet up at Himanshi's place?"

The party… We've hardly discussed it. That's why I'm certain my friends are different from all the other people at school, who won't shut up about it, and it's still a week and a half away.

I seek out Tara across the cafeteria.

She's in mid-chat with Avani and Jatin, but it's like she intuits that I'm scoping her.

We catch each other's eyes. She's a hundred feet away from me, but her smile has me seeing stars.

"Ground control to Ved," says Himanshi.

"Huh?"

Nitin scratches his scruffy chin. "Are you bringing a date?"

"I'm going with Tara." Kanan side-eyes me.

"And her friends. Sorry, I should've said something sooner. I'll still chip in my share for the car." It's going to be murder on my bank account; nonetheless, it's the right thing to do.

"No worries." He waves me off. "We were expecting twelve, but they only had a ten-seater, so we're chill."

He's not the most talkative or the sharpest, but he is nice. I can see why Tara liked him.

THE WHOLE 'CONVERSATION over dinner around the dining room table' thing is actually pretty great. Amit Uncle and Kavita Aunty are always attentive. They care about how our days went and about how each other's days went. I missed it that week when Amit's uncle was in Japan. When he got home, we fell right back into it, like a family.

Tonight's discussion is heavier than an average Wednesday's; there are a bunch of topics to cover. Kavita Aunty's firm is taking on a high-profile case—some cricketer got caught cheating on his wife with a Bollywood star. There was photo evidence of the affair slapped all over the tabloids.

The wife, Kavita Aunty's client, is petitioning for divorce and aiming to suck every last drop of blood from her husband's body; we unanimously support this endeavor.

Cheaters are the worst.

Amit Uncle's new game, Terror in the Streets, a zombie-hunting first-person shooter, is going live on Black Friday. It tested well, especially in the Asian and European markets, but there are still glitches to iron out.

His staff is in a frenzy.

Tara and I received the results of all of our midterms. Her GPA went up to 8.9.

Mine dropped to 7.75, brought down by tennis, which I'm lucky to have gotten as I am a bumbling oaf who can barely get the ball over the net.

She has completed and submitted her application to the university. My application portfolio is almost finished. I'm still trying to choose the last five photos for my portfolio. I'm leaning toward a few that I took of Jim Corbett; the eeriness of them stands out from the ordinariness of the rest—a touch of pretty-ugly to counterbalance the conventional beauty. "It's weird; this year feels like it's flying and dragging simultaneously," I comment.

Kavita Aunty gets it. "That happens when there are big changes on the horizon. It's excitement mixed with a hint of fear."

"Damn, Mom, you're like a philosopher," Tara sniggers.

"Hey! Your farewell party is next weekend, isn't it?" Amit's uncle questions

Tara pushes some rice around her plate with her spoon. "Yup."

"Are you excited?" He elbows his daughter in the teasing way dads in movies do.

"I don't have anything to wear!" Tara's tone is whinier than I'm used to, and it's such a stereotypical teenage girl thing to say. It's darling coming from her.

Kavita Aunty is amused by it, too. "There's an easy fix for that. I'll give you my credit card, and you two can go shopping this weekend. Take your friends; have a girls' day!" To me, she says, "I'd offer to come with you, but she gets flustered when I gush over dresses."

"We'll go on our own. I don't want anyone to see my dress until the day of the party."

Smart. Girls at our college live by the credo, 'Imitation is the sincerest form of flattery? Everyone wants to copy the Queen Bee. Their efforts are fruitless; no one measures up to Tara.

Amit uncle's eyes bug out as if he was smashed in the head with a baseball bat.

"Are you going with boys? Because I'll need to meet them first." He flexes his right bicep. "Fatherly duties and such." He's joking, and sort of isn't.

It's awesome that someone's eager to take on fatherly duties for me. And I want to bang his daughter. Fuck a duck...

Tara cracks. It's a miniscule wince, imperceptible unless you were watching it. Unfortunately for her, I was watching it. "There will be boys at the party. Neither of us is going with one." She glances my way.

Kavita Aunty reaches across the table and pats Uncle's hand. "I think we already know her boyfriend."

Tara's soul vaults out of her body, and I'm pretty sure I'm having a stroke.

"Who, who?" Amit uncle prods his wife, giddy as a schoolgirl.

"Kanan."

The name is a defibrillator for Tara's stopped heart. She's relieved Kavita Aunty didn't say, our daughter—as am I—though annoyed that she said Kanan.

It makes sense. Kanan is the only person Kavita Aunty's seen me hang out with. If I let her stand uncorrected, Tara will not be pleased. "I'm not, we're, he's... no, he's my friend. Regular friend." The brain is damaged; send help!

Kavita Aunty shows a pout. "That's too bad. You'd make a cute couple."

Oh God, that's just going to make it worse. Tara's anger is rising. What a raw nerve to poke! She pushes her chair away from the table and snatches her plate.

"Thanks for the nosh, Mom."

I do the same. "Yeah, thanks, Kavita aunty." We don't thank her enough.

I shadow Tara into the kitchen. The saloon-style panel doors swing open and close.

"That blew." She tosses her silverware into the sink.

I misinterpreted her reaction. She wasn't angry; she was upset. A smidge green, but more covetous of my openness than Kanan's, led her parents to assume we were dating.

You could have come clean. Oh my God, what? Why would I suggest that? I like being close to her; I like having a warm place to sleep and adults who give a shit about me. They're fine with me having a boyfriend, but me seducing their kid is an altogether different thing. Who knows how that would go over? Set aside the violation of their trust; I'm a mudlark with nothing to my name and an uncertain future. They have a kingdom, and she is their heir.

I can't worry about this now. I have to say something comforting. Better make it good. 'I love you' would be good. Not that!

"You don't ever have to be jealous of anyone. I'm yours. Entirely. You know that, right?"

"I do now."

She should've known about it ages ago. She isn't clairvoyant after all. I have to use my words more often. "I'm happy exactly as we are. I don't need anything or anyone else but you."

The Lip Bite. "You have to go upstairs. Double-time." She steps closer to me and whispers in my ear, "I want to kiss you." I scramble out of the kitchen and jet up to her room.

Chapter 39

Dress shopping comes in third on the 'Top 10 Ways to Torture Vedika' list. Having to spend more than half a minute in a small space comes first, and silent treatments are second. On the flip side, Tara is thrilled. Moreover, she's basking in it. We killed an hour in Pacific Mall, another hour in another mall—she did find a Western dress she really liked there, but it was 16000, and she scoffed at that price tag. She made an adorable gah! noise and said, "Not for something I'm going to wear once."

She decides to stray from the department stores and take a stab at the handful of smaller shops. Ritu Designs is the third store we visit. The instant we stroll in, she gasps and gravitates toward a fuchsia-to-rose gold ombre sequined dress; it's singular, one of a kind. She inspects it front and back, checks the price tag, and beams. "This is it." It's dress number four of the day, although she wasn't this certain about any of the others.

"Try it on." I don't have to see her in it to know it's going to make her blue eyes pop like whoa.

She steps out of the dressing room and strikes a pose, hand on her hip, elbow bent—straight out of a fashion magazine.

"What do you think?"

The dress was pretty on the hanger; it was breathtaking on her. It hugs her curves in all the right places. The plunging neckline shows enough cleavage to qualify as scandalous. She's got C-cups, at minimum.

Argh. The short hemline is also something to behold. I lean forward in my chair. "I think that is a dangerous dress."

A suggestive grin. "Does it make you want to get me out of it?"

Yep, right here, if I'm honest.

"Your face right now!" She points at me and doubles over laughing. "This is definitely the one."

I'm carrying her garment bag. And the bag containing her sparkly new shoe pumps. This is what the boyfriend in hetero couples must feel like—a pack mule. Please, you love it.

"You haven't looked at any dresses yet, and I know why," she says.

"Let's hear it."

"At first, I thought it was because you didn't want to use my mom's credit card, but you're also not a dressy kind of girl." Nailed it. The whole damn thing. "Correct on both counts."

"My mom will be pissed if you don't let her pay for your outfit, so that's settled." Her mouth twists like it does sometimes when she's working on logarithms.

"I have a solution to the dress problem!" She takes my hand, entwines our fingers, and drags me to the nearest escalator. We're in a congested-ass mall in the middle of the afternoon on a Saturday. Does she realize that she's holding onto me, or was it a spur-of-the moment reaction to her excitement?

She knows her friends won't be here. And mine aren't the type to hang out in a place like this.

"Where are you taking me?" It could be to the seventh layer of hell; I don't care as long as her hand is in mine.

"You'll see when we get there."

We went into a store called Spruce. It's way more my style. The clothes here are dapper, tailored for women who prefer a more masculine approach.

We're greeted by an employee who gives us a chipper, "Hi! Can I help you ladies find something?" She ogles us and spends a significant amount of time on our clasped hands. Heat rises in my chest as I steal a glimpse of Tara. She understands that this woman has us pegged and still does not let go of me. Is this… Are you winning?

Tara goes, "She needs a cord set, with round or V neck design if you have it, and"—she takes a gander around the store, points to a collarless button-down—"that kind of."

The woman and I share a look. We're both flabbergasted. "Dang, girl, you want an application?" she asks.

I chuckle.

"What color are you looking for?" Tara leaves that up to me. I consulted her anyway. "You want me to say black, don't you?"

Now she's flabbergasted. "How did you know that?"

"It complements fuchsia." I wink at her and make a click with my tongue.

"You guys are too cute. What size are you?"

"Four," Tara and I reply in unison. I am agog. She shrugs. "I've spent months checking you out."

Holy sh*t, she said that aloud, clear as water! All I can manage to stammer out is,

"As long as I don't have to wear a typical girl's dress."

Tara responds with a smile.

My cord set shirt has a round collar per Tara's request—I'm standing in front of the full-length mirror in the fitting room, checking myself out from different angles. Not bad. Not bad, hell! This thing was made for me.

"Come on, I want to see!" Tara calls through the curtain.

I step out into the waiting area.

Her stare is penetrating—pupils dilated, mouths ever-so-slightly open. I've seen this look from her before—lust. We're humming the same tune. "You like?"

She gives me a slow nod. "Mmhmm. A lot."

"I'll take it," I say to the salesperson. I don't give a goddamn what it costs; wrap this bitch up; it's mine.

As we're leaving the store, I take her hand. She allows it without a balk. We walk, digits laced together, all the way to the car. "I'm a little surprised by this..." I tap my pointer finger against her knuckle.

"Girls hold hands with their friends all the time."

Girls like us are rarely friends—a girl as femme as her and one who's so noticeably... Bhavya said it best: full bi.

When we hold hands, we look like a lesbian couple. I know she knows that. "The woman at Spruce probably isn't the only person who guessed that we're more than friends today."

"You're more important to me than the opinions of strangers. I have to show you that."

"I—" Nope. "I like that. Thank you."

"Me, too. And you're welcome."

Chapter 40

The week is a blur. It's already Friday afternoon. I'm thankful that my midterm exams are over. If they'd been this week, I'd have flunked every one of them.

I did manage to finish up my college app. I submitted it about two minutes ago; it's whirring its way across the interwebs to some admissions rep's inbox. Ever the plucky conqueror. There is nothing left to do but wait. Here's to dreaming big! It's the only productive thing I've done in the past six days. I was useless in the Photography Club yesterday. We went around the room showcasing some of our portraits, and I couldn't come up with anything to say about mine—the pictures of the famous women from Diwali night.

The buzz about the farewell party has been all-consuming; none of my teachers managed to friggin' teach anything because none of the senior students were interested in learning anything. God, how bad is it going to get in May after the final term exams? The literal last party for us is stupidly nervous. It's preposterous.

I survived an emotionally abusive home, yet here I am, shitting myself because I'm going to a farewell party tomorrow.

It's made me realize that I am incapable of being normal. I've taught myself to believe that normalcy is overrated and that because I had an atypical childhood, I'll be better prepared than my peers to deal with real-world grown-up stuff. Who'd have thought that something as natural and grown-up as falling in love would screw me up?

The problem is that I want the night to be perfect, but I know nothing ever is. Perfection doesn't exist.

Isn't there something about flowers that I'm supposed to take care of?

That's it! Corsage, or wristlet. Corsages are the things that get pinned to the gown, right? No, that'll leave holes in her pretty, pretty dress. Wristlet, then. Fuck, will I even be able to get one this late? Why didn't I think of this sooner?

I check the time—four twenty-two—and get to googling. The nearest florist, Sweet Somethings, is half a mile away. It closes at five. Run your ass.

I fly down the steps, nearly ram into Tara at the bottom, and cause her to spill a bit of the drink she has in her hand.

"Shit, Scrawny! Where's the fire?"

"Sorry!" Her parents aren't home. I give her a kiss. Screw the undercover protocol; I almost killed her. "I'm going for a jog." In a pair of jeans?

"Oh-kay." She doesn't call shenanigans, even though she knows she could.

I'M SWEATY AND WINDED. Compose yourself; you have business to conduct. I strip off my hoodie, tie it around my waist, and rest my arms on my head to catch my breath. I gotta start working out; this is pathetic.

Sweet Somethings' automated glass doors swish open. A middle-aged woman in a blue apron holding a tall exotic potted plant appears before me.

"Hello," she greets me as she places the pot down on a tiered display riser. "Are you picking up an order?"

I read her name tag: Anjali. "No. I need to place one. It's last minute."

"I'll see what I can do for you. Come on in." The shop is teeming with flowers and plants. I feel like I've stepped into the Secret Garden; it's otherworldly. "What is it you're looking for?"

"A wrist corsage."

"Ah. You must go to St. Mary. We've been taking corsage and boutonniere orders for weeks."

"Yeah. I'm new at this. I, uh, forgot to get one for my friend." Huh. I referred to Tara.

"Oh, dear. You'll be without a friend by tomorrow night!"

Lol. "You see my problem."

"What's her favorite flower?"

I know this! She's mentioned it before.

"White lilies."

"And what color is she wearing?"

"An offensively bright pink."

She chuckles. "A stargazer will pair beautifully." She opens the door of a refrigerated case, plucks out a large lily, two small white roses, a sprig of greenery, and a handful of baby's breath, then arranges them. "How's this? Wrapped in pink and white ribbon."

It's very Tara. "She'll love it."

"Great. I'll set it. Give me a few minutes." She vanishes behind the counter into a back room, where another man is putting together a colorful bouquet.

"HERE YOU ARE. Keep it somewhere cool until you give it to her." He hands me the wristlet in a plastic container.

I stare at it. Elegant. "How much do I owe you?"

"Nothing. Don't tell my wife." He winks and signals in the back room.

I get it. He sees a good friend in me. I see an older version of myself in him.

Someday I'm going to be a middle-aged woman who has a wife. Whoa, that's gonna be wicked. "Thank you."

"You're welcome. Enjoy your party." I turn to leave, then pause. "Um, actually, can I get a bag for this, please?"

It must be an odd request; his brow furrows. Flowers are meant to be seen.

Whatcha going to say, 'I'm fucking my friend, so I have to hide it if I want to surprise her?' I'm not fucking her. I'll never 'fuck' her; that implies sex without emotional attachment, which would not be possible with Tara. "If you have a bag, that is."

He reaches under the counter and presents me with a plain brown paper sack.

"Good luck."

Chapter 41

Tara and her mom are getting their nails done. Afterward, they're going to a salon. Tara refused to tell me what hairstyle she'd chosen. I know she'll be stunning, however she wears it. Aunty asked me weeks ago, when she made the appointments, if I wanted to join them. Tara knew my answer before I gave it.

I should've gone. Waiting around the house has me anxious as hell. It's going to be a long afternoon. Uncle detects it—for a man, he's remarkably in tune with women; he was meant to be a father of daughters. He's on the couch, working on his laptop. He slips his headphones down around his neck. "Hey, kiddo, mind giving this sequence a play-through and letting me know about any glitches? I've been looking at it too damn long."

It's bullshit, but I adore him for it. "No problem."

He takes his headphones off, hands them to me, and shifts the laptop onto my knees. "Use the arrow keys to run, the trackpad to aim the gun, and tap it to fire."

"Cool."

I'm no gamer. Still, I welcome the distraction. The graphics are high-definition buildings on fire, plumes of smoke stretching toward the sky, horrified people fleeing the city, and gnarly zombies zooming at you from every direction.

The scenes are immersive, intensified by the soundtrack of dissonant string instruments and heart-pounding beats. The gameplay is smooth, which is good for a novice. No glitches whatsoever. He might be a genius.

He's going to make a shitload of money on this. Good for him, doing what he loves and making money for it. I can only hope to be so fortunate.

Tara and Aunty arrive home around four. She manages to dodge me; I don't get to see her until she's all dolled up. She yells to me from the top of the stairs, "We're leaving at seven!"

Three. Whole. Hours.

We meet in the hallway outside our bedrooms. The first thing I focus on is her hair—a rose gold and diamond headband, loose curls flowing down her shoulders and her back, like a caramel waterfall.

Next is her makeup: glittery, bright-pink smokey eye, black mascara, and a hint of wing to her eyeliner. Her eyes are unbelievable.

Soft pink cheeks and a slick, neutral lipstick. Draped around her neck is a simple laureate necklace with a pink teardrop-shaped pearl resting in her cleavage and a shorter chain with Raina's crown ring on it. Then, the dress... "I'm calling the police. You're trying to kill me."

Her left eyebrow arches. "Have you seen yourself?"

I'm wearing a little makeup. My hair is straightened and slicked back in a low ponytail, a gender-bended Prince Charming. From the way she's gawping at me, I know all of it was the right decision. She steps to me, fingers the top button of my cord-set shirt. "I'm in trouble."

"You might be." Forgetting something?

"Oh! Wait." I dip back into my room and grab the plastic clamshell container from the bag on my desk.

Her eyes bulge at the sight of the corsage. "When did you get—"

"Last night, that 'jog' I took." She's getting teary-eyed. "Don't cry, Babygirl; you'll ruin your makeup." I slide the band onto her left wrist.

She gambles on a kiss. I can't—don't—stop her. "I love it."

"I knew you would."

"Tara, Vedika, it's getting late!" Aunty Hollers from below

"Ready?"

"Yes," she replies.

"You're both so beautiful!" Aunty squeals as we reach the landing.

Uncle is in hyper-dad mode, snapping picture after picture of us with his cell phone.

"Dad, please."

"Just a few! For posterity."

Tara rolls her eyes at his dorkiness but complies. We pose beside each other, smiling.

"Let's get one with all of us together," he says. He sets the autotimer and props the phone up on the console table, then rushes to the stairs. We all cram in close to each other: Uncle next to Tara and Aunty next to me. A red light blinks three times.

"Everybody smile!" The flash goes off. He hurries back to the table, scoops up the phone, and examines the photo. "Looks great!" He shows it to me. It does. We look like a family.

"I wish Raina were here," Tara says, not melancholic, simply conscious of her absence.

Uncle squeezes her shoulder. "She is, honey. In our hearts."

The moment is ruined when Aunty notices the corsage on Tara's wrist. "That's lovely."

Major oversight! I was so excited about the prospect of buying her flowers—I've never done that for anyone—that I didn't stop to think about appearances.

Tara covers my ass. "I figured I deserved it, even if I'm going solo." She is damn clever. It smarts: People buy flowers for their significant others all the time, a proud display of affection, yet I can't. Another 'maybe someday'?

A car horn blares outside. Uncle and Aunty see us out.

There's a long white stretch car at the curb. I ogled Tata. "You didn't leave anything."

"This wasn't me; it was Avani. It's the squad's last party."

I didn't realize how much this not-quite-farewell means to them. On a scale of one to ten, Kanan's enthusiasm over it comes in at a solid six.

Then again, he's more level-headed than most. "I understand that." I open the door, usher her inside, and climb in after her.

"Have a good time!" Aunty calls us.

Uncle waves.

THE INSIDE of the car might as well be a nightclub. There are blacklights built into the interior roof and floor, and the music is pumping through the speakers at a deafening volume. It's Avani, Jatin, Meera, Shreya, Kritika, and her 'Bae' whose name I can't remember, Kartik, and another girl, Diksha.

All I want to do is hold Tara's hand, like other couples are doing. I won't reach for her in front of her friends. I beam, make small talk, and laugh to keep myself preoccupied.

We reached the entrance. Lots of kids are already clambering for photos. Any other time, I'd be among them, but I left my Nikon at home. Tara is too exquisite to keep looking at through a viewfinder. I want my eyes to capture her and burn the memory of her and this night into my mind.

We pile inside the grand lobby—there's a four-tiered crystal chandelier hanging from the ceiling between two winding, marble staircases. A maître d' in full penguin suit greets us, "Welcome to the Farewell. Upstairs to the Great Hall, please."

THE LIGHTS in the Great Hall are low, and the whole room is decorated in our college colors—fabric streamers extending from the chandelier in the center of the room to all the corners, four intricately braided balloon arches, one on each side of the square dancefloor. The round tables are adorned with layered black and orange cloths and topped with towering centerpieces of bright, exotic flowers. There are laser lights flashing. The music is blaring. It's like something out of a movie. I'm overwhelmed by it.

"Are you okay?" Tara asks.

"This is surreal." I hear the astonishment in my voice.

She gives my arm a rub, then says to everyone, "Let's find a table."

HALF AN HOUR Or so into the evening, Tara suggests I go find Kanan and say hi. I was going to do that anyway, but it makes me happy that she says it. They're becoming more comfortable with each other day by day, and I'm relieved. I love both of them. Platonic love is another new concept for me—less scary, just as brilliant.

I've been missing out.

I spot Kanan at a table on the other side of the room with Mani, Bhavya, Himanshi, and Nitin. He's wearing a black suit with an electric blue shirt and a black skinny tie—very debonair, and he knows it. "You look fly," he says to me as I take a seat in a vacant chair beside him.

"Thanks. You're not bad yourself." Then to the others, "You all look amazing."

A round of thanks

"Having fun?" Kanan asks.

"Yep. You?"

"Yeah." He gets close to me so he can keep her voice low. "I'm glad you didn't have to come crying to me."

"So am I."

"See you out there?"

"Definitely."

WE DANCE and dance for what seems like hours—sometimes just the two of us, sometimes with her friends, and sometimes with mine. Every song is catchier and more infectious than the last. It occurs to me for the first time that I really like to dance. And I've got some pretty sick moves. At the moment, our two friend groups are mingling together on the floor—all of us having fun, no cliquey garbage getting in the way. Bhavya and Shreya are working on it, and it is a spectacle. Kanan and I are facing each other, and Tara's behind me. I take a chance and lean my head back against her shoulder. She puts her hands on my hips! Spence gives me an eyebrow waggle. He throws her finger up, makes a little circle in the air, and mouths,

"Turn around."

Thanks for the hint, buddy. I got this.

I do a quick spin and am eye-to-eye with Tara. We sway together, our bodies obeying the push and pull of the pulsing beat. It feels like we're alone in the room.

My God, the way she moves—sensual undulations, as if she was born for this. She's glimmering under the laser lights, dewy with sweat. I'm the one who's in trouble; her hips, stomach, shoulders, neck... I want to touch her and kiss her everywhere.

The tempo shifts and throws me off. The tune is Christina Perri's

"A Thousand Years." It's too slow for us to dance to. Shame. This is a great song.

All the groups that have been dancing together break into couples. The kids who are here stag move off the floor—it's not even a thing to second-guess for any of them. Not so much for me. I side-step in the direction of our table.

Tara clutches my elbow. "No."

"It's a slow song."

"I'm aware." That grin! Coy. She slinks her arms around my neck and holds me so close to her that I can feel the rise and fall of her chest as she breathes. I'm a train wreck; I have no idea what to do with myself. "This is the part where you put your arms around my waist." I do. She leads, and I follow, step by step. Totally her puppet.

Yes, I am. It's fantastic.

I can't stop looking at her. She doesn't take her eyes off of me, either. This is what I wanted—the most socially acceptable thing a couple can do in public. So why is there a knot in my gut—not the good kind?

A blink is all it takes; I see that every person in the room—students, teachers, wait staff—has their gaze glued to us.

"People are staring." I hitch my chin at the tables.

Tara's attention does not leave me for a millisecond. She brings her lips close to my ear. "Let them stare."

I can feel the wonderment in my eyes as I look at her again. The expression on her face—it's the same one she had at the Diwali party, when I stopped myself from going there and had to explain why. I wish I knew how to describe it or what to call it. I'm overcome with the most intense ache to kiss her. That would be too much.

The song approaches its end, with piano and violins hanging in the ether. No, not yet!

I worry that its fade will make her regret her decision. It doesn't. She takes my hand and places her fingers in the spaces between mine. How seamlessly our hands fit together, as though they were made for one another, is nature's grand design. Don't get sentimental. Screw that. This isn't a mall full of strangers; she's declaring to the entire school that I am hers and she is mine. This is massive for me. I'm going to enjoy it.

"Ladies and gentlemen," the DJ's voice streams through the sound system,

"Please make your way to your seats; dinner is being served."

The Brigade is silent as we gather in our chairs. Meera has her elbow on the table, hand up, chin resting in her palm, and her mouth hidden behind her fingers. It doesn't do much to conceal her smirk.

Jatin nods at me, Secret Bro Cipher, for 'Respect, bro! Kritika reaches over to Shreya and gives her shoulder a light smack.

"You owe me twenty bucks, bitch!" All of Tara's friends fall into hysterics. They've known this whole damn time! An open secret. It is hard to believe with this group of girls that nobody dared to inquire about it.

Tara brings my hand up to her lips and gives it a gentle kiss. And for a moment, everything in the universe is perfect.

The car dropped us back around half past midnight. I hop onto the curb first and help Tara out of the car. Avani calls after her, "Get it, you thirsty girl!"

"Shut-the-fuck-up," she blurts, and she slams the door. Even in the darkness, I can see her skin flushing.

I have no expectations. "Hey…" I snake my arm around her waist and peck her on the forehead. "No pressure."

"I know."

The lights inside the house are off, save for the nightlight at the top of the stairwell. All around us is stillness and shadow.

She takes off her heels and places them near the shoe rack in the foyer. I slip my white flats from my feet and leave them next to hers.

We creep up the stairs. "Thanks for tonight," I mutter when we reach my room.

"I enjoyed every minute."

"Thank you."

I give her a kiss. "Goodnight."

She lets out a low, disbelieving breath.

"Seriously, that's all I get?"

"How much do you want?"

"Everything." Her hand shoots out through the dimness, and she tugs me to her by my jacket. I enveloped her. Her mouth is in my mouth, our tongues tangling in a graceful polonaise.

Not in my—Raina's—bedroom.

I should've booked a hotel. Presumptuous.

I push us away from my door, and we shuffle, still kissing, to her room.

She closes the door behind her and presses her back against it.

If we're going to do this, I want to see her. Every. Last. Inch. I switch on the desk lamp. That lustful glare has returned. Alright then. I beckon her with my finger.

She's in my arms, and we're kissing again. Her lips are frenzied, starving for mine. I couldn't slow her down if I wanted to.

She unbuttoned my shirt, relieved me of both, and then unclasped my bra and ripped that away, too. She combs over me, honing in on the long, thin scar over my heart. She goes to run her finger across it. I encircle her wrist. "Don't…" She's surprised but doesn't falter.

"You're perfect, you hear me?"

I kiss her so hard that it knocks the wind from both of us.

I shed the rest of my clothes, pull her close, and unzip the back of her dress; it falls down around her feet, and she kicks out of it. I'm staring at her. Perky breasts, toned abs "You are gorgeous."

She smiles and kisses me again.

I walk her backwards to the bed. We collapse onto it. I'm on top of her, reveling in her lips and running my hands over her breasts and stomach. My fingers creep beneath the elastic band of her pants. She tenses up.

"Maybe we should stop." I try to push myself away. She doesn't let me go.

"I don't want to stop."

I searched her eyes. She means it, although there is something... "Aww, sweetie, you're nervous." I kiss her cheek.

"I'm clueless, and you're so... not."

Yes, but it is meaningful. It's like they were dress rehearsals, and it's finally opening night.

"We just have to let each other know what feels good, okay?"

She nods and raises her hips, allowing me to get her fully naked.

I kiss her lips, nuzzle her cheek, and nibble on her earlobe. She gasps. I lick a trail down her neck, her clavicles, and brush my tongue over her nipples, her ribs, and her flawless abs.

She's already breathing heavily.

I slither down her body and spread her legs. I kiss, then nip, the insides of her thighs. Closer, closer. I taste her. She's ready.

My tongue finds her sensitive spot. I tease her at first, give her time to get into it. Her muscles go taut. I will work harder.

Tighter, and tighter still. I start to suck.

"Harder," she murmurs. I oblige her and increase the pressure. She paws at the back of my head and pushes down a little. That's it, beautiful, show me how you like it.

She's rocking against me. Her soft moans grow more and more constant.

"Don't stop. Please, Vedika."

My name… Her voice begged me. I'm not stopping; I'm gonna make damn sure she finishes.

I glide my fingers into her and work her insides to the rhythm of my tongue. I feel her throbbing. Almost. "Oh God. Oh my God." Her legs quiver. She pulls my hair. Clenching. So close. I pick up the pace. Come on, baby girl. She bucks up to my mouth, and her back arches. "Aaahh!" There it is.

She collapses, her whole body shaking.

I crawl up the bed, flop down beside her, wipe the sweaty bangs out of her eyes, and then my own.

Gradually, her breathing returns to normal.

I grin. "That was the best orgasm of my life, and it wasn't even mine." A cackle charges out of her, and I quickly cover her mouth. "Shhh. Your parents!" I say it through my own tittering.

She quiets down and pulls my hand away.

She kisses me and wicks the remnants of herself from my lips. "There's something I want to try."

"What is it?"

She whispers it into my ear as though the walls might overhear her.

I'm impressed. "That's advanced."

"I saw it in a video once. It got me so turned on."She blushes.

There is no reason for that anymore. "Let's do it."

"Yeah?" Her eyes sparkle with anticipation. She scooches up the mattress and plumps a pillow under her head.

"You're sure?" I look down at her.

She's glaring at my pelvis, biting her lip. "Hell yes, I am." She wraps her arms around my thighs and thrusts her face into me.

My body doesn't wait for my brain to give it directions; it just starts grinding against her. She releases my legs, reaches up, cups my breasts, and massages me.

Pinches. God!

She's making circles with her tongue in the most incredible spot. "Right there." I'm about to say, 'a little faster,' but she speeds the cadence—just a touch—on her own. It's as if we've done this a thousand times before, like she already knows exactly what it takes to get me off. "Yes, like that!"

She has me panting. My knuckles are white, wrapped so tightly around the bed rail. I'm not going to last much longer.

The tension inside me is building and building. All of my muscles feel ready to snap. I'm starting to quake. Heat spreads to every corner of my being. Oh shit, I'm gonna… "Fuck, Tara!"

That's it. I'm spent. My breath is ragged. I fall sideways off of her.

She turns to me. I watch her lick her lips. She slings her arm across my torso and wrenches me to her. "That was in-tense."

"I'll say, God."

"Did you really co—"

"Yes!"

She looks so proud of herself. She should be. I kiss her shoulder.

We've been quiet for a long time, folded around each other. I play with her hair and wrap wispy tresses of it around my fingers. I am so content. Sex is different—better—when you're in love. I don't think I'll ever get enough of her. "Ready for round two?" Her eyes go wide. "Ro-round two?"

"Unless you don't have the stamina."

Challenge proposed.

She pushes herself up on her elbow and squints at me. "Oh, you're going to learn today."

Challenge accepted! I kiss her and whisper into her mouth, "Show me what you got."

Chapter 42

I woke up at 5 AM. My body is hot, even though I am bare-ass nude. Last night we... Twice.

And you're still in her bed. Shit! We fell asleep! I throw the covers off and attempt to get up, but she grabs my forearm.

"Don't panic. It's still early." She motions to her nightstand. The digital clock reads 5:05. "Good morning." She leans in and kisses me. It is a very good morning. She takes her fingers through my tousled hair.

"You're precious when you're sleeping, all curled up in a tiny ball."

I have to smile at that. "How long have you been awake?"

"Not long." She sucks in her bottom lip.

"Are you—" regretting it? "Alright?" She was so into it last night, but...

"I'm great. I was—could you hold me?

Just for a little bit."

It's Sunday morning. We have at least an hour before Uncle and Aunty get up. I lie flat on my back and open my arms wide. She crashes into them, and I embrace her. She nuzzles her nose against my neck. I feel her breath and sweet, tender kisses on my skin. I could do this and want to do it every morning until the end of the day.

"Do you know the first thing I noticed about you when my parents brought you home?"

"My cute ass?"

She chuckles. "That was the second thing. The first was your eyes, golden brown, like honey. I thought they were beautiful.

And sad." She lifts her head, cups my cheek, and makes me look at her.

"They're better now. I don't ever want to see them like that again, because I... She hesitates, but only for an instant. I thought she was about to say I love you, but she said, "I really liked you and wish we could stay together."

My eyes welled up without warning. I don't know if she will ever accept me like she was with Kanan in front of everyone. She has her whole life in front of her, and I don't want to ruin it.

"Same here."

I kiss her so deeply. I can't.

Then there's the sound of the door swooshing open, Aunty cooing, "Knock, knock! How was the"

Holy-fucking-shit! That's right, the bedroom doors don't lock. I moved away from Tara faster than I have ever moved in my life. My breath leaves my body with such swiftness that I am sure I am going to die right here on her bed, naked as the day I was born.

"Mom!" She yanks the sheet over herself and grips it so firmly that her fists are red.

Aunty's expression... Shock and confusion. There's no disgust, but that's cold comfort. "Both of you, living room. Five minutes." She disappears.

"Fuck, Fuck, Fuck, man." Tara leaps to her feet, clawing for a T-shirt from the pile of folded laundry on her desk chair. Her face is a death mask.

"That did not just happen. What are we going to do?"

I'm standing next to her now. "I'm so sorry. I should've gone back to my room when I first woke up."

"Let's go downstairs fast."

"It'll be okay." Please, God, or it has to be okay!

Kavita Aunty stood in the living room, her face contorted with a mixture of anger, disbelief, and profound disappointment. The room seemed to grow colder as the weight of her discovery settled in. She couldn't tear her eyes away from the sight of her daughter and me, their entwined fingers and tear-stained faces revealing a truth she hadn't been prepared for.

Aunty's voice trembled with a mixture of rage and sorrow as she struggled to find the right words. Her eyes, once filled with unconditional love and understanding, were now brimming with a mixture of hurt and anger.

Aunty (furious and heartbroken): "Tara, how could you? After everything we've talked about, after everything we've tried to instill in you... I can't believe you would make this choice."

Tara's heart ached at the pain in her mother's voice, and I felt the weight of her disapproval like a heavy anchor on her soul. The room seemed to close in on them as Aunty's fury filled the space.

Aunty (voice raised, her words laced with anger and sorrow): "This is not the life I imagined for you, Tara. It's not the path I wanted you to take. Do you have any idea how this will affect our family, our reputation, and our lives?"

Tara, overwhelmed by her mother's outburst, tried to speak, but words failed her. I, too, was at a loss; her guilt and shame were nearly unbearable.

Aunty's anger intensifies. "You have betrayed the values we hold dear. I don't even know who you are anymore."

Tears welled in Tara's eyes as she realized the depth of her mother's anger and disappointment. Aunty's reaction was not just about their relationship; it was about the fundamental breach of trust and the shattering of her expectations for her daughter's life.

As the room filled with the tense and suffocating silence of anger and sorrow, the three women grappled with the profound and painful realization that their relationship had irrevocably altered the dynamics of their family.

Tara, overwhelmed by the intensity of the moment, finally found her voice. Her eyes filled with tears, but she spoke with unwavering determination.

Tara, with her voice quivering "Mom, I love Vedika. I can't help it. It's real, and it's the most honest thing I've ever felt."

Aunty's face, etched with a mixture of anger, shock, and heartache, couldn't bear to hear these words from her daughter. In an outburst of frustration and despair, she raised her trembling hand and slapped Tara across the cheek.

The room seemed to reverberate with the sound of the slap, and the pain on Tara's face was palpable. I gasped, her own eyes brimming with tears.

Aunty's voice raised. "Don't you understand what you've done? You've torn this family apart. You've shattered my dreams for you."

Tara, her cheek stinging from the slap, struggled to hold back tears, her heartache intensified by her mother's disapproval and anger.

Tara (softly): "I'm sorry, Mom. I didn't mean to hurt you, but I can't change how I feel."

The room was filled with oppressive silence, and the tension was too heavy to bear. The relationship between Tara and her mother had fractured, and the path forward was uncertain, leaving them all to grapple with the profound changes this revelation had brought into their lives.

After the emotional confrontation and the slap, Tara felt a deep sense of despair and frustration. She couldn't bear to stay in the house any longer, suffocated by the weight of her mother's anger and disappointment. Without a word, she turned and made her way to the front door.

Mrs. Kapoor, still emotionally charged and struggling with her own feelings, watched as Tara reached for her car keys. I stood by, my heart torn between my love for Tara and her desire to respect the family's boundaries.

Tara's mother, her voice filled with sorrow and desperation, asked, "Where the hell are you going?"

But Tara, unable to articulate her feelings any further and too hurt by the recent events, continued on her path to the door. She opened it and stepped outside, leaving the house behind, the door closing with a heavy finality.

As the door clicked shut, Kavita and I were left with a profound sense of uncertainty and heartache, not knowing where the future would lead for their family and Tara's relationship with me.

"You just packed your bags right now... You can't stay here, not even for a day. I am calling Amit; he will book your tickets for Delhi."

"Aunty, please, Lis..." as I spoke with teary eyes.

"Just pack your bags now," she yelled at me.

Chapter 43

In the dimly lit room, I sat amidst the scattered remnants of my emotions. Tears streamed down my cheeks as I packed my bags, my heart heavy with concern for Tara.

I ruined everything. I finally got the family that loves me, and I fucked up everything.

It had been an agonizing hour since Tara had left, and I couldn't shake the growing sense of worry.

As I folded a piece of clothing, my hands trembled, and I whispered Tara's name, a silent plea for her safety and well-being.

Suddenly, the ringing of her mother's phone pierced the room's silence. Kavita's voice, stricken with urgency and anxiety, echoed from the other side of the door.

Aunty yelled from the living room, "Vedika, get the car now!" "Tara met with an accident," and she started crying out loudly.

My heart raced as I rushed to obey her command.

"Where is she?" I rushed to take my jacket, and we left home. I called Amit uncle while driving to reach the hospital as soon as possible.

I and Aunty arrived at the hospital in a frantic rush, our hearts heavy with anxiety and dread. We couldn't comprehend how a seemingly simple family disagreement had escalated into something so catastrophic. Desperation etched on our faces, we rushed to the reception desk, where I breathlessly asked for Tara's whereabouts.

The receptionist pointed them in the direction of a somber group of doctors huddled together, engrossed in a serious discussion. We hastened in that direction, their footsteps echoing through the sterile hospital corridors.

As we approached the group of doctors, their faces wore expressions of grave concern. My heart pounded as I sought any sign of hope, but the expressions I saw in the doctors' eyes sent shivers down my spine.

The doctors informed us of the grim reality. Tara had been involved in a devastating accident, struck by a truck. Her condition was extremely serious, and they were fighting to stabilize her.

Aunty overcomes shock and fear, unable to process the magnitude of the situation. Her eyes welled with tears as she tried to absorb the severity of Tara's injuries and the uncertainty that now clouded our lives.

"I cannot lose her." She said this while crying.

"Nothing will happen; she will be okay." I tried to calm her.

In that hospital corridor, our world had shifted irrevocably, and the painful wait for news about Tara's condition began.

After thirty minutes, I saw Amit uncle running towards us with a scared face. "What happened? How did this happen? Is she okay? Where are the doctors?" He shoots a canon of questions at us.

Doctors are treating her. I said it with teary eyes.

In the small, sterile room adjacent to the intensive care unit, I, Kavita, aunty, and uncle sat in grim silence, the weight of despair pressing upon their shoulders. The hour that had passed since our arrival at the hospital had felt like an eternity, filled with anxious pacing and whispered prayers.

Two doctors, their faces etched with the heavy burden of news to deliver, entered the room. The atmosphere grew colder as they began to speak.

Doctor 1 said with a heavy sigh, "We've done our best to address the internal bleeding, but I'm afraid the bleeding remains uncontrollable."

Doctor 2 She said solemnly, "Tara's condition is extremely critical. It's a matter of hours. We are trying our best."

Tears welled in my eyes as I saw Aunty and Uncle's faces crumple in despair. The room was filled with the sound of their heart-wrenching sobs, the realization of an impending loss taking its toll.

My hands trembled as I grasped the gravity of the situation. My heart ached with guilt and remorse for the role I had played in this tragic turn of events. I had never anticipated the devastating consequences of their relationship, nor had I intended for Tara to be in this condition.

The doctors' voices, though gentle, felt like a relentless wave of despair crashing over them.

Doctor 1 said compassionately, "If you want to see her, you can see her."

Uncle and Aunty rushed towards the ICU room. I decided to stay in the corridor only.

How am I supposed to say bye to her? That's not how I imagined our future would be. My eyes are brimming with tears, and the overwhelming weight of guilt bore down upon me, making it difficult to breathe. In that poignant moment, my heart was a tumultuous sea of emotions, a storm of remorse, love, and desperation. I looked at Tara's pale face through the small window, once filled with life and laughter, now lying so still and fragile. Every memory of our time together flooded my mind—their laughter, their secrets, their stolen moments of love. I love her. But it would be better if I leave. I do not want to cause her more pain.

Amit stood by her bedside, his strong and calloused hands now trembling, gently running through her hair, a gesture that had once comforted his daughter when she was a child. His face, etched with sorrow and despair, is moist with tears that freely stream down his cheeks. Beside him, Aunty stood, her eyes filled with anguish and her trembling lips silently forming prayers. The room is heavy with the collective weight of their grief, their hearts aching as they face the stark reality of losing their beloved daughter.

Tara's parents had always envisioned a bright future for her, filled with happiness, success, and love. But now, their world had crumbled, and their dreams lay shattered. The room was filled with the distant hum of machines monitoring Tara's fragile condition, a harsh reminder of the fragility of life.

As Tara's father continued to run his hands through her hair, his touch was a silent plea, a ditch effort to convey his love and his longing for her to wake up and return to the world of the living soon. They were a family bound by love, now facing unimaginable pain for a daughter who had been the center of their world. Their tears fell without restraint, and the room seemed to echo with their shared grief.

After some time, Amit uncle comes outside, wiping his tears.

"You should meet her last time," he said.

I had no courage to go inside; I had already lost my parents. I don't wanna lose her. She was my home. It's all happened because of me.

I walked into the room. The moment Aunty saw me, she left immediately with anger and teary eyes.

My fingers reached out to gently touch Tara's, my heartache intensifying with the realization that this might be the last time

I'd feel the warmth of her hand. My love for Tara and the guilt I felt for their relationship overwhelmed me and shattered me, and I was lost in the anguish of a moment. I just wished I could rewind, but I knew I could never change. It all felt like a bad dream.

"Baby,"

"I never imagined it would come to this. I never wanted to bring you harm or cause pain to those you love. I wish we could turn back time and undo all the pain we've caused. If I could trade places with you, I would do so without hesitation. You don't deserve this; none of you do."

"I love you, Tara, and I always will. I wish I could have said it before. I never meant to hurt you, your family, or myself. I hope you can find it in your heart to forgive me one day. You are the most beautiful and precious person I've ever known. I'll carry the weight of this good for the rest of my life, and I'll always remember the love we shared, even if it was imperfect and complicated. I wish you recovery, healing, and all the happiness you deserve. When you wake up, I won't be here. But you will have to move on and start a new life. You may be with a boy this time. Okay?" I said it with teary eyes and a smile on my face.

I bowed her head, my shoulders shaking with grief. I leaned down to gently kiss Tara's forehead, a tear falling from my eye to land softly on Tara's cheek, a final goodbye to the love of my life.

With a heavy heart, I left the room, leaving a piece of my soul behind. The door closed with a soft click, and as I walked down the sterile hospital corridor, my tears flowed freely, leaving a trail of love and heartache in my wake, forever etching Tara's memory in the deepest chambers of my heart. I left and decided not to come back here again.

www.ingramcontent.com/pod-product-compliance
Lightning Source LLC
La Vergne TN
LVHW041015150826
845672LV00001B/98

* 9 7 9 8 8 9 1 8 6 4 1 5 3 *